ALSO BY JAY CRONLEY

WALKING PAPERS

WALKING PAPERS

JAY CRONLEY

Random House 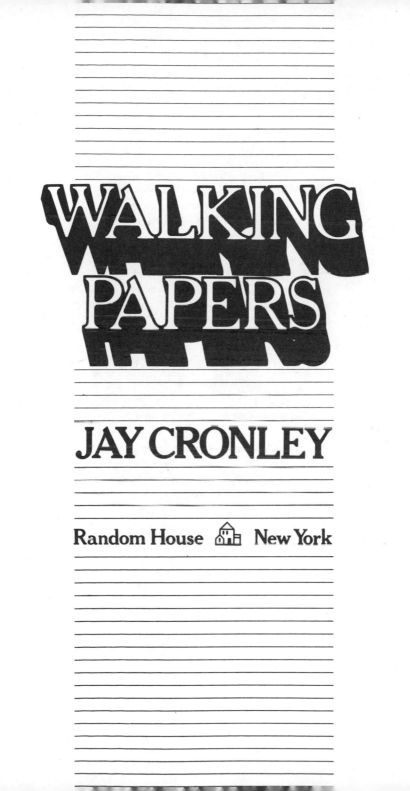 New York

Library of Congress Cataloging-in-Publication Data

Cronley, Jay.
Walking papers.

I. Title.
PS3553.R544W35   1988   813′.54   87-43234
ISBN 0-394-56947-4

Manufactured in the United States of America
24689753
First Edition

Dedicating a book is a lot of fun because it is the only page exempt from editing. Some day, I hope to put a collection of lost paragraphs here. In the meanwhile, this is for Mel Berger and Irene Webb, best friends who have a way with words.

PART ONE

1

John Grape decided to go to the ballet, after all.

There always seemed to be one going on somewhere. Any art form in a storm—that was his new motto.

He had been to a ballet once, something about a big red bird—some woman covered with feathers. She had bigger shoulder blades than breasts; a figure that wouldn't turn heads in a men's prison.

"Fifteen minutes," a bailiff said, opening the doors to Courtroom 101.

John Grape knocked an ash from his cigarette into a round container topped with sand and walked across the hall, dodging lawyers and their victims, to where his wife had just sat down on a wooden bench.

She was reading *The Wall Street Journal.*

They had disagreed about a few things before, but never so . . . *expensively.*

She had moved out now and again, but never to court.

Deloris sat next to her attorney. They both looked up. They both frowned.

"You don't have to speak with him," the attorney said to Deloris, who nodded.

"Bum a smoke?" a short man in a ragged denim jacket said to John Grape, who handed over a cigarette.

"Where have you been?" John Grape asked his wife.

She had been somewhere for sixteen days and seven hours.

4 "I've been to Europe," she said.

"Bum a light."

John Grape flicked on his lighter.

"What have you been doing in *Europe*?"

"Trying to put my life back together."

"Nice place, Europe," the short person who had come to court with empty pockets said. "I hear."

"You win," John Grape said to Deloris. "Let's go home." He smiled. "Then to a nice ballet."

Deloris stood and folded *The Wall Street Journal* under her arm.

Her lawyer shielded her from John Grape, and they walked toward court.

"Goddamn it, come back here," John Grape said.

They didn't come back there.

John Grape sat on a wooden bench and smoked.

"Maybe she's not bluffing this time," he said.

"What have they got you on, anyway?" the man in the frayed jacket wondered. "They got me on forgetting to put a new transmission in a car. A simple oversight."

They had John Grape on more personal matters. They had him on lying drunk upon occasion—like when he couldn't think of a perfect idea to write a novel about.

They had him on what they called antisocial behavior—merely for banishing Deloris's friends from his property when he was trying to write.

They had him on throwing furniture around once in a while.

They had him on working hard. In other words, they had him on trying to hustle a buck.

"Based on my experiences here," the man in the denim jacket said, "saying '*You win*' usually gets their attention better than that."

"If she's not bluffing, she's making a big mistake."

John Grape stood and looked around.

"Don't let them strip you of your pride and dignity," the alleged mechanic said; and then he wandered off to explain how easy it was to mis-

take an expertly crafted rebuilt transmission for a new one, particularly if   5
a couple of lightbulbs had burned out in your place of business.

John Grape backed out of the way of some other alleged perpetrators
and sucked more refreshing tar and nicotine into his lungs.

He didn't belong here.

He belonged in his house.

He felt like a lower form of life that had been carried inside on somebody's pant cuff.

He put out his cigarette and went to tell his attorney that it didn't appear
that Deloris was bluffing. His attorney had already come to that conclusion
because he was sitting at a table in a courtroom.

John Grape never cared much for court.

For openers, you couldn't smoke.

He wondered what they gave a condemned person after sentencing—
gum?

Court was the worst place he had ever been.

And he had been to Florida.

Still, he would have given anything to be in Miami, where people wearing bricks were not considered legally dead until they had washed ashore
three times—this, to hold down the much-publicized crime rate.

The only thing he had liked about Miami was the way it had made him
feel young again. But it turned out that he had felt young again by default.
Almost everybody else was holding onto something. Almost everybody
else was old.

John Grape had been in court once before, three years ago Thanksgiving
week in fact, which figured, given the way his luck had been running.

That court appearance came as a result of a novel he had written, and
the subsequent shooting involving a man named Otis Otterbein and a
woman named Helen Shields.

Otis Otterbein shot Helen Shields in the butt; just nicked her, actually.
Based on the X-rays entered into evidence, it was almost impossible for the
untrained eye to tell whether Helen Shields had been harmed by a bullet
or a splinter. But she sued John Grape for $125,000 nevertheless, claiming
that he had ruined her social life, had ruined her sex life, had caused her

6   to stutter, had caused her to put on twenty-five more pounds, and had caused a number of other physical and psychological ailments and infirmities that deprived the poor woman of the prime of her life and turned her into a member of the living dead.

And, of course, her butt hurt.

The lawsuit, and trial, concerned a novel called *Class Act*. The book was about a mousy little fellow, the class whipping boy, who got more than even with all the bullies by turning their fifteenth high school reunion into a robbery. The central character in the novel waited until everybody got drunk at the reunion dance, then produced a gun and stole what his classmates had been showing off—jewels, mostly.

The novel tipped the scales at just under five pounds. It came in at 432 pages. The book had its moments, but as one critic said, that left seven hours and ten minutes of reading time unaccounted for.

John Grape would have been the first to admit that it was a tad long.

But there was no need for everybody to get so goddamn . . . *mean*.

A critic in Chicago wrote that when he was halfway through Chapter One, he became concerned that he was having a stroke and almost rushed himself to a nearby clinic. This was the critic's awkward way of saying that the opening chapter, which contained three dream sequences, was a little long and confusing.

Very funny. The best review was from Otis Otterbein, who thought the book was terrific—so terrific, in fact, that he bought a pistol and robbed *his* fifteenth high school reunion.

Shooting Helen Shields, the former class president, in the butt in the process.

When Otis Otterbein took the witness stand, he held up a copy of *Class Act* and testified, "Yeah, I read it. Three times. And a hell of a fine book it was, too."

"Before or after you shot Miss Shields?" an attorney asked.

"Before. After, the police took all my stuff."

John Grape would have swapped verdicts in a second with the birdbrain who loved the novel.

Otis Otterbein, who testified under oath that John Grape had messed up his head, got four years.

John Grape had to pay Helen Shields $17,500.

The judge ruled that the novel was directly responsible for all the pain in Helen Shields's butt and a little of the anguish in her head.

Not wanting to turn the next reunion season into one big bloodbath, the publisher recalled the remaining copies of *Class Act*, which took about an hour and ten minutes once the major reviews had made the rounds.

That was bad. But this was worse.

John Grape sat down, stood up, sat down, and then loosened his tie.

Somebody said, "The divorce is granted," and hit a mallet on something hard.

People directly involved in the proceedings began shuffling around stacks of paper.

"What in the hell is going on here?" John Grape said.

He took his glasses from an inside sport coat pocket and put them on and squinted at the sons of bitches wearing grins on the other side of the courtroom. He saw them with some difficulty.

He had slept on his glasses a few nights ago, busting the right lens. So now there was no right lens.

"You're divorced," said John Grape's attorney, whose name was Larry.

"Now wait just a goddamn minute."

"Keep your voice down." Larry pushed the sleeves on his suit coat up. "It's time to get serious."

John Grape didn't feel altogether well. The previous night, a lot of people had gathered in the apartment next door, and at around 2 A.M., it sounded like they chose up sides and had a handball tournament. He'd had to swallow whiskey directly from the bottle in order to get some sleep, and as a result, he was a little jittery. The sudden appearance of strange objects made him jump. He had jumped most recently when he looked to his left at a clock and caught sight of his own nose.

"So she's not bluffing."

Larry shook his head no.

"So I am divorced."

Larry nodded.

"I may kill her."

Larry put down his pencil and said, softly, "John, this is neither the time nor the place for jokes."

8   "Who's kidding?"

Larry looked at where John Grape's right lens should have been.

John Grape took off his broken glasses so he wouldn't seem incapable of extreme seriousness *"Now* who's kidding?"

Larry picked up his pencil and returned his attention to the stack of papers in front of him.

John Grape put on his glasses, his *glass,* and looked across the courtroom at his wife, his *ex-wife.*

Deloris yawned. Her attorney, whose name was Shupak, leaned back and exchanged pleasant conversation with a bejeweled member of the gallery.

"They're laughing," John Grape said.

"Put them out of your mind," Larry told him.

John Grape wondered how you did that—he hadn't brought a chainsaw to court.

"Eighteen years." That was a long time to be married. A lot of memories that were no longer applicable. A lot of *furniture.*

"Eighteen damn years."

"Nonsense, you'll be out in six months," Larry said, fiddling with some more papers.

On the way to court, Larry had stopped at a place across the street for two quick bloody Marys.

The time was 9:45 A.M.

John Grape hoped that his attorney, whom he hadn't seen more than a couple of times since the trial about the class president's butt, had turned into an alcoholic, that the two fast bloody Marys were no indication of what Larry thought of their chances with respect to the unpleasant business that lay ahead.

Once the judge had spread a half-dozen pieces of paper in front of her, she asked for everybody's attention and said it was time to go to work.

"This is the settlement hearing," Larry whispered.

The settlement hearing got off to a poor start when the judge, a woman named Jane Brace who wore her hair pulled tightly into a bun, gave Deloris the house.

It was a very nice house, too—on five wooded acres in Woodridge, which was in Connecticut, forty and a few miles from Manhattan.

The house had started out as part of a water mill. Then in the 1920s a bootlegger converted it into a gin mill. That person's name was Leo the Oaf Lima, and he occupied the place on what was now known as Whisper Lane until 1934, when he died of Ford's Syndrome; one Saturday in October, six black Fords ran over Leo as he was raking pine needles off the front yard.

The property stayed in the family until the early 1960s, when the last of the Limas, Buddy the Nose and his brother Anthony, were shot dead in the basement. This altercation allegedly concerned a dispute over gambling revenues. But the real estate agent was certain that the Lima brothers, womanizers of some repute, had simply been murdered in their sleep by a disgruntled husband or two, as though a slaughter of this nature somehow made the house more livable.

John Grape got a great deal on the house, which was mostly stone, and on the hundreds of birds, the stream that cut across the back yard, and the many dozens of healthy trees.

He had paid $150,000 for the five-acre package seven years ago.

The house needed work.

After John Grape had it rebuilt almost from the ground up, he put a redwood deck out back.

He had the stream rechanneled so that it passed within twenty-five yards of the master bedroom.

He loved the place.

Losing it in forty-five seconds pissed him off.

As instructed by his attorney, he had tried to prepare himself for the worst; but when the judge said that Deloris could have the house and moved right along to the next item on the agenda without so much as clearing her throat, John Grape threw a pencil onto the table in front of him and said, "Goddamn it."

The pencil bounced off the table, struck the floor, and hit the judge's bench.

"Did you throw that?" she said, rising slightly from her chair.

Larry stood quickly and said, "He dropped it, your honor."

10

"He dropped it *forward*?"

"It spun when it hit."

"Mr. Grape."

"What," John Grape said.

"What, *your honor*," Larry whispered.

"What, your honor."

"*Stand up*, John."

John Grape stood, but continued to stare at the table below him.

"What did you say when you *dropped* your pencil?"

"Goddamn it. Your honor."

"That's what I thought you said."

The bailiff put John Grape's pencil back on the table.

Larry put the pencil in his briefcase.

"Mr. Grape, if you continue to use language like that, I will be the *second* to find you in contempt."

Shupak put his hand in front of his mouth, since grinning shamelessly at another's misfortune was considered tasteless.

"God being your first judge."

The attorneys approached the bench.

Larry said, "Based on Caswell versus Caswell, 1983, the *degree* of incompatibility is not to be considered a factor in the distribution of property."

"Is there any *new* business?" Judge Brace said.

"We contend that the award of the house to Miss . . . Worth . . . is unreasonable and excessive."

"Noted."

"We request that the house and the property be sold, with the revenue split."

"Get real," Shupak said.

"I deem the settlement in question, the house, to be fair and just, and to stand as rendered," Judge Brace said.

"Thank you, your honor."

"How'd we do?" John Grape asked when Larry returned to his chair.

"Our hat's in the ring," Larry said.

"So much for the goddamn hat, we'll never see it again."

Judge Brace gave John Grape the northernmost two acres, which was very big of her, even though this plot of ground only contained about twenty-five big rocks and ten or twenty trees.

The stream didn't come near this part of the property.

And John Grape couldn't develop the land without Deloris's consent, or until she sold her adjacent holdings.

"Would you like to buy some rocks?" John Grape whispered to Mort Goldberg.

"No thanks, I'm married to one," Mort said from his seat on the front row of the gallery. He was John Grape's literary agent.

He sat alone on that side of the courtroom. He wore jeans and a sweatshirt and needed a shave.

About thirty expensively dressed people sat behind Deloris. John Grape thought that warranted an objection or two. He thought everybody should have been ordered to spread out. But Larry said there was no such thing as *prejudicial seating.*

Next, to go with the house, Deloris got the mimosa tree that was in the middle of the front yard.

Upon hearing this bad news, John Grape took the end of his tie and wiped some perspiration off his forehead.

"Easy," Larry said.

He thought they had a good chance to get the tree, despite the fact that it was securely anchored in the ground.

The mimosa was John Grape's favorite.

He had nursed it through some bad times, once wrapping the trunk with plastic when bugs moved in from the west.

It won a ribbon from a gardening magazine because of its perfect conformation.

Deloris had never watered the tree. She had never pruned it. She had never chipped ice off the branches. But she got it because Shupak introduced evidence from a horticulturist who said the mimosa probably wouldn't survive a transplant.

"Furthermore," Shupak said, nodding at John Grape, "he lives in an apartment now."

"Not by design, you son of a bitch," John Grape said under his breath.

12   ". . . also gets custody of Duffy," Judge Brace said.

"*Who?*" Larry sorted through some papers.

"The stupid dog," John Grape said.

"Oh."

"Mr. Tompkins?"

"Your honor?" Larry stood.

"Am I to understand that you and your client aren't particularly interested in what's going on here?"

"We're more than interested, your honor. We're *concerned.*"

"Then will you please quit talking."

"I apologize, your honor. Miss Worth has been awarded so much so quickly, I was simply searching for a clean piece of paper on which to write it all down."

"The court reporter is quite proficient," Judge Brace said.

"At this point, your honor, I'm not certain that my client will be able to afford to have the record transcribed."

The judge said she would speak more slowly.

"My heart goes out to you, old friend," Mort Goldberg whispered to John Grape.

"It's all right, I didn't like the goddamn dog anyway," he said.

The next important item to be considered was a request for $20,000 that would be used to further a career cut short by motherhood, *that* old standby.

Deloris considered herself a promising painter and wanted to be paid so she could study art.

Larry was quick to his feet.

"There's no cause for a room and board allowance, since by definition, any alimony would cover that."

"Miss Worth is supposed to *commute* overseas?" Shupak said.

"We pray against it," Larry replied.

John Grape, who was getting a headache, and who seemed to be getting nowhere by sitting calmly while his belongings were being handed out like party favors, stood suddenly and said: "She can't draw."

"I'm *sorry?*" Judge Brace said, turning her right ear toward John Grape as though she hadn't heard him correctly.

"She can't draw."

Larry sat down and turned his chair away from his client to show the court he didn't condone this rudeness, either.

Judge Brace frowned and said, "You're saying Miss Worth is not a very good artist?"

"No, I'm saying she's terrible."

A few of the minks sitting behind Deloris coiled into striking position.

"I see," Judge Brace said.

"Thank you, I appreciate it," John Grape said, bowing slightly.

"So in other words, Mr. Grape, one of the more qualified institutions of higher learning would be the perfect place for Miss Worth to *learn* to draw, wouldn't it?"

John Grape opened his mouth.

Eventually, he closed it.

"Ouch," Mort Goldberg said. "Low blow."

Many people approached the bench this time.

John Grape was first in line. He asked if he could speak with Deloris for a minute.

"As you can probably tell, my client has been under a great deal of stress," Larry said, trying to explain this most recent interruption.

Judge Brace asked, "Is this about something that remains to be settled?"

She glanced at a sizeable list of items still to be distributed.

"Yes," John Grape said.

"Might it speed this up?"

"Yes."

Shupak shrugged.

Larry looked at the floor.

Judge Brace tapped her pen on the bench. "Mr. Grape, you've caught me at a very good time. I have to use the restroom."

She called for a five-minute recess.

Shupak sat beside Larry.

"What's one tree, Alex," Larry said. "The manager of the place where John lives said he could put the mimosa in the courtyard."

14   "Larry, as far as I can tell, it's the principle of the thing," Shupak said, straightening the knot on his silk tie. "Just between us, she's still pretty set on punishing him to the fullest intent of the law."

Larry looked at his notes. "We'll give you the twenty-four inch Sony console and the grandfather clock for the tree out front."

"My first impression is that we have a good shot at the Sony."

"You can't have all *four* television sets."

"You can have the Casio."

Larry squinted at his list. "The Casio is a black-and-white with a *two-inch* screen."

"Inch and a half."

"We'll take it," Larry said.

Deloris scooted her chair back toward the gallery, sighed, and said to a friend of hers named Bonnie, "I don't know about this."

Bonnie leaned across the railing, picking some lint off Deloris's skirt and said, "The gray is perfect."

"I'm not talking about what I'm *wearing*. We had no idea we'd get so *much*. Maybe this isn't such a good idea after all."

Deloris glanced up at the judge, who had just returned from the restroom and was smiling softly at her.

"So give him a few pillows back later," Bonnie said.

She said she knew exactly how Deloris felt. She had been through a similar ordeal. Sometimes you couldn't help but feel pity, even for somebody who was real boring. What a person had to do at times like this was ask herself how often she had moved out during the last couple of years.

"Eight times," Deloris said. "No, nine."

A person had to ask herself when he had been sober for an extended period of time, when they had last *talked,* or had some fun.

"Maybe it'll change once he gets another decent book written," Deloris said.

A person had to ask herself if she wanted to be sacrificed to another's *so-called* craft.

"I don't want to influence you one way or the other," Bonnie said. "You

can call these things off anytime. And, he'll still be there, after the divorce.
But I'd have shot him, long ago."

"Excuse me," Marie said as she sat down next to Mort Goldberg. "What
have we got here anyway?"

Since Marie's retirement from the phone company, she had taken up
watching trials as a hobby.

"A divorce," Mort Goldberg said.

Marie smiled and took a candy bar from her purse. "It's dull out there."
She nodded at the door. "Arsonist due south. Some car thieves on the other
side. This the settlement hearing?"

Mort Goldberg nodded.

"Where do we stand?"

Marie offered Mort Goldberg a corner of her candy bar.

"The woman got the house." Mort Goldberg snapped his fingers.

"Nice house?"

"A showplace. Creek. Trees."

"What's going on, a little begging?"

"Something like that."

"That the poor guy?" Marie pointed what was left of her candy bar at
what was left of John Grape.

"That's him."

"What caused it?"

"The divorce?"

Marie nodded.

"Offhand, I don't think she likes him much."

"There anything specific to hang your hat on?"

"Well," Mort Goldberg said, accepting another bite of chocolate, "for
openers, John passed out in a whorehouse on their eighteenth wedding
anniversary. I mean, for *closers*."

Marie raised her eyebrows, whistled softly, and wiped chocolate off her
upper lip.

"It's not as bad as it sounds."

"So you're a friend of his."

"John's a writer, a novelist." Mort Goldberg sighed. "He was in the

16 whorehouse researching a book, you know, getting some atmosphere. The women he interviews are punchy, they've had their skulls driven against the headposts on beds once too often. John gets depressed. He comes to the conclusion that having some whores killed off by a garden-variety lunatic is a rotten idea. It's happened at least a thousand times throughout the course of fictional history, . . ."

"Marie."

"Marie. So he has a few too many beers, passes out in the living room. Writing novels is tough work."

"You'll get no argument from me," Marie said. "Thank God for the greeting cards that come all written out, that's what I say."

"Anyway, John said it was like entrapment."

Marie cocked her head to the right.

"What was?"

"Forgetting the anniversary. He said his wife, his *ex*-wife, hadn't mentioned the exact date in months."

"Save my seat."

Marie said she was going to get a friend of hers named Betty, who was upstairs wasting her time on a murder trial.

John Grape reached up to remove a cigarette that should have been between his lips and wondered what he could say that would make Deloris quit taking his stuff and let him come back to where he belonged.

He had been restrained from entering his own house since the evening the three whores wearing skirts that were about seven inches long rolled him onto the front lawn—which was right at a month ago.

In the meantime, he had written Deloris mushy poems; then, when she didn't reply, he'd ring her up and threaten to drag her out of his house by force, if necessary.

Being thrown out was enough to confuse a person.

"I don't know what to say," John Grape said, feeling around by his mouth for the cigarette that wasn't there. He sat in Shupak's chair, and kept a civil distance. "Things are getting out of hand, aren't they."

Deloris wore a wool suit he had never seen and a four-year-old frown.

"We have to get on with our lives, John," she said.

"I want to go home, goddamn it."

"What about *me*?"

"You can come too."

John Grape smiled at what he hoped was a joke.

"Why don't you mind your own business," he then said to Bonnie, who was eavesdropping from her seat on the first row of the gallery.

"Why don't you get a job," Bonnie said. "Quit pretending you're a big-shot writer."

John Grape made a fist out of his right hand.

"Don't you dare strike me," Bonnie said.

"John," Deloris said, shaking her head, "You don't care anything about me. Nothing matters except your work."

"*What* work," Bonnie said.

"You're just afraid to be alone, that's all," Deloris told him.

John Grape gave Bonnie a murderous look and said to his new ex-wife, "Don't let eighteen years go to waste."

"I thought you wanted to talk about the settlement."

"I want to talk about us."

"You've had . . . years."

A button popped off the part of the shirt that was stretched across John Grape's substantial stomach. He picked up the button and said, "We can have the divorce annulled."

The judge hit her gavel on something.

Shupak asked for his chair back.

"What happened?" Larry asked.

John Grape shrugged and said he wasn't sure. "I asked her not to divorce me."

"John, you have to understand this. The mare is already out of the barn."

"A button popped off my shirt."

"These things happen," Larry said.

Deloris got $12,500 so she could study art at the school of her choosing. Larry acted like they had found a great deal of money on the sidewalk. He grinned and wrote *Now we're getting somewhere* on his notebook.

18   What had happened, though, if you wanted to get technical, was that John Grape had just lost $12,500 more.

When Deloris was awarded $117,460, Larry dropped *his* pencil.

John Grape reached inside his sport coat for some cigarettes, shook a Barclay out of the pack, put it between his lips, then rubbed the back of his neck.

The bailiff's eyes widened.

The court reporter blinked at the numbers she had just written—the $117,460.

Deloris and those in her entourage smiled.

"This is an old-fashioned ass-kicking," Mort Goldberg said. "Maybe there's a book in it."

John Grape rolled the cigarette around between his lips.

"Don't light that thing," Larry said.

"They're talking about my *brains*," John Grape said.

Judge Brace told everybody to get quiet.

The $117,460 was approximately half of what John Grape had earned from his big book, *Unnatural Causes*, a mystery novel he had written eight years ago.

The novel was made into a motion picture, starring Robert Redford.

The paperback rights were sold for $50,000.

All told, counting overseas reprint deals and television money, John Grape had earned—after commissions to his agents—a quarter of a million dollars for his first book.

A quarter of a million dollars was a lot of money eight years ago February.

It would also be a lot of money twenty years from next June.

"This is the low point of my legal career," Larry said.

You could tell by the judge's expression as she explained her decision— she seemed to twinkle—that this was what the judging business was all about: precedents, or, in other words, publicity.

Deloris had asked for half the profits from the novel, claiming that without her help, the book would never have been written, the movie would never have been made, and John Grape would still be teaching the alpha-

bet to college freshmen. She swore under oath that she had helped with
the big twist that appeared near the end of the novel, and that eight or ten
other bits of advice showed up in print and on big screens everywhere.

Deloris claimed to have co-written the novel, sort of verbally.

John Grape had, in fact, asked her several questions about the book.
It was like he was thinking out loud.

To the best of his recollection, she had replied, several times, "That's
good, honey," or, once, "Don't you think that scene is a little corny?"

For which she was suddenly being paid $117,460.

"Makes a person think twice about taking work home from the office,"
Marie said to her friend Betty.

John Grape stood up, took the cigarette out of his mouth, pointed it at the
judge, and said, loudly, "I think part of the problem here is that she's a lesbian."

Judge Jane A. Brace, who had never been called a lesbian in one of her
courtrooms, didn't like it one bit.

"Sit down this *instant*," she said to John Grape.

He chose instead to light his cigarette, take a puff, and cough.

"It's my house," John Grape said to anybody who cared enough to listen.
"It's my money."

"Your honor," Shupak said, rising. "The court needs to be aware that Mr.
Grape is capable of outbursts of extreme violence."

"Pardon me, but I think I missed something," the court reporter said.

"Nobody is fucking me out of my house," John Grape said.

"Oh."

The court reporter blushed.

"*Bailiff*," Judge Jane Brace said.

The bailiff ordered John Grape to sit down and to drop his cigarette.

"I *told* you that you'd never change," Deloris said, as though she had
only been testing him up to this point—as though she had been thinking
about giving him a few more rocks.

John Grape had to smile at that as he walked toward where Deloris and
Shupak stood very close together.

He said over his shoulder that they were going to have to work a lot

20　harder than this for his money; and to show the court that he was not kidding around, he tipped over the table in front of Deloris and her attorney.

Papers flew every which way.

Deloris jumped back.

Shupak, who couldn't have weighed more than 150, gamely attempted to stand his ground. He had withdrawn a pen from his vest and held it in front of him the way you would a sword. He pushed the tab at the top of the pen and jabbed the writing end at John Grape, but he didn't stand a chance.

He was pinned beneath the table, which had come to rest upside down on his stomach and legs.

One of Deloris's friends leaned over the railing and swung a purse at John Grape, but he saw it coming and punched it with his fist.

The purse seemed to explode.

John Grape stepped onto the table and moved toward Deloris.

Shupak's eyes snapped shut.

The bailiff's name was Tucker.

He was sixty-three years old.

As a bailiff moves toward the Halloween of his or her years—mandatory retirement—he or she is spared the rough stuff like murder trials, and put on divorce detail, where all a person usually has to do is keep the Kleenex box full and transport exhibits from the tables to the bench.

Therefore, Tucker was slow to react to all the contempt that suddenly surrounded him.

Once it became apparent that he was going to have to do *something*—as John Grape stepped on poor Mr. Shupak, for instance—Tucker unfastened the strap that held his gun in its holster.

By this time, the judge had redirected her wrath toward the bailiff and was demanding that he stop John Grape by force; Shupak had rolled out from under the table and was crawling for the door; the court reporter was running for the judge's chambers, carrying her dictation machine under her right arm; Marie and Betty sat with their arms around each other; Larry was stuffing papers into his briefcase; Mort Goldberg was making notes in case there was a book in this; John Grape was smoking and telling

Deloris from a distance of about six inches that you shouldn't take money that wasn't yours; and Deloris was telling John Grape that he couldn't write another decent book if he lived to be a hundred and ten—or forty-three, the way he was smoking.

Tucker took his pistol from its holster, released the safety, and stepped over a table leg and one of Mr. Shupak's shoes, certain that the newspapers would overreact if he shot an unarmed man in divorce court, and one who had just been skinned, to boot.

So he decided to unload a warning shot into the ceiling and brought that off without a hitch, except for the cloud of dust that settled onto those remaining in Courtroom 101.

"My God, it's *asbestos* dust," somebody yelled.

"Well, *fuck*," Tucker said, putting a handkerchief over his mouth.

"You're in contempt, too," the judge said.

Some bailiffs from nearby courtrooms carried Shupak out the front door and John Grape out the back door. Shupak experienced a great deal of pain when he took a deep breath—a busted rib, somebody guessed. Four bailiffs—one on each limb—bore John Grape down a dark hallway.

"We had our moment in the sun, don't you forget that," Mort Goldberg said to Grape, who shouted that he would burn his house down before he'd let queers and shyster thieves take it from him.

Judge Brace remained at the bench, making furious notes.

"This is one for the books," Larry said later to Mort Goldberg. "A judge suing a defendant."

2

They all got together in a small room around a corner and down a hall from some jailbirds. Larry was in charge of being upbeat. Mort Goldberg was going to nod enthusiastically and say, "Yeah," whenever possible.

Larry chattered as he worked on some forms pertaining to John Grape's release from the cell he had occupied with a man named Hatcher, who had been arrested for robbing a church after the eleven o'clock service the previous Sunday. Larry and Mort Goldberg were very concerned about John Grape's emotional well-being. They had met for a pot of coffee before they saw him and decided to act optimistic and pretend he was better off than he really was.

So Larry told him about a woman who had adopted a foreign boy between the start of a trial separation and the day divorce papers were filed. The punch line of this true story that was supposed to make John Grape feel like it could have been worse was: This guy had to pay child support for a kid he had only seen twice.

John Grape didn't seem to find that too uplifting.

"The person I was in a cell with held a gun on a priest," he said. Then he took a long drag of a Camel nonfilter.

Whereas Barclays blended nicely with society, they didn't quite fit jail. Behind bars, you needed something with a kick to it, something to take your mind off the fact that you were behind bars and surrounded by maniacs. Since his incarceration, John Grape was up to nearly three packs of Camels a day.

"Then last month," Larry said, still trying to brighten the dingy room, "I represented a man who had been making up sons and daughters for the income tax deductions. A son here, a daughter there. He made up eight kids down through the years, John. Then one morning his ex-wife came across all the old tax forms. It was like she hit the Irish Sweepstakes. She sued her husband for a considerable amount of child support, so he was faced with the prospect of serving years in a federal penitentiary for tax evasion, or coming up with around thirteen hundred a month for eight *ghosts*."

"Now there's somebody who could use a skill to fall back on," Mort Goldberg said, smiling. "Like writing."

John Grape ground out his cigarette and said, "Is killing her a book?"

Larry excused himself to file the forms.

"Is it?" John Grape said.

"John, listen to me." Mort Goldberg wished he had somewhere to go. He thought about excusing himself to use the bathroom, but assumed he would be too frightened, here in jail. "I know things look a little rough now, but all you've got to do is lower your standard of living a smidgen, you'll be all right."

"That's not funny," John Grape said, starting another cigarette.

"It was a suggestion, not a joke."

"*Is* killing her a book?"

Mort Goldberg glanced over his shoulder to make sure they weren't being overheard. "John, I don't think this is the right attitude to take on the street."

"Is it?"

"Stories *about* murders, sure, they're books. But stories *by* murderers, before the fact, that's a whole other arena." Mort Goldberg grinned. "Offhand, John, I imagine I'd have trouble getting you an advance, seeing as how that would make the publisher an accomplice."

As a first offender, John Grape got off with four days in jail and fines totaling $3,500.

24   Plus what the broken furniture cost.

Plus Shupak's medical bills.

John Grape probably wouldn't have had to serve more than a couple of days in jail had his first offense not been followed by his second through eleventh offenses.

They got him for disorderly conduct, contempt of court, using obscene language in a public place, wanton destruction of property, and smoking in a No Smoking zone.

But Judge Jane Brace hadn't come after him for questioning her sexual proclivities . . .

They paid John Grape's fines and almost ran outside for some fresh air.

It had just started sprinkling.

They stood under two umbrellas as Larry brought John Grape up to date with regard to what had happened while he was out of action and out of pocket.

A junior member of his law firm had learned that Judge Jane Brace shared a condominium with a professional Roller Derby skater. Named Marsha Lewellyn.

"A lesbian judge in divorce court," Mort Goldberg said, shaking moisture off his right shoe. "Rotten piece of luck."

Larry said that as far as he could tell, it didn't matter much one way or the other because there was no legislation in force that made a judge's sexual preferences relevant. The law was supposed to be immune to matters of the flesh. Mort Goldberg begged to differ. He found this bit of news to be a great miscarriage of justice.

"She makes out with a girl friend ten minutes before she carves up John," he said, shaking his head, "now that's what I call sex discrimination."

Larry said his firm would continue to check into the matter. Meanwhile:

"They want the first month of alimony and child support set aside in a separate account. When a person demolishes a courtroom, it's standard procedure. You've already paid tax on the book and movie money she gets, so I'll see what I can do about getting those funds released as quickly as possible. Here's a list of who gets what. We're appealing everything that's marked."

John Grape stuffed the piece of paper into a pocket without looking.

Larry guessed that John Grape would come out of this with around $30,000, maybe a few dollars less.

"That's almost more than I have in the bank," Mort Goldberg said.

"It's a disgrace, and we all know it," John Grape said.

Larry blinked at a crack of lightning. "There's one more thing that isn't on the paper. If your daughter goes on to graduate school, you're responsible for seventy-five percent of the tuition, books, and room."

Mort Goldberg said he thought it was *child* support, not *adult* support.

"It's like the continuation rule in pro basketball," Larry said, turning up the collar on his raincoat. "When a guy gets fouled at the free-throw line and then goes on in and stuffs it. With college, once they start, you're usually in the boat."

"John," Mort Goldberg said, stepping away form some rain that was making a puddle, "I've got a real good feeling about this. Did we ever talk about my need-equals-creativity theory?"

John Grape sneezed.

"Once a person gets a few bucks, he gets complacent, he gets lazy. He can't write a lick. I'm in the business forever and I know for a fact that abject poverty brings out the best in a writer, not any theory or work habits. So go home and write me something good, maybe one of those locked-room mysteries where somebody gets killed even though it can't happen."

"Home?" John Grape said.

"But don't use the character Redford played in the movie," Larry said, putting on some gloves. "She gets half of any written or filmed sequel."

"What home?"

"It's all relative," Mort Goldberg said.

"So," Larry said.

"Well," Mort Goldberg said.

Larry took his umbrella and went left.

Mort Goldberg took his umbrella and went right.

John Grape stood soaking up the rain.

3

ohn Grape sat in his apartment wondering what he was going to do with the rest of his life.

He didn't feel like writing.

He felt like eating a Sarah Lee Banana Cake.

The reason he didn't feel like writing was that he couldn't think of anything to write about. This had never stopped him before. But it stopped him now. He had been working for two or three months—who could remember—on a variation of a perfect murder. Things seemed to have been proceeding smoothly enough—who could tell for sure—until John Grape reached the point where he needed a reason for a perfect murder to happen. A motive. Greed, jealousy, insanity, he'd take anything. But nothing fit. His plan the last few days was to wait for divine intervention.

He couldn't *believe* he was divorced.

Music noise coming through the wall to his left confirmed it.

That wall seemed to have been made of thin pizza crust.

He played another quick game of *If Things Get Bad Enough, I Could Always* . . .

. . . leave the country.

. . . learn a trade.

. . . commit a crime.

Things had worsened since the last time John Grape had played the game. He had played it this morning when he went to the kitchen to scare up some breakfast. He discovered that the roles had been reversed. Breakfast had scared him. Dozens of mealy bugs had taken over his box of grits.

Unable to think of anything more productive, John Grape squinted through some cigarette smoke, and some grease smoke from the kitchen, at a rented television set that had a slightly crooked picture tube.

He watched a pregame football show.

"I'm ready," a young man said, grinning mindlessly at the camera.

He was a quarterback for the Philadelphia Eagles, a rookie starting in place of a man who was out with kidney stones. He winked and sprinted off to the right. Pretty soon, he ran back in front of the camera, heading in the other direction.

"It looks like Jeff is a little nervous," an announcer said. "He just ran to the wrong bench."

"Get him a map," John Grape said.

He had bet fifteen hundred dollars on the Eagles, who were at home with the Dallas Cowboys, those chumps.

Dallas was favored by six points.

John Grape despised Dallas.

His mood suited Philadelphia, a team that believed in the old-fashioned work ethic and was not opposed to spilling blood. Dallas, on the other hand, pussy-footed around. It could play a game on a garbage dump and come out unsoiled.

Another reason why John Grape had bet a lot of money on the Eagles was because on Monday Night Football, the home team getting points covered more than Julia Child.

First, he had bet two hundred dollars, which was what he usually bet on a sporting event. But nothing happened. No tingle, no rush of adrenaline, no sense of competition, no danger. All John Grape felt was the desire to be elsewhere.

A bet was supposed to take your mind off your troubles.

But John Grape's troubles were so numerous—the rented sofa on which he sat seemed to have been covered in gunnysacks—he had bet five hundred more on Philadelphia.

Even with seven hundred dollars on the line, the racket coming through the wall took the edge off what should have been a very exciting time.

28   He had no choice but to call his bookmaker and add eight hundred dollars.

Finally—a little peace.

There was nothing like having fifteen hundred bucks you couldn't afford to lose on a twenty-two-year-old who didn't know where his team was sitting to take your mind off the trials and tribulations of everyday life.

Compulsive gambling was very underrated with respect to its therapeutic value.

The only time compulsive gambling was a problem was when a person bet on the wrong team.

There is no such thing as a sick winner.

John Grape found it mildly disconcerting to note that things had deteriorated to the point where a three-hour flight from his world now required a fifteen-hundred-dollar deposit.

So he had another beer.

He should have made his bet fifteen seconds before the kickoff.

He had made the last of it ten minutes before the kickoff and was now faced with the prospect of killing eight minutes and thirty seconds in a place that vibrated when a truck went by.

Time passes very slowly in an apartment filled with cheap furniture and several kinds of smoke.

John Grape thought about thumbing through a book Mort Goldberg had sent. It was written for men experiencing a mid-life crisis.

There was wishful thinking.

This felt like a *late*-life crisis. John Grape put the book under a short leg on the coffee table. The name of the place where he and the smoke sat was the Shadybrook Apartments.

"Where is the brook?" John Grape had asked the manager on his first visit, the manager a woman who had the slumped posture of a person who has been called out of bed at 4 A.M. to check out a shooting once too often.

"It runs underground," Mrs. Carson had said.

"Where's the shade?"

"Indoors."

The Shadybrook Apartments were sixteen units over sixteen units, with a birdbath in the middle. They were located on the outskirts of Norwalk, six miles and a few blocks from his house.

In the beginning, he had settled here so he wouldn't have too far to move back. Now, he wouldn't have too far to carry the gasoline and torch. John Grape had made a serious mistake when he went shopping for an apartment—he had gone during the day, one Thursday around noon.

All was tranquil then.

There was a very good reason for that.

Everybody was inside, catching up on their rest after a full night of raiding and narrow escapes.

Most evenings, the courtyard at the Shadybrook Apartments resembled the infield at the Indy 500 on race day; people congregated there to drink beer and work on engines. As far as John Grape could tell, much of the work involved the sanding of serial numbers. At forty-two, he was far and away the most senior of the residents. At forty-two, he was elderly.

The football game started as he was picking up his telephone to bet even more on the Eagles.

He could always gamble for a living. Turn professional. He had been an amateur gambler for some while.

He guessed the way a person turned pro was by betting more money on more games.

But he soon reasoned that if he were going to be a professional gambler for more than one night, he was going to have to learn how to deal more effectively with stress.

As the rookie Eagle quarterback began throwing passes that landed nearer his own feet than a receiver's, John Grape spilled beer on himself and burned a small hole in the rented sofa.

Just before the first quarter ended, Dallas missed a short field goal and John Grape threw his fist into the air and pulled a muscle in his neck.

And early in the second quarter, after the rookie quarterback fumbled two consecutive snaps from his center, John Grape got so mad, he could feel the pulse beating by his temples, which couldn't have been healthy. Still, things picked up.

As Philadelphia attempted a forty-five-yard field goal with nine seconds

30   remaining in the first half, John Grape sat quietly, his arms stretched across the back of the rough sofa, a cold beer between his legs.

The score was 9–7, Dallas.

John Grape's fifteen-hundred-dollar bet was looking better all the time.

He could really use three points at the end of the half—Dallas would go to its dressing room depressed, trailing by one.

He was one cool customer as Philadelphia's field goal attempt landed on the Dallas half-yard line.

It was quite possibly the worst field goal attempt in the history of professional football.

The only thing to be said for it was that the kick went in the proper direction. Most of the time.

"It's a good thing close only counts in horseshoes," an announcer said.

The broadcast booth and the rest of the nation fell silent.

After a bit, the announcer said, "What I meant was that if close counted in field goal attempts, the Philadelphia kicker *still* wouldn't have gotten anything for that feeble attempt. Somebody has already come closer, that's my point."

"Yes, Dallas has already made three field goals," another announcer said.

"See, *that's* closer."

John Grape had some more beer and wondered why the network was not required by law to put this message across the bottom of the screen: *The Surgeon General has determined that listening to these voices causes chemical dependency.*

The halftime entertainment was provided by a group of women who should have been coming out of cakes at a coaches' convention instead of trying to promote pep.

So John Grape went to the kitchen and sat down at his typewriter and knocked out a few lines.

In this apartment, his electric typewriter seemed very much out of place. For one thing, it worked.

Being in the same room with a novel-in-progress was like being at a racetrack with a couple of extra bucks in your pocket.

At the races, you had to make a bet in case you were walking around lucky without knowing it.

A writer should try the keyboard upon occasion to see if he has been sitting around brilliant.

John Grape wrote, *She killed him for his money.*

He sat back, had a sip of beer, and smiled.

Not a bad day's work.

Two six-packs and fifteen or twenty cigarettes later, John Grape stood, swaying slightly, in front of his rented television set.

He stared at a blank screen.

He shook his head.

Players had been flashing on and off the screen for fifteen minutes.

"We seem to have lost our picture again," an announcer said.

"So we'll continue to talk you down," another announcer said. "You're missing some pretty exciting stuff. Incomplete pass."

"No, he *caught* the darn thing," somebody said.

"I believe you're right."

"He's at the fifty . . ."

"Who is?" John Grape tossed an empty beer can aside.

". . . the forty . . ."

"He might go all . . ."

The audio part of the broadcast became scratchy.

". . . fumble . . ."

". . . penalty . . ."

". . . probably illegal use of . . ."

"Wait, hold everything . . ."

The sound went off.

John Grape paced back and forth in front of the fuzzy silent screen.

He had no idea where his bet stood.

The last he had heard, the game was still close.

"We're back," an announcer said. "Finally."

"In a way," another announcer said. "We're back in *spirit.*"

32   John Grape recognized this voice as the one who had been glad close only counted in horseshoes.

"What Ben means," the first announcer said, "is that we're back with the audio portion of our telecast."

"He means *broad*cast," Ben said. "Since we have no picture."

"Some cable broke," somebody said.

"What's the damn score," John Grape said.

"The score is twelve–ten, Dallas," the first announcer said.

John Grape stopped pacing.

He smiled.

"Good," he said.

"There's a time-out. Dallas has the football on Philadelphia's one-yard line."

"Bad," John Grape said, wincing. "That's worse than bad. It's horseshit."

"It's more like the ball is on the six-inch line, not the one-yard line," Ben said.

"I won't pay," John Grape said. "That's simple. So they'll break one leg. It won't cost fifteen hundred for a cast, I'm home free."

"It's fourth down," the first announcer said.

"Wait a minute," John Grape said, starting a cigarette.

"And there are only twenty-two seconds left in the game."

"I'm back in it." John Grape began pacing again. "Twelve–ten. Fourth and one. Twenty-two seconds. They kick the field goal, Dallas wins fifteen–ten." He grinned. "The mafia owes me fifteen hundred."

Ben said, "I'd go for the touchdown."

"*Why?*" the first announcer said.

"Because he's a numbskull," John Grape said, sitting on the edge of the rented coffee table, which was more comfortable than the sofa.

"Because you get more for a touchdown than you do for a field goal," Ben replied.

"Did I tell you," John Grape said.

The first announcer said, "But if they don't make the touchdown, Philadelphia has all its time-outs left and could win the game with a long field goal."

"True," Ben said. "But kicking from inside the one rubs me the wrong way. I *still* think Dallas will go for the touchdown."

"Here comes the kicker onto the field," the first announcer said.

"I'm rich," John Grape said.

The only way he could lose his fifteen-hundred-dollars bet on the Eagles plus six points was if Dallas scored a touchdown.

He was going to use his winnings to fix up his apartment.

He was going to fix it up with somebody else.

He was going to sublet it and *move*.

Moments passed. There was still no picture.

"There's the snap from center," the first announcer said. "The ball is down."

John Grape smiled at the snowy screen and held his arms up, a referee signaling a successful field goal.

"*Blocked, blocked,*" Ben screamed.

John Grape said, "Huh?"

He lowered his arms.

"It wasn't blocked," the first announcer said. "The holder dropped the snap from center."

"The clock is at eighteen seconds," Ben said. "Seventeen . . ."

"The kicker picked up the muffed snap from the center."

"Fourteen, thirteen . . ."

"He's rolling to his left."

"Twelve . . ."

"He's going to try a pass."

"Ten . . ."

"Somebody *tackle* the son of a bitch," John Grape yelled. "*Intercept* it."

"It's *complete.*"

"Nine, eight . . ."

"He's at the five-yard line, the four . . ."

"What?" John Grape said, swatting at all the numbers coming from the speakers of the rented television set as though they were bees out to sting him.

"Seven, six . . ."

"The three, the two . . ."

"Five . . ."

"He's at the one . . ."

34 "Four, three . . ."

"He's diving for·the end zone."

"Two . . ."

"Goddamn it, who's winning? Is he running or dancing?" John Grape yelled.

"*Touchdown*," the first announcer said.

"One . . . there's the gun ending the game," said Ben, who had been counting down the time. "I *told* you they'd go for it."

"We'll be back with the final statistics," the first announcer said.

"No you won't," John Grape said.

He rose from the coffee table, lifted his right foot, and kicked in the screen on the rented television set, raising his arms like a referee, and wondered why he had done that, since there hadn't been anything on it lately.

4

John Grape worked five, no *six*, times harder than he had ever worked before and then went to find a younger blonde.

All but the elder blondes were spoken for, so he had to make do with a younger brunette.

He settled on greed as a motive and worked an average of fourteen hours a day for two weeks about the variation of a perfect murder that had *best seller* written all over it.

It took John Grape two hours and twenty minutes to get a date at a club called TGINS, which stood for Thank God It's Not Sunday.

The club was closed Sunday.

A lot had happened since John Grape's last date almost two decades before. The girls had stayed the same age. He had not.

He had forgotten what day it was and wore a suit. It was some Saturday. In the suit, he felt like a parent. He would have felt less conspicuous wearing a horned Viking hat and animal skins.

Most of the women John Grape smiled at or said hello to frowned at the size of his stomach.

As the afternoon wore on, nice looking people of a similar age paired off, leaving John Grape first at one end of the bar, then the other.

A bartender asked if he were a cop searching for a runaway.

36   Two hours and twenty minutes was a long time to look for a date in a club full of single women.

A female of indeterminate age beat John Grape out of twenty-five dollars on the pool table.

Her name was Shirley. She was skinny and had big eyes inside a small head. She reminded John Grape of a Mexican hairless.

Shirley cleared the pool table of solid-colored balls, plus the eight ball, in roughly three minutes; it took that long because she stopped to show John Grape her false teeth.

He finished his fourth or sixth drink at the bar and was about ready to return to his apartment and work on his novel when a woman named Marilyn challenged him to a game of video blackjack, with the person accumulating the most make-believe dollars buying the next Drambuie.

"I don't drink Drambuie," John Grape said.

Marilyn told him that would not be a factor.

"Meaning you're going to win?"

She smiled and said her last name was Champion. She wore nice clothes. She was no Miss Georgia. Nor was she Miss Antarctica. She was more handsome than beautiful. She had clear eyes and good skin and a healthy glow.

John Grape didn't know what to think.

He hoped he was not about to be mugged.

"Ladies first."

He stuck four quarters into the video blackjack machine.

Marilyn blinked and said she hadn't heard that one in years.

"I've been in here a couple of hours," John Grape said. "I'm desperate."

Each player started with a thousand dollars in pretend money. Marilyn Champion bet six hundred dollars on the first of three hands and was dealt a six and a king by the machine—a total of sixteen. The dealer showed a trey up, with the hole card down.

Marilyn reached for the *Hit* button.

John Grape said, "I don't want to seem pushy, but maybe you should stay with the sixteen."

"Gamble a lot, do you?"

John Grape lowered his head and nodded.

"You lay the points last Monday?"

John Grape thought back and shook his head. He had taken the New Orleans Saints plus eight points when they played at home against the New York Giants.

"You were on the *Saints?*"

The Giants had won, 35–2.

"For a while," John Grape said.

Marilyn raised her eyebrows.

"I was drunk by the half," John Grape told her.

She grinned and hit her hand of sixteen with the five of diamonds.

Marilyn Champion was thirty seven and six months divorced from a man named Chuck Martinelli, who owned a public relations firm. She was a stockbroker. She had decided that life was too short, or *long,* she wasn't sure which, to spend lurching from one cocktail party to another, so she left Chuck to his concepts and double-breasted pajamas and was casually looking around for a normal male to share some time with when the mood struck her.

She had tried a club or two comprised of mature singles, the majority of whom were anxious to prove that they hadn't been divorced because they were terrible at sex.

Not that there was anything *wrong* with sex.

She simply enjoyed it more as a journey than as a destination; if John Grape knew what she meant.

He was fairly sure he knew, and if it turned out he didn't he'd sure as the devil ask around.

Marilyn found the fact that John Grape was an important novelist fascinating. She had read *Unnatural Causes,* and even had a tape of the movie.

"We could always go to my place and watch it again," John Grape said, pleased that he still recognized a flirt after all these years. "I'll tell you about what happened behind the cameras."

"Great," Marilyn said, scooting her chair back. "I'd love to."

"Wait," John Grape said, remembering where he lived. He swirled his drink and watched the ripples. "I forgot a couple of things. My apartment

38   is . . . well, it might be a halfway house for all I know. And I don't have a VCR." He smiled weakly. "Divorce."

"She got it?"

"No. I got it. I kicked the television in a week ago Monday when Dallas got that late touchdown."

"You were on the *Eagles?*"

"No, every time I win, I like to destroy the equivalent dollar amount in merchandise so I won't get overconfident."

Marilyn Champion scooted her chair back to the table, studied John Grape at great length and said, "I'm very particular about whom I invite to my apartment."

"I could always stand in the hall and watch my movie from there."

"I cannot tolerate people who misuse themselves."

John Grape picked up the pack of Camels beside his drink and wadded them into a ball. He said he quit as an example of how much he valued her company. He said smoking was only a hobby, anyway.

"You also need to quit chewing your fingernails."

"Done."

Marilyn smiled and handed John Grape her check.

It was for $38.50.

"I bought a guy a drink," she said.

"Of what, rare blood?"

Marilyn said she liked a man with a sense of humor.

John Grape waved at a waiter. "Don't worry, I'll behave," he said to Marilyn Champion.

"I'm not worried in the least," she replied.

Thus far, dating reminded John Grape of being married.

During the ride in Marilyn's car—a new Buick—John Grape did some things he couldn't remember having done in a long time.

He made conversation. He said he was going on a diet. He was witty. He could have been charming, for all he knew.

He wondered why he hadn't made a similar effort with Deloris toward the end of their marriage.

Then he came up with a very good reason: He hadn't *known* it was the end of their marriage.

They sat on Marilyn's sofa and drank champagne.

Her apartment was full of brightly colored furniture—the leather sofa on which they sat, close together but without touching, was orange. But John Grape wasn't about to complain. He had forgotten that they still made leather furniture.

He had a bite of Brie; this cheese was better than what you squirted out of a tube.

He took off his shoes and put his feet on a leather ottoman. They were watching his movie.

"This scene gives me goosebumps," Marilyn said, nodding at the screen.

John Grape's story was about a woman who had grown tired of living with an unpleasant person who knocked her around, so one afternoon she murdered him, having first paid a terminally ill immigrant a considerable amount of money to admit to the crime.

The scene playing on the VCR was about twenty minutes from the end of the film.

A man in prison clothing, the immigrant, spoke quietly with his wife.

"It's true," the immigrant said. "I'm better. The tumor, it shrinks with the new treatment. But you have the money."

"It's not enough," the man's wife said. "The babies and I, we want *you*."

Marilyn hit the *Freeze* button.

"He admits to a crime he didn't commit, takes a fortune from the murderer so his wife and family will be set for life, marches off to die, only he doesn't, he gets *better*. John, it's the best I've ever seen."

John Grape had a sip of champagne, which beat white wine made in Arkansas, and said he got to see them film a lot of it. "Denver. Bob Redford is a nice guy. Not outgoing. Not tall. But solid."

"*Bob?*"

John Grape nodded.

"And it came from up there?" Marilyn scooted closer to him and touched his left temple.

"I'm working on a new novel that's even better. It's trickier. *Finally*."

40   "It's almost scary being in the same room with the person who thought of that. Being on the same *sofa*."

"You should be in the same head sometimes. Writing is hard."

Marilyn said it was a distinct pleasure to be with a man who used his mind for something besides a launching pad for cheap cons. She put her champagne glass on the coffee table and said she was going to slip into something that would make John Grape less comfortable.

"I have my creative moments, too," she told him.

Marilyn Champion reappeared a few minutes later in the doorway that led to the bedroom.

She wore a black floor-length nightgown.

"Hi," John Grape said.

Marilyn said, "*Yeah.*"

John Grape jumped.

"There's *this*," Marilyn said, turning her back to him as she squatted to flick on a stereo that was to the right of the doorway. "And there's *this*." She rose to her toes and clasped her hands over her head and struck a pose, giving an impression that somebody should have been lying unconscious at her feet.

Loud drumbeats came from the stereo speakers.

Marilyn turned to face John Grape, shook the gown off her shoulders, and made twenty or thirty muscles.

She's had some terrible childhood experience, John Grape thought. I remind her of her father. She's going to beat me up.

A bikini was underneath the gown.

The bikini top was little more than a couple of eye patches joined by a piece of thread.

The bottom resembled an untied bow tie, worn lengthwise.

Marilyn Champion's biceps, which were the size of tennis balls, were several times larger than her breasts. From the neck down, she appeared to have been put together on an assembly line.

"*Now*," she said, leaping forward on a drumbeat.

She handed John Grape a trophy she had won at a body-building contest a few weeks ago.

He made whimpering sounds and put the trophy beside him on the sofa.

The routine with which Marilyn Champion had become New England's best middleweight body builder lasted more than five minutes and featured poses that showcased her stomach, on which you could have scrubbed wool socks.

When each new muscle was thrust at him, John Grape couldn't think of anything to do except drink faster and applaud politely. He tried to remember how many stairs he had climbed getting in here and used his peripheral vision to search for emergency exits.

He would jump out of a window at the first opportunity.

She should have warned him.

He wondered what going to bed with a female body builder would be like. He guessed it would be like going to bed with a soft-drink machine.

He never got the chance to find out.

When Marilyn squatted like a baseball catcher, John Grape reached into his suit coat for a fresh pack of Camels. He put a cigarette in his mouth, held a lighter to its end, took a long drag, and wondered what ever happened to old-fashioned romance.

As a wisp of smoke left John Grape's mouth, Marilyn Champion turned off her stereo and moved softly yet powerfully to a window, which she pushed open with a little finger.

"There is no place in my life for anybody who has no willpower," she said.

"The way it seems to work is that you either have willpower or you don't."

John Grape took another puff on his cigarette.

Marilyn stepped back as the smoke floated toward the window.

Muscles rippled on her forearms.

An ash fell onto the wooden floor.

"John," Marilyn said, "I hate smoke. I hate it so much, I want to kick you in the neck."

"I'd appreciate it very much if you wouldn't."

John Grape looked around for something with which to defend himself, found nothing, then stepped quickly toward some curtains.

Marilyn took two big steps at him.

42   "Stay back." John Grape brought his cigarette to his lips. "You come any closer, I'll blow smoke on these curtains. The smell will be here for days." Marilyn stood still in the middle of her living room.

John Grape inched his way to the coffee table and grabbed what was left of the cheese; then he backed out of the apartment, holding Marilyn Champion at bay by placing two more cigarettes in his mouth and a lighter just under them.

5

John Grape sat up in bed from a hot sleep at 3 A.M. on a Thursday like any other with a new thought in mind: What if your book stinks?

He sincerely hoped this wasn't the case as he got out of bed and stumbled toward the kitchen, where he sat down at the table and reread the opening of his novel-in-progress, the variation of a perfect-murder story, which was 110 pages long, or about one-third finished.

The novel began: *She hated him.*

True, it had a subject and a predicate, not to mention a direct object.

But *damn*, it was a little . . . *short.*

The opening had seemed much more effective in the light of day.

Now it seemed rather flat.

He wiped perspiration off his forehead with a blank piece of copy paper and skipped ahead, landing on page 68.

There he had written: *His brains flew out of his head and for a brief instant looked like meatballs as they splattered against the kitchen wall.*

Oh, Lord God, John Grape thought, this does not look good.

The great majority of instants *were* brief. Brains like meatballs?

He got a beer from the icebox and paced around the kitchen, afraid to look at another alleged sentence. Four sips of beer later, he peeked inside the manuscript at page 94.

"Did you kill your husband?" the detective retorted.

44 Retortec'?

What ever happened to *asked*?

John Grape pushed up the sleeves on his nightshirt. There was no reason to come apart. All great works of fiction were rewritten, sometimes frequently. John Grape began fixing his novel, frequently.

He rewrote his novel for sixteen hours and produced two pages. It was tough and choppy going. The sentences averaged only five words. He was obviously pressing.

That he was having difficulty writing what he considered to be a great idea suggested that it was time to forget about pride; help, that was all he needed, counseling from a trained specialist. So on the one-month anniversary of his divorce, he got on with life by seeking advice from a psychiatrist.

He told Dr. Everett Mathison, who had a degree from Harvard, among other places, what it felt like to have been great once.

It felt swell at the time.

Then it felt bad.

Before John Grape had been great, he had taught writing at a nearby university. It was a tough way to make a living because you had to take orders from people who couldn't write their way out of a Roadrunner cartoon. The English departments at most major universities were full of people who spent their waking hours writing biographies of obscure people. They played it safe—they'd rather be reviewed by the *New England Quarterly Digest of Literature*, circulation thirty-two, than risk their ninety-five word sentences with critics from newspapers, many of whom, at least a *few* of whom, were nearly normal human beings.

Journals like the *New England Quarterly Digest of Literature* were written, edited, and read by people who worked in English departments; so the whole field of writing and reviewing obscure biographies was pretty much an inbred proposition.

If you got real lucky, you could even review your own biography about somebody like James Joyce's neighbor. Generally speaking, people who reviewed their own books got terrific notices; or at least *one* rave. Such a thing had happened to a professor who had an office two doors down from John Grape. Writing under the pseudonym of Gregory Chesterfield, an English teacher named Sid Potts wrote that his own biography of Chester Allen Arthur's mother had, "wit, charm, and motion-picture possibilities."

He got caught when he forgot who he was and signed the seventy-five dollar check he earned for writing the review: *Best wishes, Greg Chesterfield.*

John Grape had written himself out of this sideshow, working mornings and nights and between classes—a paragraph here, a page there, it all added up.

His last magazine-writing class included a man who wore a pith helmet to class; a brunette named Corbett who took a pistol from her purse one day after class and asked John Grape to please keep it for her because she could no longer trust herself; an elderly woman named Honeycutt who couldn't hear much; and a young woman named Martindale who wrote every other sentence with different colored ink.

After you have been great once, you experience the desire to realign your life so that you can be great full time instead of part time; so when John Grape received a lot of money for the motion picture rights to his novel, he quit teaching.

He shortly learned that plenty of free time did not guarantee success, or even literacy. He learned that you needed great ideas in order to sustain life as a novelist. He began to damn all the writers who had been born back before all the great ideas were gone.

He had almost come to believe that the composition of something reasonably worthwhile was like a religious experience. Perhaps writers were like disciples. Perhaps from time to time, God would bless a writer by passing along an idea with which to entertain the masses. Otherwise, why couldn't John Grape think of something original any damn time he wanted?

He told Dr. Mathison about the three books he had written after the *Class Act* trial.

One concerned the murder of some helpless little kids at a summer camp, a story that turned into a comedy halfway through and never got off the ground; the second novel was about a gang of bumbling crooks who

46   stole the statue of George M. Cohan from where it stood on Broadway in New York and then held it for ransom, the problem there being that the City wouldn't pay more than a couple of hundred dollars for George's safe return; and the third book was about a con artist who opened a literary agency to hustle some quick money, then became entangled with the tortured lives of dozens of promising writers.

Robert Redford returned the last novel with a quotation from the scriptures about undying faith.

None of these novels was much good. On a darker note, none was published.

On a more pleasant note, none was held against John Grape at a hearing questioning his sanity.

John Grape found himself explaining to Everett Mathison that writing three or four thousand double-spaced pages of drivel could really take it out of a person. And strain a marriage.

He had become aware of the many harmful side effects of accidental or premature greatness, as it related to the creative process—premature hangovers, premature coughing, and premature loneliness, just to name a few.

Hell was full of people who had been great *once.*

So John Grape had come to the conclusion that the search for something original to write had driven him to the edge of madness.

He told Everett Mathison about the divorce in great detail.

Then he told him about his current place of residence where just that morning, gunshots had rung out at dawn as the result of a little lovers' quarrel in Apartment 4 which, according to the officer in charge of crowd control, had turned into a hostage situation by the time the complex was evacuated. He never got around to mentioning the slight problem he was having with his work-in-progress—his inability to read it without gagging.

Dr. Mathison was pretty brave about the whole thing until he heard that the toilet in John Grape's apartment had gone on the fritz.

Then he buried his face in his hands.

"What are you doing?" John Grape asked.

"Never disguise your emotions," Everett Mathison said. "I'm crying."

John Grape had just depressed a highly respected psychiatrist.

He left ten minutes before the session was to end, saving fourteen dollars.

Based on Dr. Mathison's reaction, John Grape guessed that he was even unluckier than he was crazy.

He went straight to an emergency room and presented himself to a young woman, Rosemary French, her sign said, who sat at a desk behind another sign that said:

IF YOU HAVE CHEST PAINS, PLEASE MOVE TO THE FRONT OF THE LINE.

The IRS was going to love this—writing off a brain scan as a business expense.

"I'd like to have my head examined," John Grape said.

"What is the nature of your injury," Rosemary asked, putting on her glasses so she could see if there was any blood.

"None," John Grape said in reply to the question about an injury. Then Rosemary read from a form, word for word. Seeing as how every other patient was a potential malpractice suit, you couldn't be too careful. Nobody who worked for a hospital ad- libbed much; everybody played it by the book.

"Mr . . ."

"Grape, John Grape, like the flavor."

". . . are you in *pain?*"

"Not externally, no."

"Have you suffered a blow to the head?"

"No."

"Mr. . . . Grape." Rosemary put her pen beside the form. "This is an emergency room."

"And I don't feel well."

Rosemary sighed and picked up her pen. "Address."

John Grape gave it without enthusiasm.

"Occupation?"

"Self-unemployed."

Rosemary cleared her throat. "At what?"

"Couldn't you tell? Stand-up comedian."

Rosemary squinted, straight-faced.

48

"I'm a writer," John Grape said.

"Nature of . . . emergency."

"Incompetence."

"Incontinence?"

"No, in—"

"Impotence?"

"Incompetence!"

Rosemary played with her wedding ring.

John Grape said, "I don't want my temperature taken. No wheelchair. No frills."

"You want your head examined."

"That's exactly it."

"Method of payment? Medical plan, hospitalization group number?"

"Cash."

John Grape was told to have a seat and sat between a woman holding a screaming child and a vagrant.

"Beats hanging around the library all to hell, don't it," the vagrant said, mistaking John Grape for one of his own.

Barely.

He waited in a folding chair for around fifteen minutes while the emergency room staff took care of more pressing business like skinned knees and colic.

Then he was interviewed by a nurse carrying a clipboard.

She sat beside him and asked how he was feeling.

He said he was feeling sort of stupid.

"Dizzy spells?"

"No."

"Headaches?"

"The usual."

"Vomiting?"

"No."

"Seizures?"

"No."

"Trembling?"

"No."

"Blurred vision?"

"No."

"Chest pains?"

"No."

"Neck pain?"

"No."

"Mr. . . ."

"Grape."

". . . Grape. We could use a symptom."

"The mind drifts."

"Light-headed?"

"Empty-headed."

"People with symptoms have priority."

"Let's go with headaches."

John Grape sat quietly for another half hour.

Then they hooked wires to his head and rolled him under a machine that looked like something out of a science fiction movie. They monitored brain waves and took a few pictures.

According to the intern in charge of brains, this was John Grape's lucky day.

"You've got the mind of a twelve-year-old," the intern said, laughing at his joke. There was nothing wrong with John Grape's head, at least from the outside looking in.

"I might have known," he said, yanking off the hospital gown.

The intern said most people reacted a little more joyfully when they got to go home upright.

"I'm a writer. I've been having trouble concentrating. I thought there might be something misfiring up there. The wrong kind of food, some vitamin deficiency, too much whiskey."

The intern checked John Grape's tests again. "No, this is as good as it gets."

John Grape nodded and started putting on his clothes.

"Sorry," the intern said.

John Grape returned to his apartment and took a stiff brush and two cans of Lysol to it.

50 He opened all the curtains, cleaned out the icebox, scrubbed the oven, polished the bathtub, removed leftovers from the living-room floor and carried them and a waist-high stack of newspapers to the garbage bin, washed the dish, showered, and put on new jeans, new tennis shoes, and a new denim shirt.

He made a pot of fresh coffee and put a new ribbon on the typewriter.

He started to rewrite his novel.

He wrote: *She loathed and despised him.* This suited a psychological thriller more than *She hated him.*

As he completed the first sentence, the telephone rang.

He thought about letting it go. He couldn't take any more bad news. But there wasn't any bad news left. Maybe it was Deloris, wondering if he'd like to stop by for lunch. He turned off the electric typewriter and picked up the receiver.

"Send one of your books," John Grape's daughter said. "I need it quick."

She was calling from the private university in Massachusetts where she was a freshman.

Loud music was playing in the background; loud music, or somebody was sharpening tools.

"Ly," John Grape said.

"What?"

"Quick*ly*."

"Right. Now don't send the book about the nut who robbed his high school reunion. Send the *good* one."

"What's the rush?"

"I'm failing English."

John Grape pushed his coffee cup aside and demanded to know how anybody could fail a course based upon a person's native language.

"The teacher is an Arab," John Grape's daughter said.

"And you want to bribe him with one of my books?"

"I want to suggest there's untapped potential, you know, in the genes. Send it Federal Express, okay?"

"You're hoping nobody would fail the daughter of a person who wrote a book that was turned into a major motion picture?"

"Right. There's something else. I owe three and a quarter."

"Where," John Grape wondered against hope, "does the period go?"

"After the hundred. When you park in the faculty lot, it's forty bucks an hour."

"Obviously you haven't been parking in the faculty lot by the English building."

"I've been parking next to Theory of Team Sports."

"Interesting career possibilities," John Grape said, shaking his head. "Be a referee. Marry some volleyball player."

The line went dead.

John Grape called the telephone business office in the city where his daughter went to school and learned that she owed two and a quarter on last month's bill.

He didn't have to ask where the period went.

6

ort Goldberg had seen and heard it all.

He saw and heard it all the first month he was a literary agent, and he had been observing the reruns for twenty-eight years. The faces changed. The eyes didn't.

The same thing behind all those eyes. The desire to get lucky.

He frowned at his desk, covered with manuscripts, the most prominent being an epic about life in a small town, a 750-page monster that had been dragged in by a frail woman named Gladys Livingston.

Mort Goldberg hated novels about small towns for obvious reasons. Small towns were small because nobody wanted to live in one of those goddamn places. So along those lines, who could *possibly* want to read about bumpkins? There had to have been at least 15,000 novels written about small towns and their inhabitants; and Mort Goldberg was sure that he had read approximately 14,750 of them.

Mrs. Livingston's novel was about growing up down south.

"Dear Gladys Livingston," Mort Goldberg said into a tape recorder. "I read your novel with great interest. I think it needs a little more work. By this, I mean that we need to feel more atmosphere during the first . . . two or three hundred pages." Mort Goldberg picked up page one. "It could also stand some punctuation."

Mort Goldberg rubbed his eyes, then read the last page, page 750.

A young girl was talking to some birds on this page.

More to the point, the birds were talking back.   53

"Gladys, goddamn it, can't you *needlepoint* or anything?"

Mort Goldberg pushed the *Erase* button, scooted Gladys Livingston's book aside, and picked up a veritable quickie, a 498-page spy novel written by an engineer who had taken early retirement so he could write the story that had been rattling around in his head for thirty years.

"Mister Clayborn," Mort Goldberg said into the microphone, "what if I took early retirement to *build bridges*? See, listen, the reason everybody thinks writing is easy, the reason why everybody thinks he can write a book, is because people with enormous amounts of God-given skill *make* it look easy. Only it isn't, George, it's harder than anything, as your manuscript clearly indicates."

Mort Goldberg erased that, too; then he scooted John Grape's most recent effort front and center.

It was a twenty-page outline and the first thirteen chapters of a novel.

The package had arrived by courier a few days ago. Mort Goldberg glanced at the first page of the outline, then he took a big bottle of Pepto-Bismol out of his top desk drawer and had a few swallows.

"Is he still there?" Mort Goldberg said to his phone.

"Unfortunately," his secretary replied. She glanced out of the corner of her eye at John Grape, who had been waiting an hour and five minutes.

Mort Goldberg said he couldn't believe it.

"You talking about me?" John Grape tossed a magazine aside.

The secretary said, "No."

"Then why did you look directly at me when you said *unfortunately?*"

"I had to look somewhere, Mr. Grape."

"Does he look dangerous?" Mort Goldberg asked his secretary.

"Medium," she said.

"We need some metal detectors around here, put that in a memo."

John Grape stopped in the doorway of Mort Goldberg's office and knocked on the frame.

"John," Mort Goldberg said as he cleared a space on his desk, "You're looking . . ."

He was planning to say *good.*

54 But when he saw John Grape, he was rendered temporarily speechless. John Grape was unshaven, wore overalls, a stocking cap two sizes too small for his head, and tennis shoes. He started a cigarette from one still burning, brushed an ash off his beard, and coughed. He looked over Mort Goldberg's head and said, "What's that?"

This was framed on a wall: *His eyes shone brightly like two mice in the happy cheese of his face.*

Pleased to be off the hook about John Grape's appearance, Mort Goldberg grinned and said, "It's a pick-me-up. Every time I'm reading something and I don't think it can get any worse, all I have to do is look up. Immediately I know, there's worse."

John Grape looked around for an ashtray, then flicked the end of his cigarette into a pocket of his overalls.

"*Happy cheese of his face.* It was from some mystery novel. That line could put a smile on *anybody*."

"It's some line, all right," John Grape said.

"Yes sir, makes a person's own troubles seem insignificant."

"Did *I* write it?"

"Oh no, John, absolutely not."

"Whew," John Grape said, clearing some manuscripts off a chair.

"So." Mort Goldberg wondered what he was going to say next. He had planned to have his secretary tell John Grape that there was an emergency meeting that had just been called, one that was going to last well into the evening.

Blessedly, his phone rang.

"He snuck in while I was in the bathroom," Mort Goldberg's secretary said. "I guess I could always ring the fire alarm."

"Be my guest," Mort Goldberg said.

He hung up and shuffled some manuscripts.

"It doesn't work," Mort Goldberg's secretary said a few seconds later.

"What doesn't?"

"The fire alarm."

"Unbelievable."

"And I can't think of anything else to ring."

"I can. Your neck."

"So I guess you're on your own."

"An atrocity."

"Sorry."

Mort Goldberg couldn't think of anything to do except apologize for the delay and try to think of somebody to call and negotiate with for six hours.

"Today is Diet Book Day," he said. "Twenty-eight years and they still give me diet books. But that's okay, I'm pretty good at them. Here's the problem, John, it's why you had to wait so long. Monday, we're having the offices painted, so this *morning* becomes Diet Book Day. Monday is usually Gothic Romance Day, you with me so far?"

John Grape shrugged.

"You know why Monday is best for the Gothics?"

John Grape had no idea.

"Nobody can think straight Monday." Mort Goldberg smiled. "Anyway, with the place closed Monday morning, this *afternoon* becomes Gothic Romance Day. Diet books before noon, Gothics after. Very hectic. I have to make a couple of calls."

John Grape said that was fine—he had all the time in the world.

Mort Goldberg told his secretary to get an editor named Sam Bacon at Doubleday.

"For real?" she said.

"Did you know," Mort Goldberg said, waiting for the call to go through, "that I have *six* women living in a place called Oklahoma, writing Gothics?"

There was hardly any way John Grape could have known that.

"Six, it's a considerable percentage of the population in a city called Tulsa. Must be the wind, John, that's the only thing I can think of. Somebody's hair is not blowing on page one of a Gothic, you're screwed. I'm in Tulsa a year ago visiting my stable of Gothic Clydesdales, the front page of a newspaper from Ciudad Juarez, that's three thousand miles to the south, blows by. The wind in Oklahoma must inspire these women, it's the only explanation."

Mort Goldberg blinked as somebody came on the other end of his call.

It was an assistant to the editor he wanted. He told the assistant that he wanted to talk about a Gothic called *Cinnabar's Revenge.*

56   He was put on hold.

"The *names* in these Gothics." Mort Goldberg loosened his tie. "You know what cinnabar is? I looked it up. It's some sort of rock. It's *ore*." Mort Goldberg covered the bottom of his receiver more completely. "Rhapsody, Season, Pride, Fortuity . . . there's a guy named Jeep in one I skimmed last week. There were no *Jeeps* back when this book was set, for God's sake. You know my all-time favorite? *Roget*. Honest to goodness, John, somebody named a character after the guy who wrote the *Thesaurus*, which is where they get all those names in the first place."

John Grape put out his cigarette with the thumb and first finger of his right hand and deposited the remains into a pocket.

The editor at Doubleday came on the line.

Mort Goldberg had a good idea—he switched the call to a speaker box on his desk so John Grape, bless his heart, could hear for himself about the kind of fiction that was consistently bringing in solid money these days.

"*Sam*," Mort Goldberg said to the box on his desk, "you're about to make a fool of yourself, letting *Cinnabar* go for thirty thousand."

"Mort, I'm glad you called," the editor said. "We're having trouble with the ending."

"I think you're being picky here, Sam."

"You don't think the ending is too *depressing?*"

Mort Goldberg scooted a copy of *Cinnabar's Revenge* toward him and scanned a few pages. "I think you're confusing drama with depression, Sam. The woman's book sold out in places like Tibet. It's hard to go against the grain, looking at those kinds of numbers."

"You don't think having two people shot with the same bullet as they embrace after not having seen each other in twelve years is a bit *much?*"

Mort Goldberg, who had read *Cinnabar's Revenge* in about fifteen minutes when it came in two weeks before, turned to the last page to refresh his memory. "But Sam," he said, "they're only *wounded*." He flipped another page or two. "And they get all healed up in the Postscript."

"I'll give you thirty-two five Mort, and that's it."

"Sam, what are you worried about with endings. Nobody *reviews* these damn things."

"We're concerned about negative word of mouth."

"You think somebody's going to *admit* to having read this?"

"Thirty-two five, Mort."

"You're committing professional suicide."

"Thirty-five, and that's our last offer."

"I'll tell the author you're a good Christian, maybe that will help."

Mort Goldberg disengaged the call and told his secretary to get Gloria Golden out in Oklahoma.

"You just sold a Gothic Romance for thirty-five thousand *dollars?*" John Grape said.

Mort Goldberg shrugged. "It's why I wanted you to hear the conversation. There's no rule that says *women* have to make all the Gothic money."

"I would never degrade myself in such a manner," John Grape said, chewing the nail on his right thumb.

Mort Goldberg said to his writer in Tulsa, "Gloria, I think we need to talk about pseudonyms."

She said, "You don't like Gloria Golden?"

"I love it. It's just that when you're so prolific, its pretty hard to get top dollar for two or three books under one name at the same time. We need to cover all the bases."

"And you think I need *another* pseudonym?"

"At least one, yeah."

"What do you think about Diedre—long e's—Duncan?"

"It's perfect."

"You don't think Duncan is too . . . common?"

"No, trust me on this Gloria, Diedre . . . listen I forgot your *real* name."

"It's Agnes."

"Agnes. Duncan is great. Let's go with it on this next book."

"You're sure we can't get more than thirty-five thousand for *Cinnabar?*"

"There's no need to be greedy, we'll pound them the next time."

"The new book is almost finished."

"Fine, fine."

Mort Goldberg said so long to his Gothic Romance writer who wrote novels he couldn't read, living in a place he couldn't conceive.

"Duncan is a perfect name for her," he said to John Grape. "Reminds me of a yo-yo. A Duncan yo-yo, remember when we were kids?"

• • •

Mort Goldberg couldn't think of anybody else to call, or anything to do except to get this over with, so he turned his attention to the first page of John Grape's outline.

He grinned without seeming to mean it, then skipped ahead to the last page. "What we have here is a . . . is a . . ."

"Perfect *nonmurder*," John Grape said.

". . . nonmurder."

"Right."

"Okay, John."

"A *play* on a perfect murder. A variation. A twist."

"Ergo, a *non*murder."

"Yes."

Mort Goldberg swallowed hard and took off his tie. "Now John, it says here in your outline that this guy drops dead of a heart attack."

John Grape smiled and nodded.

"And this woman, his wife, comes out of nowhere . . ."

"Out of the next room."

". . . the next room and, and . . . *shoots him*?"

"You bet," John Grape said. "Is *that* original?"

"Blasts a *dead man*?"

"Nice twist, am I right?"

"With a shotgun?"

John Grape nodded and smiled some more.

"Is it hot in here, John?"

"No."

Mort Goldberg loosened the top button on his shirt. "Air conditioning must be busted."

"It's forty degrees outside."

"Bear with me." Mort Goldberg went back to the first page of the outline. "Guy drops dead . . . woman shoots dead guy."

"Right."

"John."

"What."

"*Why?*"

"To make a natural death look like a murder."

"John," Mort Goldberg said solemnly.

"Every other time, you see murders made to look like natural deaths."

"Johnny."

"*What*, damn it.

"Why in the name of everything good the human race stands for would somebody want to make a natural death look like a murder?"

"Good question." John Grape stood and stretched. "I had some trouble with that side of it."

Mort Goldberg wished a meteorite would hit the building.

"To cover up a robbery," John Grape said.

"Of her own *dead husband?*"

"That's correct."

"John . . ."

"Don't start that again."

"A robbery of what?"

"Money, Mort."

Mort Goldberg stacked all the pages together. "So in other words, this *nonmurder* is planned, some woman walks along behind this guy with a bad heart, a shotgun up her dress, waiting for him to drop dead and hoping he doesn't do it in front of Macy's?"

"It's mostly spontaneous."

"Mostly spontaneous." Mort Goldberg shook his head. "What about the coroner, those people can take an eyelash and tell you what killed a person. You going to kill off the damn coroner, too?"

"Maybe I will," John Grape said.

Mort Goldberg put John Grape's outline and manuscript in an envelope and slid it across his desk. "John," he said softly, "I'm in the business twenty-eight years, this is the most heartbreaking moment."

"It grows on you," John Grape said, frowning at the envelope.

"John, this wouldn't grow on a piece of old goddamn *cheese*."

"Meaning . . ."

"Meaning this is the worst idea I've ever heard of. Not only does it not make any sense, it's giving me a stomachache."

60   "I'll work on it some more."

"It's only because we're dear friends I can say this. *Don't* work on it."

John Grape blew a smoke ring at the ceiling and wondered aloud what Mort Goldberg would have advised a casual acquaintance.

"A life of crime," Mort Goldberg said.

John Grape leaned forward, picked up his outline and manuscript, then scraped four or five Gothic Romances, the telephone, and the speaker box off Mort Goldberg's desk.

As the last of the pages fluttered to the floor, Mort Goldberg told his secretary to bring a rake.

They went into the park and sat on a bench and spoke frankly about John Grape's career as a novelist.

"You plan to keep on writing?" Mort Goldberg wondered.

"That's a rotten goddamn thing to say," John Grape said.

They both drew in the dirt with sticks.

"I can't date. I can't write. All I can do is eat."

"I'll send over a few diet books."

John Grape threw his stick at a squirrel.

"Stop that," an old woman sitting on a nearby bench said.

"Mind your own goddamn business," John Grape told her.

"I sentence you to eternity in hell," the old woman said.

"I'm there. I'm throwing sticks at helpless animals and yelling at hags."

Mort Goldberg patted John Grape's back and said that if writing were easy, everybody would be doing it.

"Everybody *is* doing it."

"True. But most of them are doing it very badly."

"This is all her fault," John Grape said.

"The magic will be back one day," Mort Goldberg said.

They sat quietly for a couple of minutes.

Then John Grape said, "How about this. These people kidnap Miss America. Hold the whole *country* for ransom."

"Jesus *Christ*," Mort Goldberg said, jerking his head back as though a wasp had flown in front of his face.

"You don't like it?"

"It's a little . . . downbeat."

"I make it a comedy."

"That would help, all right. I read the other day they're doing a Broadway musical about alcoholism. Anything's possible I guess, John."

"A madcap fucking comedy."

"Give me an original way to pick up the ransom, we've got a shot."

"They rob court."

Mort Goldberg said, "Huh?"

"Some big trial where the evidence is a lot of drugs worth a fortune, or maybe even money itself. Diamonds. Whatever."

"The guys who take Miss America do this?"

"No, somebody else."

"Oh."

"We may have to take the chaperone, too."

"We're back to Atlantic City?"

"Miss Congeniality, we take a bunch of them."

Mort Goldberg stood and stepped away from the bench. "John, here's an idea. A little vacation, some fishing."

"Or rob some police station, where they keep all the valuable evidence pending trials. We rob the police station."

Mort Goldberg said he was going back to work.

John Grape had another stick and was making notes in the dirt about the novels he was going to begin work on this very evening.

Mort Goldberg crept away.

John Grape yelled out that he was sorry about scattering all the Gothics.

"Forget it," Mort Goldberg said, waving. "They'll probably read better restacked together at random."

7

Okay, she had made her point.

She had wanted a few things changed. John Grape stood corrected. It was time to acknowledge receipt of the message.

Say hello, that's what he'd do.

No big deal.

Hi, what's up.

Make a date for lunch, something like that.

No pressure. No obligation. Just hi.

But according to a recorded voice, John Grape's old telephone number was no longer in service. A new number for Deloris Worth was unlisted.

Drop by.

Knock.

Pull himself together first.

He stood in front of the mirror over the bathroom sink, brushing his hair left to right, same as always. But this time, it hurt more than usual. It felt like he was sanding his head.

The problem was easily identifiable: The hair at the crown of his head was thin; thin, as in almost nonexistent. He damned the top of his head and got a hand mirror and a tape measure from the medicine cabinet so he could update the damage.

He measured what was fast becoming a bald spot. The spot was now two and a half inches in diameter.

It had only been two and a *quarter* inches in diameter when he had moved into this apartment.

Next, he measured the distance from the tops of his eyebrows to his hairline, and compared this reading with an old mark on the wall.

He had lost another fourth of an inch up front. At this rate, he would be combing his hair with a toothbrush inside six months.

He tried to cover the spot where the hair was thin from several directions, first going straight back. That didn't work. He appeared to have been standing behind a jet engine when the pilot hit the switch. His hair went up, not back.

After that, he brushed his hair diagonally across the top of his head from the left front to the right rear. This created a swirling effect as his hair moved sideways from the part on the left side, then back and across some of the bald spot.

The new style was the best he could do; if he stood perfectly still in his bathroom, having just trained and sprayed his hair for ten minutes, the casual observer might guess that the bald spot was only an inch and a half in diameter, not the two and a half.

He turned sideways and looked at himself in the mirror.

He wore only boxer shorts, the waistband of which was obscured by an outgrowth of fat. His center of gravity had shifted downward six inches since the last time he had looked.

He reminded himself of a candle that was melting.

He turned away from the mirror and looked over his shoulder at the reflection of love bumpers that extended all the way around. He pinched and poked a few places. Even the undersides of his fingers were fat. He seemed to have been pumped full of air, like a Peking duck. Smiling at himself in the mirror, he had a hard time believing how stained his teeth had become from all the cigarettes and coffee and, probably, smiling.

He quit smiling.

John Grape spread a large towel on the bathroom floor and got down

64   and did push-ups until his heart started pounding and his arms shook under the strain.

He did two push-ups.

Then he rolled over onto his back, caught his breath, and did some sit-ups. He was better at them. He was able to knock off three before his pulse tried to jump out of his ears.

8

H e had a picnic on the curb across the street trom his house, dining on two quarts of beer, a pound of cheese, and a roll of salami.

This was a delicate bit of business.

John Grape had to decide if he should apologize or assert himself. He had some salami. He'd figure out the right way to handle this soon.

From where he sat wondering about what he should say, he could see dozens of birds circling the wooded hill behind his house. He loved birds, the goddamn cute little things, the way they turned in counterclockwise circles when they bathed in the stream out back. And when the dog would quit barking, he could hear the water from the creek as it broke over the rocks not far from his bedroom window.

"Be quiet, you're ruining my picnic," John Grape said to Duffy, the Scottie, who stood on the other curb and barked louder.

Deloris had won the dog at a raffle that provided aid to starving artists who were starving because they couldn't draw.

The dog was named for what it did best, which was sit on its duff.

"I'm warning you for the last time," John Grape said, putting a hunk of cheese on his picnic basket.

The Scottie showed its teeth and yapped some more.

"Have it your own way," John Grape said, standing.

• • •

66 Two deputies from the sheriff's office sat in an unmarked Chevrolet four-door about a quarter of a mile from John Grape's picnic.

They sat on a hill.

The driver, whose name was Rucker, raised some binoculars to his eyes and said, "There he goes again."

"What?" the other deputy, Ed, said.

"He kicked the dog right in the butt."

"It wasn't self-defense?"

"Ed, a person *committing* a crime is not entitled to that sort of protection under the law. Self-defense is reserved for the victim."

"I say we let him be," Ed said. He was married. "What have we got on him, anyway?"

"So far, we've got kicking a dog. We've got trespassing. Sitting on that curb violates a condition of the divorce decree. Public drunkenness. Maybe vagrancy. You name it, we've got it. Loitering. Littering."

"He's only lonely, that's all."

"We've had a complaint filed," Rucker said, adjusting the binoculars. "A divorce stretches a man thin. There's no telling what's inside that picnic basket of his."

"I bet it's only Spam."

"So what happens if while we're sitting here ignoring a complaint, he produces a weapon from the basket and starts killing people."

"I'm not taking the poor guy to jail, that's all I know."

"Ed, you keep talking like that, you can *accompany* him."

They stopped the Chevy next to where John Grape sat, still drinking beer and eating cheese. It was almost dark.

"How's it going?" Rucker said. "We're with the sheriff's office."

John Grape smiled. "Have you ever wondered why little birds turn in counterclockwise circles when they take a bath?"

"No," Rucker said. "Not hardly."

"I just figured it out. Instinct. Instinct, thought, what's the difference?"

"That's a real good question," Ed said. "Don't you think?"

"It's got possibilities, I guess," Rucker said.

"That's my house over there."

The deputies nodded.

"See the gravel around the front flowerbed? Hauled it in myself. Took a week. See the mimosa? Won a prize. You like redwood?"

"Who doesn't," Ed said.

"Oversized deck out back, right by the creek."

Rucker asked, "John, where's your car?" John Grape pointed across the street at a green Mercedes in the driveway.

"The . . . other one."

"Flat tire."

"How'd you get here?"

"Bus."

"John," Rucker said, "now I don't want you to take this the wrong way, but you have to move on."

"Feel that?" John Grape held up his right hand. "That's my breeze. I *bought* it."

Rucker said softly to his partner, "He's babbling incoherently."

Ed said, "He's only reminiscing."

Rucker doubted it. "John, I'd like to have a look at what's inside your basket there."

He took a flashlight from the glove compartment and shined the beam on John Grape, who held a large piece of Swiss cheese in front of his face and squinted through a couple of the holes.

"John, the nicest way I can put this is that you're a public nuisance. She wants you out of here. Therefore the county wants you out of here. Therefore *we* want you out of here."

"I'm here to apologize," John Grape said.

"John, you have to quit talking about things that do not have anything to do with the price of beans," Rucker said.

"Price of eggs," Ed said. "Hill of beans."

"Deloris Worth filed a complaint against you for violating the conditions of your divorce, one of which concerns habitual loitering without consent. You're not supposed to occupy space, transiently or otherwise, which includes in or on a motorized or nonmotorized vehicle, within five hundred yards of the outermost property-line boundary."

"She *what?*"

68   "Sitting here isn't healthy, John," Ed said. "It's like throwing yourself on an open coffin."

"Let's go." Rucker leaned back and opened a rear door.

John Grape stuck his hand into the picnic basket and said he wasn't going *anywhere.*

They drove off; it was that, or reach for their guns.

Next, they threw a net from a fish poacher onto John Grape.

They had parked a few blocks away and came at him from the rear—through some pine trees.

Ed threw the net.

Once airborne, it expanded from its carrying-size of about two feet into something resembling a big blanket. The net was made out of a prickly fiber that readily attached itself to a fish's scales, or to a person's hair or clothing.

John Grape had run out of cigarettes and was crawling along the gutter in search of a workable butt when the net settled over him. He smashed the quart beer bottle he was carrying, hacked away some of the net by his feet, and began hopping across the street toward his house, where he planned to dive in through the front bay window, then play things by ear.

He carried the neck of the quart beer bottle in his right hand in case he came across Deloris.

The Scottie took up the chase, became tangled in the net, and tripped John Grape, who started rolling in the general direction of his house.

"John, come back here," Ed yelled. "This is getting embarrassing."

Rucker put on some work gloves, twisted the ends of the net together, and dragged John Grape across the front yard toward the unmarked Chevy four-door.

As John Grape slid along on his back, his arms and legs arranged at awkward angles, he decided that this was no way to live. He had tried to get on with his life by working harder, and all he had to show for it was a bigger appetite. Being netted like a common madman was just about all he needed. If they were going to put him in jail for coming to say he was sorry, he would get in a few licks first.

Only what, he wondered as the skin on his shoulders started to disappear and the stinging began, could he possibly do that would give him pleasure?

About all he could think of was to knock Deloris unconscious.

Just draw back and flatten her.

Ed, Deloris, and her best friend, Bonnie, stood on the front porch. Deloris wore a smock covered with paint smears.

"What's going on here," she said. "Who have you got all wrapped up?"

Ed said, "It's only your . . ."

"It's nobody," Bonnie said. "A panhandler."

"Oh. At *night?*"

"It's nothing to worry about. Go back inside, I'll take care of it "

"Don't be too hard on the poor fellow."

"But . . ." Ed said.

Bonnie took Deloris inside.

Upon returning, she told Ed, "I'm the one who called you."

"Oh," he said. He leaned against the front door, which was closed, and wondered if he should be taking notes.

"She's undergoing therapy. Very *deep* therapy. Hypnosis. To get over *that.*"

They looked toward the curb.

Rucker had John Grape on his feet, leaning against the back fender.

"Oh," Ed said.

"She's making remarkable progress. And she doesn't need to have any bad memories brought back to the surface at this point."

"*You* called in the complaint?"

"The law is the law," Bonnie said.

Ed took this information to John Grape, and removed a pine needle that was sticking into his neck.

"She's having you flushed from her system," he said.

John Grape cleared his throat and gritted his teeth.

"These are not my words. It's a direct quote from the. . .*co*-complainant."

John Grape squinted at the porch, where Bonnie stood with her hands on her hips.

"Like an *exorcist?*" Rucker said.

"A therapist."

"Oh."

"Those are my thoughts exactly. Anyway, she's hard at work getting over the sight of you, the sound of you. They're pretending you're *dead*. She didn't even recognize you."

John Grape asked Ed to get him a cigarette butt out of the gutter.

Ed handed him a fresh cigarette. "Look at it this way, maybe she'll forget the alimony."

"John," Bonnie said, stepping off the porch.

John Grape held the net away from his mouth.

"If you promise to stop this, I'll tell them not to put you away."

Rucker said they got paid the same, either way.

"John?"

"Yes, I heard you. Being set free would be extremely pleasant. It's hard to get much writing done in jail with everybody banging everyone else's head off the bars."

"You *will* stop this."

"Sure, sure."

"You heard him."

"We heard him," Ed said.

"Mark my words, John, if you pull anything like this again, you'll be in big trouble."

John Grape would have thoroughly enjoyed marking Bonnie's words. He would have enjoyed marking them as they left her lips. He would liked to mark them with his fists.

Instead, he thought of a great idea for a book—it would be the story of how he got his house and the rest of his stuff back.

This would be a nonfiction book, a glorious proposition; he wouldn't have to *think* anymore. All he'd have to do is put on a pot of coffee and recall certain memorable events in his recent past, such as what it felt like to have been clipped by a lesbian judge; and then the last part of the book would only be a matter of taking good notes. Off the top of his head, the only thing that concerned John Grape was the fact that there wouldn't be an abundance of sex in his nonfiction book. At least *yet.*

Hypnosis?

Pretend he was dead?

John Grape smiled; he had no idea that Deloris found the memory of him working nineteen hours a day to be so . . . haunting.

Then he wondered if he was only kidding himself again. After a person had thought up 150 to 200 book ideas that turned out to be untranslatable, it was hardly worth the effort to get too excited before you hit page two. He wondered how this idea would hold up in the light of day. Most of John Grape's ideas didn't age well; most lost their charm proportionately as the alcohol left the bloodstream. But this one was hanging in there, two or three whole minutes after John Grape had come up with it.

He couldn't stop smiling, a very good sign.

He needed to try the idea out on somebody who wouldn't take him to court, wanting a cut, after correcting a little spelling.

So he stood quietly as Rucker took the net from around his head and shoulders.

"I thought he'd be drunker," Bonnie said to Ed, who guessed that being netted had a way of sobering a person up.

"Why's he *smiling.*"

John Grape heard the question and said it was because he had been visiting with God a few minutes ago, then he threw back his head and laughed.

It didn't sound like a particularly healthy laugh.

"Damn, John," Ed said. "Stop that."

The Scottie growled.

Bonnie had obvious second thoughts about giving him the gift of freedom.

"Get him in the car," Rucker said softly to Ed. "Let's get him to the bus stop."

John Grape looked into the bus at a man sitting on the front row and said, "On second thought, I'll take jail."

The passenger had greasy hair that extended past his shoulder blades.

"On you go," Ed said.

"Everything is going to be fine," John Grape said as Rucker helped him up the front steps and onto the bus.

The front doors closed. The bus rolled off, spewing fumes.

"There a florist still open?" Ed said, glancing at his watch.

"A little something for the wife?"

Ed nodded.

• • •

"Got a second?" John Grape said to the bartender, Clarence.

The bar was around the corner from the Shadybrook Apartments.

John Grape had walked quickly from the stop where he had hopped off the bus. Clarence stood by the cash register with his arms folded across his chest.

"I believe I can fit you into my busy schedule," he said.

John Grape was sitting alone at the bar.

Two men occupied a booth on the other side of the pool table.

They had been drawing on napkins for two hours.

Clarence sincerely hoped the big *X* they had drawn on one of the napkins did not represent *his* safe. He hoped the tiny squares were not *his* back windows. He hoped the two parallel lines behind the square stood for *somebody else's* alley.

Clarence would hate to have to crack their heads open. It got so messy.

That was about the size of it, this evening.

"And you might bring me another beer," John Grape said.

Clarence looked at the clock over the cash register and said Happy Hour had ended.

"Damn,"John Grape said. "In that case, bring me a Perrier with a twist."

"You're kidding."

"Yes."

"It's a good thing. I'd have to send out."

John Grape got a second beer, introduced himself, and said he lived in the apartments around the corner.

"I hope you're kidding again," Clarence said, opening a can of Coke for himself.

John Grape smiled and said yes, he lived there and he was a writer. "Books. Novels."

Despite the fact that this bar was twice removed from any tourist traffic—it was two turns from anything remotely historic, like a statue of a Revolutionary War hero—it somehow managed to attract all sorts of worldly types. Just within the month, Clarence had mopped up after a guy who said he knew Yogi Berra real good, a guy who said he had kicked Walter Cronkite's ass back in high school, and a man who said he used to date Mamie Van Doren.

John Grape could tell that Clarence didn't believe he was a writer—
Clarence yawned—so he got into his billfold and dug out a card that proved
he was a member in good standing of the Novelists' League of America.

Clarence grinned and shrugged, as if to take his yawn back.

"It can drain the life right out of you," John Grape said, putting his billfold
in a back pocket.

"What can?"

"Writing."

"You'll get no argument from me. I get brain lock everytime I try to think
of something to say in a one-inch ad for the local newspaper. Usually, I
wind up with something like *Cold Beer Here.*"

John Grape stared off into space a few seconds, blinked, and then said,
"Where was I?"

"Being drained of life."

John Grape had a swallow of beer and said he'd like to try out an idea
for a book he had just thought of on Clarence.

Clarence nodded at a stack of paperbacks by the cash register and said
he was a pretty tough audience. "Nights like this, it's read or start bankruptcy proceedings."

"It's an . . . adventure."

"I love adventures. Westerns, adventures, and mysteries, you can't go
wrong with any of them."

"It's about somebody who gets divorced, a man."

"Right," Clarence said.

"He fights it."

Clarence frowned and wondered how you did that.

"You take it to court, challenge certain things."

"Oh." Clarence said his cousin got divorced two or three months ago.

"Did he take it to court?"

"No, he took it to an insane asylum."

Clarence excused himself for a minute to serve some bowlers who had come
in to drown their sorrows. They were evidently very bad bowlers, because they
always stopped by to drown their sorrows on the way *to* the alley.

When Clarence got back, John Grape told him that this idea was being
shared in the strictest of confidences; you could never tell who might steal

a plot and peddle it to television. He said that if what they were talking about ever got out of the bar, he'd come back and burn it down.

Clarence started to ask John Grape if he liked having teeth in his mouth, then said, "Tell me this. Will you come back and burn the place down even if I *don't* say a word about this?"

, John Grape smiled and had some beer.

"She gets the house."

"We're back to the book."

John Grape nodded. "I want your honest opinion about this. Don't worry about my feelings. I have none."

"You've got it. I hate bad books."

"It's a great house. Parquet floors. Clear creek out back. So on and so forth. She gets most of the land. Most of the money."

"In other words, he gets wiped off the face of the earth."

"He . . . loses his job."

"Right."

"Starts running out of money."

"He must have been a real horse's ass," Clarence said.

"Not particularly."

"A bum."

"Not at all."

"Then why'd she divorce him?"

"General principles. She said she had stopped growing as an individual, had lost her identity, was fed up with his drinking."

"I don't like your female lead," Clarence said. "There's nothing wrong with drinking in moderation."

"He has no friends, can't get a date."

"*Brother.*"

"His daughter is failing English."

"Christ, this a little downbeat, don't you think?"

"He has no reason to occupy space, no hope for the future."

"I've seen happier books." Clarence reached for a Kleenex.

"He will never again enjoy the peace of mind and life-style to which he had worked so hard to become accustomed."

"I may wait until this one comes out in paperback," Clarence said.

"Then, as his faith, pride, and will are about to cease to exist . . ." 75

"He *kills the bitch*," Clarence said, leaning over the bar.

One of the bowlers looked up and said, "Good for him."

"No," John Grape said, finishing his beer. "He thinks of something better. I hope."

"Something more fun than wringing her neck?"

"He remarries her."

Clarence sniffed. "I think this book needs a couple of spies, some gratuitous violence."

"There's more," John Grape said.

"Another round," a bowler said. "What is this, do it yourself?"

"That's right, just like when you're in the mood for some sex," Clarence told the bowler. He turned back to the writer.

"Just between us, I think there *better* be more to it."

Upon Clarence's return from taking the bowlers a round, John Grape said, "He quits smoking."

"That ought to teach her," Clarence said.

"He quits drinking."

"What's next, *breathing?*"

"He quits eating, loses thirty or forty pounds." John Grape squinted at some notes he had made on the bus. "Simply put, he quits doing everything she didn't like."

"Simply?"

"Gambling."

"I hear quitting things you love is hard."

"It depends on what's at stake. What if a fortune is at stake?"

Clarence shrugged. "You're turning him into a sissy."

"He gets a new face."

"A new *what?*"

"Nose. The chins go."

"Go *where?*"

John Grape looked up from his notes. "Corrective surgery."

"Oh."

"Eyes, skin. He's in pretty bad shape. Has some new hair sewn in. Gets himself all fixed up."

John Grape turned his notes over.

Clarence tightened the lid on a salt shaker.

"This is pretty sweet," he said, "but I thought she didn't like *him*, not what he looked like."

"It's no factor," John Grape said, putting his notes in the front pocket of his shirt.

"And she'll remarry him because he's suddenly such a nice guy?"

"Something like that."

"Because he quit smoking?"

John Grape nodded.

"And lost some weight."

"Yes."

"And had his face sliced open."

John Grape smiled.

"You'd think from talking to my cousin there was more to getting your stuff published than that."

"There is."

"So what's the big finish?"

"She doesn't know it's him."

Clarence took a glass from a shelf behind him and drew himself a beer. He sprinkled some salt on his wrist, licked it off, then had a couple of swallows of beer.

"You're right," he said. "That's better than killing her."

"This is the worst service," a bowler said, "that I've ever had in a bar."

"You mean *not* had," another bowler said.

"Not had," the first bowler said.

"You owe nine dollars," Clarence said. "You'll have to forgive me. We're talking literature."

"Well, there goes thirty seconds," the second bowler said.

The first bowler put $9.05 on the counter and led his team out the front door.

Clarence put the nine dollars in the cash register and the nickel in a cup and began pacing back and forth in front of where John Grape sat at the bar.

"Tear it apart," John Grape said.

"I'm thinking."

"Any weakness at all."

"This is *good*."

"You're just trying to sell beer."

"If I was trying to sell beer, I'd say it was bad."

"So you would."

"I like the motive. The *motives*. Greed. Hate. Revenge."

"Absolution."

"You've covered all the bases with motives. It's going to hurt the guy, getting his face cut."

"Yes."

"But who wouldn't be willing to hurt for a lot of money."

"Yes."

"She wouldn't recognize him?"

"No."

Clarence stopped pacing.

"That was a stupid question," he said. "*You're* the writer. Of course, she wouldn't recognize him."

John Grape frowned.

Clarence started pacing again. "You're saying people *can* change," he said.

"Yes."

"Inside out."

"Yes."

"If there's enough motivation."

"That's exactly it."

"And if they've got enough money to have all the work done."

"Yeah," John Grape said, staring soberly at his beer.

"So *give* him enough money."

"All right."

"I just thought of a scene you can use," Clarence said, topping off John Grape's beer. "He's off getting carved up, the woman, the one who tossed him out, she falls in love with some guy."

John Grape winced slightly and said there were laws governing how

78   quickly people could remarry; but there was always Las Vegas, wasn't there.

"What in the hell are you talking about?"

"I was just thinking out loud."

"About what?"

"The fact that she might fall in love with somebody."

"What do you mean, *might.* Type the damn scene in, she *does* it."

John Grape nodded.

"I like to let my characters react spontaneously, just like real people."

"Anyway, she falls in love with somebody, your guy comes back all changed and blasts his ass off."

John Grape had a *lot* of beer.

"How about this," he said. "He wins her away from the guy, charms her back."

"Boring." Clarence shook his head. "You need some blood and guts in the book somewhere. "Listen to this. While he's having his face chopped, the woman turns queer, how's *that* for a kicker?"

John Grape closed his eyes.

Clarence asked what he was doing.

John Grape said he was imagining how the character in his book would feel if he came back and discovered his ex-wife was in love with either a man *or* a woman.

He guessed the character would feel bad.

But he would always have his health, that was something.

"I never knew a writer projected so much of himself into a book," Clarence said.

"Yes, it accounts for the emotion," John Grape said.

"There's one problem with the whole structure of the thing," Clarence said after he took some drinks to three men who came in and started playing gin. "It's the one thing that could keep you off the best seller charts."

"I wouldn't be surprised," said John Grape, who was getting rather sloppy.

"The way I see it is that people don't change because they're never really desperate enough to compromise their standards, to quit doing what they enjoy."

"I wouldn't be a bit surprised," John Grape said, straightening himself on his stool.

"So there you have it."

"Where?"

"The critics will nail you on it."

"What?"

"The guy is going to quit smoking, drinking . . ."

"Eating."

". . . and he's going to start doing things . . ."

"He's hated, that's right."

"And get cut."

"You bet."

"There's the basic problem. Things could *never* get that bad, bad enough to make a person give up something like gambling, on top of all the rest."

John Grape laughed. And started a cigarette.

"I mean, it's obvious, isn't it," Clarence said, wiping some beer off the counter. "There's no such thing as desperate enough. Or somebody would have changed by now."

"Maybe nobody thought of it," John Grape said, taking some money out of his pocket.

"Maybe."

John Grape covered his tab, tipped Clarence five dollars, thanked him for the ear, and headed for the door.

"Maybe your guy is deaf and dumb," Clarence said.

John Grape waved over his shoulder and told Clarence he'd keep him informed.

"If you can make things bad enough for him, I'll buy *two* copies."

John Grape missed the door on the first try and hit his forehead on the frame.

How's that? John Grape wondered, with regard to bad enough.

9

It took John Grape the better part of two days to find a reasonably priced private detective.

Most private detectives came complete with sophisticated surveillance equipment. The one John Grape finally hired was named Louis Archibald. He came with an appetite. He ate two sandwiches during the interview, and it wasn't anywhere near time for a meal.

"Don't let this place fool you," Archibald said, nodding at his cramped headquarters. "The city is my office. This is like a big post office box. It's a place to open mail."

He said that although he hadn't written the book on divorce-related work, he had added a few footnotes. He then tried to sell John Grape a Family Pak on adultery that included color photographs and fifteen minutes' worth of videotaped discreet meetings.

But all John Grape wanted was for Louis Archibald to have a look at Deloris Worth a time or two a week in different places—a couple of hours here, a few there. No trucks with one-way mirrors. No video cameras. John Grape wanted to know what his ex-wife was up to, generally speaking.

"Cheaply speaking," Archibald said.

He was instructed to stay alert for a change in Deloris Worth's life-style. If, for example, she became romantically involved, John Grape would appreciate hearing about it.

"There's not too involved anybody can get in twenty minutes on a street corner," Archibald said.

John Grape made the point that over an extended period of time, he was certain that Archibald would be able to notice even the slightest break in routine.

"How extended?" Archibald wondered.

John Grape said it could be a while.

Archibald put down some potato chips and reached for a contract.

John Grape penned in a clause that excluded snacks from ordinary business expenses.

He wrote about being married. He wrote about having a book made into a major motion picture. He wrote about being divorced. He wrote about living in an apartment where the gas stove sometimes came on without being asked. He touched upon the all-consuming desire to think of something else great to write about.

Fun stuff, this nonfiction; until you had brought everything up to date. Once John Grape's story had caught up with his life, he had a cigarette and a cold beer and wondered what he should quit first in order to get this ultimate self-help book of his off on the right note.

He decided to quit smoking and drinking later. Gambling—that was a logical starting point.

The closer John Grape got to the time when he would have to stop doing things he enjoyed, the more nervous he became.

But he wasn't pleased about certain physical aspects of his life—there was no denying that. He could barely get two belts he wore in college around his middle. He disliked everything his current image reminded him of; so in that respect, all he had to lose was some depression. No matter what happened, he would come out of this healthy.

If his idea for getting his house and money didn't work, he could always marry some beautiful widow. Turn his magnificent idea into fiction.

Now, *there* was a chilling thought.

That becoming fit could be written off as research was a pleasant enough prospect.

82   So he got his affairs in order—he boxed and stored his belongings and made the necessary reservations—and then he went out to quit gambling.

A person couldn't quit something he wasn't doing.

10

John Grape's idea of a good time was gambling until he dropped at a place like the Gold Dust Casino.

The Gold Dust Casino was conveniently located within staggering distance of downtown Las Vegas. It was about a half mile from what there was of the city's business district. This was not the kind of neighborhood where you'd wear a mink at three in the morning; it was probably not the kind of place where you'd wear a coonskin cap, either.

The lounge act at the Gold Dust Casino was a woman who wore her heart on her sleeve, almost literally—her substantial breasts flowed over a low-cut gown and were supported more by her forearms than her bra. A card on her piano made public her name, which was Deedee McIntyre.

"Damn it," she said, forgetting the lyrics to "Moonglow."

Her piano was on an elevated platform near where John Grape sat playing roulette.

She interrupted the theme from *Lawrence of Arabia* to say to a tourist who had drunk too much, "Thanks a lot, friend, you just put a dollar bill in my *drink* glass, not the tip bowl. You ought to get out of the house, the *cave*, more."

Now wait just a minute, John Grape thought, stretching: What am I doing here?

After thirty or so seconds, he remembered.

Having some fun.

84   Putting his life back together.

Seeing as how this might be the last fun he would have for quite a while, perhaps ever, he wanted it to count.

His waitress was pleasantly mature—she seemed forty or so. She wore a skimpy maid's costume. A name tag read *Helen*.

She didn't wear the skimpy maid's costume in a particularly sexy manner; rather, she appeared to be waiting for a doctor to examine her.

"What's on sale?" John Grape asked.

"My fourteen-year-old," Helen said. "You can have him for next to nothing."

"You doing anything later?"

"Touring Europe."

"Not *that* much later. Tonight."

"Oh." Helen shifted her weight from her left side to her right. She looked at the stack of big bills, fifties mostly, in front of him and whispered into his ear, "Filling out police reports. Helping them get a line on the one who mugs you."

John Grape smiled and told Helen that he'd have one of those, nodding at her tray: *Tahitian Moonbeams, ninety-nine cents, today only.*

The card appeared to be at least a month old.

"What's in it?"

"It varies. Little umbrellas. Rum."

"And hit the songbird," John Grape said, nodding at Deedee McIntyre, who sat frowning at some sheet music. "This is my going-away party."

Helen looked around for more revelers.

"I'm giving it to myself."

"When does it start?" Helen said.

John Grape devoted ten minutes to getting a feel for the roulette wheel, losing a number of five dollar bets on red and black. He'd bet five dollars on a number inside a red circle, then the little silver ball would drop into a black hole, and so on and so forth.

There was one other player at the wheel, a man wearing a big cowboy hat. He'd bet against John Grape on every roll. After a few minutes, he was fifty-five dollars to the good, the most he had ever been ahead in his life.

"I'll let you know when I'm going to start trying," John Grape said to the guy wearing the cowboy hat.

"Trying? What do you mean, *trying?*"

John Grape lost five dollars more on black.

The man under the hat won ten dollars.

"You trying yet?" he asked.

"No, I'm just kidding around."

"Be sure and keep me posted."

The Gold Dust Casino looked more like a meeting place for the local chapter of Alcoholics Anonymous than a gaming establishment. A few fidgety people wandered about, talking to themselves. Even the people operating the tables were on the disheveled side. The man in charge of the roulette wheel—he had *Ronnie* stitched over a shirt pocket seemed to have shaved with an unsteady hand this morning, probably while the bathroom was spinning.

John Grape ordered another Tahitian Moonbeam, switched from red-black to odd-even bets, and lost seven out of eight.

Deedee McIntyre said, "I'd like to dedicate this next one to the heavyset guy in the black shirt, the one who couldn't pick the right color after the fact. From *Promises, Promises,* starring . . . what was his name, he's been around forever, Jerry somebody, composed by the guy married to Angie Dickinson a while, ah, forget it."

"Hey, bear down up there," said a man named Charlie Catalino, nick-named Pinkie because of the large diamond rings he wore on both little fingers.

John Grape finished his second Tahitian Moonbeam and slid ten one-hundred-dollar bills onto the square reserved for betting odd numbers.

"Changing a thousand," Ronnie said.

Pinkie Catalino, who was a pit boss, nodded and yawned.

"What chips do you want?" Ronnie asked John Grape.

"I don't want any chips," he said. "Just yet. I'm betting the thousand on odd."

The man accompanying the cowboy hat wished he had brought the grocery money from home; all he had brought was the medicine money.

"Pinkie," Ronnie said.

Pinkie Catalino, having just shooed away a customer who had spilled beer on a blackjack table, strode briskly to the roulette wheel and said quietly, "How about we don't call me Pinkie at the top of our lungs, in front of guests."

Ronnie shrugged. "Mister Catalino, he wants to bet a thousand on odd."

"There's a problem?" John Grape said, ordering another drink.

Pinkie Catalino said, "Heavens no, Mr. . . ."

"Grape."

"A what?" Helen said.

"It's my name."

"Oh. I thought you were ordering something *else.*"

"You staying with us, Mr. Grape?"

"*Staying* with you?" John Grape looked up at all the mirrors. "There are rooms up there?"

"We have a number of mobile home hook-ups in the back," Pinkie Catalino said. "The only such facility in town that offers *room service* to our motorized guests."

"No, I'm not . . . parked here."

"I see."

Pinkie Catalino was tan. He had a lot of hair and wrinkles. He reminded John Grape of one of those singers out of the sixties named Frankie or Bobby.

"But next time I'll stay here, I promise."

"It's no problem." Pinkie Catalino folded his hands together in front of him, cleared his throat, then asked if John Grape would please excuse him a second.

Pinkie Catalino and Ronnie turned their backs to the roulette wheel.

Ronnie asked, "What's wrong?"

"Just stand there," Pinkie Catalino told him, twisting his right hand forward and his left hand backward. "These goddamn diamond rings got stuck together."

The silver ball made eight or ten revolutions, then dropped to the bottom part of the wheel, down with all the numbered holes. It hopped a few inches into the air, then skipped over about a dozen holes before falling into the one marked twenty-nine.

"Jesus," John Grape said, "do you win anything extra for hitting your age?"

He decided not to quit gambling just yet.

Now they threw some money around in the Black Chip Club, which was a big room on the second floor, toward the front of the building.

The Black Chip Club was reserved for the serious gambler who didn't want to rub sob stories with the reprobates down below. The Black Chip Club was named for the color of a hundred-dollar chip. It had a few blackjack tables, a few crap tables, a few roulette wheels. It was decorated with the kind of wallpaper you feel—fuzzy, velvety, purple stuff. The place smelled of last year until Helen went at it with a big can of herbal air freshener.

"You're not going to believe this," John Grape said, sipping still another Moonbeam, "but I am, I *was,* a problem gambler."

"What *is* this fucking guy," Carmen "Bumper to Bumper" Trafficante, a vice-president in charge of hanging onto money, said softly to Pinkie Catalino. He replied, "Some clown that got hot."

John Grape kept talking to all his lucky friends who had come upstairs with him. "I've had eight straight losing years on pro football, never won a *dime* in a casino."

"No kidding," the guy with the cowboy hat said. His name was Bill, and he had started betting along with John Grape.

"This character has hit *how many* in a row?" Carmen Trafficante said.

"Eight, nine. Odd, black, red, goofy crap, no rhyme or reason."

"What of ours has he got in front of him?"

"Right at ten grand, Carmen, maybe a little more. The thing is, he's hot, he's got an aura. I hated to bother you, but he's got this look, he's liable to do anything."

"Aura's ass." Carmen Trafficante frowned at John Grape.

"Now where was I?" John Grape said after he ordered a round for the house.

"Losing a lot," Bill said.

88   "Yeah, I lost at everything, baseball, you name it. You know what I think? My subconscious brought me here, not for a good time, but to get the poison out of my system, to hit rock bottom, to reach the point where there's nowhere to go but up."

"*That* does it," Pinkie Catalino said, taking a step forward. "Nobody calls *my* place of employment rock bottom."

"Please don't scare him away with *our* money, *okay*?" Carmen Trafficante muttered.

Pinkie Catalino said, "What rock bottom, friend?"

John Grape looked around the Black Chip Club. "Vegas."

"See, he's only calling our city rock bottom, not the structure here," Carmen Trafficante said, faking a smile.

"A man calls my city horseshit, he's calling me horseshit."

"You don't even live in the city limits."

"I hate to interrupt," John Grape said to either of them, "but what about the thousand-dollar limit?"

"What about it?" Carmen Trafficante said.

"It's . . . cumbersome."

"Well then, fuck it," Carmen Trafficante said as he started to light a long, thin cigar that was already lit; a sign of weakness that caused Bill to nudge John Grape in the ribs.

John Grape touched the felt in front of him.

Bill, Helen, and Deedee McIntyre stood behind him, sipping drinks.

Ronnie wiped lint off the wheel.

"He hits some number on the pecker with ten grand, this place is a bowling alley, a skating rink, a used car lot," Pinkie Catalino whispered.

"I like the odds he doesn't hit a number," Carmen Trafficante said.

"How about this. We cheat his ass off."

"He's with the Gaming Commission, they're starting to send people around pretending to be players, we cheat his ass off, this place is one of those things you said, only we're not checking out bowling balls, we're in with the fucking criminals checking out tunnels."

Pinkie Catalino nodded. "So we leave it with the Almighty." Pinkie Catalino nodded some more as he closed his eyes and said a little prayer.

"Then if he hits a number, we take out a gun and shoot him."
Pinkie Catalino opened his eyes and smiled. "Good. Insurance always makes me feel better."

Besides numbers from one to thirty-six, a zero and a double zero were also on the roulette wheel.

People who bet a single number went against odds of 38to1, but collected by only 36to1; this house advantage kept Pinkie's fingers warm.

"Let's gamble," John Grape said.

He slid half of his chips onto the square with zero in the middle, and the other half onto double zero.

"It's only food for our baby," Bill said, dividing the eight hundred dollars he was ahead on the numbers John Grape had bet.

Deedee McIntyre split one hundred dollars on the zero and double zero. Helen halved fifty dollars on the same.

"What ever happened to loyalty?" Pinkie Catalino said.

"Fifty-five hundred and seventy on the zero, likewise on the double zero," Ronnie said, arranging the chips in neat stacks.

"One of those hits, we're looking at devastation to the tune of . . . two hundred thousand and change," Pinkie Catalino said.

Carmen Trafficante no longer cared about maintaining an image of quiet confidence—he yanked off his bow tie, slung it aside, and moved next to Ronnie.

"Spin it," he said.

"There's one thing I should mention," John Grape said over his shoulder. "I usually do better after I have a feel for the table." He ran his left palm over the numbers on the felt. "This one still feels unfriendly."

"Follow your instincts," Helen said.

"I'm speechless," Bill said.

Deedee McIntyre said that it had been her experience to note that wishy-washy people usually lost.

John Grape frowned at the felt, then said, "We're only betting a buck apiece this time."

He pulled the rest of the chips toward him.

• • •

90   The silver ball went:

Hop.

Hop, hop.

Hop.

Hop, hop, hop.

Clunk.

It settled into the slot next to double zero as though it had been drawn there by magnet.

Deedee McIntyre screamed, "You owe me a *fortune.*"

John Grape came to rest facedown on the felt.

"Honest to God," Carmen Trafficante said into a telephone. "This clown's got fifty-one hundred on zero and the same on the double zero, there are some others with him, my *employees*, can you believe it? Then right before Ronnie drops the ball, he pulls back, they all pull back, bet a buck each. Wanted to get a *feel* of the club table. No, the guy is alive, I can see his ribs moving. Put on something transparent, we'll go to a nice place, get something to eat, celebrate. No, not *here*, Gloria, I said somewhere nice didn't I?"

Carmen Trafficante stood beside John Grape, who hadn't moved much after ten minutes.

"How do I work this thing?" Pinkie Catalino asked, squinting at the front of an Instamatic camera as though it were a Rubik's Cube.

"You punch a button."

"Which button?"

"Punch them all."

Pinkie put the camera to his eye and started punching everything that moved.

"I want this blown up the size of a movie poster," Carmen Trafficante said, resting his right hand on John Grape's shoulder.

"More bad news," Bill said into John Grape's ear. "It came up twenty-two, even, you lost another grand. You've got one thousand of their money left in front of you, plus five grand of your own. What's the plan?"

Bill put his ear near where John Grape's mouth touched the felt.
He listened, nodded, and said, "Right."
He moved ten hundred-dollar chips to the odd square.
"Bets down," Ronnie said.
Bill, Helen, and Deedee McIntyre made bets on even.
Ronnie spun the wheel and dropped the ball.

Two guys wearing tan jumpsuits with Gold Dust Casino on their backs carried John Grape out the back way—down the service elevator to an alley full of boxes.

Helen flattened a few of the boxes and the big men in jumpsuits put John Grape on top of them.

"I want ten percent of what everybody won betting against him," Helen said.

"He cost me two grand when he chickened out up there," Deedee McIntyre said.

"Let's have it."

Deedee McIntyre handed over sixty-five dollars.

Bill gave Helen eighty-two dollars.

She added twenty dollars of her own to the small roll, and tucked the money into an outside pocket on John Grape's sport coat.

"So much for the rumor that drinking too much is a bad thing," Bill said. "He passed out while he still had eight hundred dollars of his own money left."

Pinkie Catalino told a security guard to stay in the alley until John Grape woke up—just another example of the personal touch that made the Gold Dust Casino the perfect place to visit after a catastrophic divorce.

PART TWO

1

ohn Grape stood at the edge of some desert outside Phoenix, wondering if he had lost his mind, not that it would be any great loss.

Books devoted entirely to losing weight sometimes sold millions of copies, that was one thing to remember.

He blew a drop of perspiration off his nose, looked at a cashier's check for $33,789.34, shook his head, and put the document on which his net worth had been recorded in a pocket before a buzzard swooped down and stole it, mistaking it for something edible.

He had kept the cashier's check in a safety deposit box at a bank while he was in Las Vegas. It was a good thing. Otherwise, he'd have probably bet $33,000 on a game of Keeno. It's doubtful he would have won. He had left right at $4,800 cash at the Gold Dust Casino. Not bad at all. He figured he must have been hot at the tables. Judging by the way he felt, $4,600 of the $4,800 had to have been spent on whiskey.

Arizona reminded him of his attic—there didn't seem to be an abundance of air present.

Warm sunshine hit his face. He stood in front of a group of buildings that were surrounded by a chest-high wall. According to the cab driver who had brought him here, stucco repelled the heat. It didn't do much for John Grape either.

The buildings reminded him of a retirement community or even a

96   minimum-security penal facility. The roofs were tile. The main gate was wrought iron. Lots of sand was behind him—sand and lizards.

If it was this warm in *February*—it had to be at least 75—John Grape wondered about July. You could probably fry a chicken on the sidewalk then. The brochure advertising this place hadn't concerned itself with average summertime temperatures, obviously because there was nobody to record them.

He wondered what people did for a breeze out here.

Ran, he guessed; that, or put the convertible top down and headed north.

He looked at his watch. It was ten minutes until noon—check-in time.

He smoked one last Camel and threw the remainder of the pack onto the desert, but was immediately uncomfortable with that decision; so he strolled onto the sand and buried the remaining dozen cigarettes, carving a hole in the hard earth with the heel of his right loafer.

He measured the distance from the buried Camels to the street—twenty-three feet—and marked the spot against some kind of growth on the horizon, a mound that could have been in another state or country, as the horizon seemed a two-day drive away.

A person couldn't be too careful here on Uranus, where the convenience stores were far and few between. John Grape finished a can of Budweiser and walked toward the front gate. There was a sign over it that read: *Sunrise.*

There wasn't a cloud anywhere.

Moving about under a cloudless sky make John Grape feel edgy. It was as though he was walking around in a big glass room that didn't have any curtains.

There was no place to hide.

"Hi, welcome to Sunrise, I'm Skipper," said a blond young man as he swung open the front gate.

"Hi, I'm Annette," John Grape said.

The joke flew over Skipper's head and died a fast death out with all the centipedes.

"Annette?"

Skipper raised his eyebrows.

"The Mouseketeers. They used to introduce themselves Hi, I'm Patty, Hi, I'm Jimmy, at the first of the television show."

"Right," Skipper said with mock understanding and real enthusiasm, even though it was obvious that he had no idea what the man was talking about. "Over here, please."

He walked to a little hut and signed John Grape in, presenting him with a packetful of maps and policy statements that sounded like sermons.

"There another way out of here, Skip?"

Skipper, sensing another joke, laughed.

"Well, *is* there?"

"Uh, sure."

Skipper hadn't run away with the circus. He had probably been born backstage at an *Up with People* concert. During the registration process, he offered John Grape some shriveled orange things. "Steamed apricots." Steamrolled was more like it.

John Grape chewed until his jaws got sore, then deposited the endless slow-food snack in a garbage can.

Before setting off on a quick tour of the facilities, Skipper smeared some white stuff on John Grape's nose for protection against the sun. The tour, taken at a dog-trot, featured quick looks at the golf course, tennis courts, and swimming pool. It ended in the managing director's office.

Wolfgang Zimmering had started Sunrise thirteen years before—built it with his bare hands, John Grape assumed, judging by the man's physique.

He wore a tan T-shirt like some skin he was about to shed. The only things about him that were not in perfect condition were his hair and eyes. He wore glasses. There was a crew cut on top of his head. He sat behind his desk, glowering at John Grape's file—his personality profile.

During the thirteen years he had owned and operated one of the most respected health resorts in the world, and during the previous ten years when he had served as Director of Fitness at a spa in Stuttgart, he had never seen anybody like this man—anybody *alive.*

And although he was in the business of dealing with the sloven at close quarters, wasting time on the hopeless was another matter.

There were several cigarette burns on the questionnaire John Grape had mailed in; and also a number of smart-alec answers to serious questions like *What are your hobbies?*

John Grape had answered: *Sleeping.*

"It will surprise you to know," Wolfgang Zimmering said, looking over the top of his glasses, "that we are within a month of being the same age."

"Who's the oldest?" John Grape wondered.

"You are, by . . . nineteen days."

"Well, you can't take it with you, that's been my motto. Up to now, of course."

"Take what with you?"

"Good health." John Grape grinned.

Wolfgang Zimmering made a note on the file and turned to page two.

"You smoke?"

"Socially."

"You drink?"

"Drank. Smoked. You're looking at the new me."

"You are grossly overweight."

"It's a good thing you don't charge by the pound," John Grape said, sensing a personality conflict in the making.

"You don't play golf or tennis."

"That's *bad?*"

Wolfgang Zimmering tapped the file on the desk.

John Grape said, "Can we go off the record?"

Wolfgang Zimmering closed the folder.

"I'm starving to death."

Wolfgang Zimmering rose to a height of about six three and walked to a window overlooking a swimming pool where a women's exercise class was in progress.

"Mr. Grape," he said over his shoulder, "we are very serious about becoming well here. This is not a decoration." He nodded at a sign over his desk that said: DISCIPLINE IS THE SECRET OF LIFE.

John Grape covered two coughs.

"Please remember this. Truth is a conduit to wellness." Wolfgang Zimmering leaned over his desk and looked seriously into what remained of John Grape's eyes. "And the truth of the matter is that I am concerned about your attitude."

So this was what the brochure meant when it said you'd feel right at home here, John Grape thought; this guy was everybody's *Mrs.*

John Grape ate a raisin from a bowl on the managing director's desk. Then he had another raisin.

Then another.

Then ten or fifteen.

Wolfgang Zimmering moved the bowl, sat down, and reopened the file. "If you are not completely serious about becoming well, or if you are not capable of dealing with the truth, you should leave with your full deposit."

John Grape made a muscle with his right bicep.

He got a cramp and rubbed it out.

"Ouch, goddamn it," he said.

"You have applied for two weeks here. The program commences with a physical examination. If you choose to leave prior to the completion of your session, you will be required to pay approximately ninety percent of the full tuition."

"There a machine around here where a person can get a little extra burial insurance?" John Grape asked.

Three doctors and two nurses looked down at him as though he had just slithered out of a garbage dump. Which, so to speak, he had.

He lay on an examination table, wearing only baggy boxer shorts.

"Well, what say we have a go at it," a doctor said, pushing up the sleeves on his smock."

"I wouldn't be surprised if Sandcastle sent him here," a nurse said. "As a practical joke."

Sandcastle was a spa on the other side of town.

They almost had to drill to find a heartbeat.

One of the doctors found a pulse in John Grape's neck, followed it downward a bit, then lost it in his chest.

Various tests revealed that John Grape had high blood pressure, a high cholesterol reading—high everything except self-esteem.

When they put him on the treadmill, there was no speed low enough and he was repeatedly flung off the back; finally, they had him walk in place for about two minutes.

"Stop him, *quick*," a nurse said when three or four needles on gauges entered red zones.

After the tests had been completed, a dietician and physical therapist sat down with Wolfgang Zimmering to discuss an appropriate course of action. Usually, the computer produced customized exercise and diet programs in forty seconds. This time, it took three minutes, the equivalent of something like 950 man hours.

John Grape had planned to catch up on his rest after the exhausting physical examination—his first in a dozen or so years.

He ached all over. Even his stomach was sore.

They had stuck his stomach with a number of instruments, trying to get a body-fat reading. First, they used something that resembled tweezers without success. Then they tried prongs, the kind large men used on blocks of ice before air conditioning and freezers. About all they could think of to compare his body fat with was a marble wrapped inside a big sponge.

They wouldn't let him rest.

Shortly after he had settled into his room, which was like a Junior Suite at a Hilton or a Hyatt—it was barely big enough to comfortably accommodate one person named Junior—a man from the class where you learned how to quit smoking stopped by with literature, a needle, and an extension number to call in a panic situation.

"You could save everybody a lot of trouble by bunking in with me," John Grape told the person who helped you quit smoking.

This man then gave John Grape a shot of nicotine, which would satisfy his desire for a cigarette while sparing his lungs further punishment.

He left behind ten cigarettes made out of lettuce.

They tasted like mud and could have used some creamy Italian.

Next, his dietician, whose name was Rita, stopped in with his menu for the first few days.

He was limited to 1,350 calories a day, not, as he first thought, an hour.

There wasn't much to discuss.

He got orange roughy tonight.

He seemed to be on the orange diet; if it was or had ever been that color, he could have at it. Rita gave him a vitamin shot. It was not an entirely unpleasurable experience. Rita gave him the shot in the right hip. He had a big hip, but she had two good ones. Also, good calves.

It was a shame John Grape had debts older than she was.

After that, his roommate popped in between golf lessons to introduce himself.

"Hi, roomie," this person said. "Sheldon Hammond."

Sheldon Hammond appeared to have just stepped off the cover of *Birdwatcher's Digest*. He wore Bermuda shorts with knee socks color-coordinated to a yellow shirt.

"Care to play eighteen?" he said.

"Eighteen what?"

"Fairways. Greens. Holes. Weedy fields."

"I despise golf," John Grape said.

"Well then, we probably have a lot in common, the difference being that I play."

Sheldon Hammond was an endodontist from Dallas who had dropped in to lose six ounces, get a nice suntan, and slice open a few hundred golf balls. He was a regular, having been to this mecca of fitness five times within the last three years.

After he introduced himself, he walked to the window, opened it, and took a few deep breaths of clean desert air while admiring the scenery, which he said was like a great painting in that you saw something different each time you looked.

John Grape looked into his daydream about cigarettes and beer.

The scenery outside their window was some very green grass followed by some brown sand, and a few of those mounds, way off.

"The sun must make everything seem different, the way it reflects off the desert."

"No, I think it's different every time you look because of all those lizards shifting around," John Grape said. "So you're a dentist. I hear there's a lot of instability in that field."

102   "I'm an endodontist. Root canals only."

"It's the cleaning and filling and pulling that sends a person around the bend?"

"Not necessarily."

"You bring your bag with you?"

Sheldon Hammond turned from the window.

"I've got a lower tooth here in front that's been throbbing a little."

Sheldon Hammond shook his head no—he hadn't brought his instruments. Then he excused himself to go carve up a few fairways.

There was John Grape's out: If Sheldon started talking about divots, birdies, and pin placement, he'd mention bleeding gums.

Right after he met his roommate, a physical therapist named Clark showed up with John Grape's customized exercise program.

Clark was only about five and a half feet tall, mostly chest. He didn't change expression much and reminded John Grape of an assassin. "Here," he said, passing out some clothing that had trouble written all over it; it was a sweatsuit with the name of the place on the back.

They made him exercise the *first day*.

They made him walk.

According to the computer, anything else might tax his heart to dangerous limits.

First, they weighed him at a lackluster 232.

"No good," Clark said.

Along with his muscles, Clark also watched his words.

Then they put John Grape in a rubber suit and made him walk 100 yards; and, after a two-minute break, they made him walk 250 *more* yards.

"You must walk faster," Clark said as John Grape started his 250 yard march. "Or . . ."

"Or *what*, goddamn it," John Grape said, blinded by perspiration.

"Or we walk more."

The last twenty-five yards, he walked as fast as he could and got very dizzy. He also got a cramp in his right thigh, so he had to hop the final few yards on his left foot—*anything* to keep from walking to the other end of

the track again, which was near the golf course and all the more a health
hazard.

As Clark rubbed the cramp out of John Grape's leg, almost removing
skin, somebody from the medical staff took a heart reading and reported
to Wolfgang Zimmering, who had bicycled over from the administration
building, that there was a very good chance Mr. Grape would pull through.

He spent fifteen minutes in a steam room.

He had a rubdown.

"You're like pizza dough," the masseuse said.

He took a shower.

He ate dinner.

You had to squint to see dinner.

There wasn't much of it.

Everybody in the dining room sat beside one of his or her own. John
Grape sat beside a fat woman from Oregon. She had been there eight days.

"What'd you weigh when you hit town, four hundred?" John Grape
asked.

The fat woman from Oregon moved.

John Grape dragged himself to his room after dinner, looked at his
schedule for tomorrow, which included five minutes on an Exercycle,
watched Sheldon Hammond putt a golf ball across the floor, missing a
chair leg he aimed at twenty-two times; then decided to take a moonlight
stroll into the desert, maybe for fifteen hundred miles or so, straight east.

2

The morning of John Grape's third or fourth day at Sunrise, he was called to the principal's office. He couldn't remember exactly how long he had been there because he was too tired to count. He was taken from the class where a person learned how to live without cigarettes.

This class was going all right. Most days, they showed everybody jars containing black lungs taken from dead people. The class was just before lunch; consequently, nobody asked for more sushi.

Many people got nicotine shots. Those who hadn't smoked for a couple of weeks got nicotine gum. Three or four people had signed up to be hypnotized, and they seemed to be doing better than most. One fellow who had been hypnotized told John Grape that each time he thought about smoking, he threw up, thereby solving two problems simultaneously—this man had lost ten pounds in one week, mostly right through his mouth.

Skipper had interrupted the down-with-smoking class and asked John Grape to please follow him.

John Grape's profile suddenly appeared on a wall in Wolfgang Zimmering's office.

His hands were in his pockets. He was trying to appear casual at sundown, out by the front gate.

Rita sighed.

The next slide that Wolfgang Zimmering projected onto the wall showed John Grape on his hands and knees, digging in the desert for cigarettes with a knife he had borrowed from the dining hall.

"What is this?" John Grape said.

Wolfgang Zimmering said, "Quiet please."

The third slide showed John Grape on his back in the desert, using a rock for a pillow as he blew a smoke ring.

"See, what happens is that exercise . . ."

Wolfgang Zimmering moved on to the next slide.

". . . makes me nervous."

He was now shown in one of the maintenance sheds, playing poker with an assistant greenskeeper, a bottle of cherry vodka between his knees, a stack of dollar bills on his side of the orange crate that was being used for a card table.

Wolfgang Zimmering shut off the projector and turned on the lights.

Rita lowered and shook her head.

Clark squeezed a rubber ball.

"Those guys working on the golf course beat me out of seventy-five bucks," John Grape said. "I think your greenskeeper deals seconds." He fiddled with his right sweat sock. "Listen, if I'm going to get paddled, she can do it." He smiled at Rita.

Nobody replied.

"All right, let's get it over with," John Grape said, crossing his legs.

"To what do you refer?"

Wolfgang Zimmering pulled out his top desk drawer.

"The lecture."

"You misunderstand."

Wolfgang Zimmering opened John Grape's file and then began typing numbers into a computer to his right. "We do not wish to discuss what we have just witnessed. Rather, we wish to *forget* it."

"Great. You smoke a couple of packs for twenty-five years . . ."

"Two packs a day for twenty-five years is *three hundred and sixty-five thousand cigarettes.*"

". . . it's not like giving up sunflower seeds."

106   "Mr. Grape," Wolfgang Zimmering said, turning off the computer, "this is not a . . . Howard Johnson's. How can I put this. Your tuition does not entitle you to sin at will. The simple fact of the matter is that in less than one week, you have become a very disruptive influence here."

"You put me in with that slap-happy dentist, what do you expect. It's like the *Howdy Doody Show* in there. A lousy sparrow flies by, he jumps up and down for joy."

"Mr. Hammond is an *endodontist*."

"He's drilled one too many dry holes, if you ask me."

Wolfgang Zimmering slid an envelope across the desk.

John Grape picked it up and said, "What's this?"

"Clark will drop you off at the nearest bakery."

John Grape opened the envelope and took out a check.

"It's your deposit, *in full*."

"Damn," John Grape said, "I've flunked out of charm school."

Five minutes later, Wolfgang Zimmering said, "Please bear with me."

He made a note or two as he read from the bylaws.

"As this has not come up before, I want to be quite sure about the procedure."

John Grape had eleven raisins, his allotment for the spring.

"Yes, I was quite right the first time."

Wolfgang Zimmering put the bylaws back into a file cabinet.

"You're telling me that somebody has to *vote* on whether or not I will be permitted to continue to piss away a thousand dollars a week?"

The managing director frowned.

"*Spend* a thousand a week," John Grape said.

"The executive committee, yes, should you wish to resubmit your application for continued residency."

"Let's run it up the fig tree," John Grape said.

He hoped the greenskeeper was on the executive committee; the greenskeeper would sure as hell vote to keep him around.

That greenskeeper had four tens and then four kings on consecutive hands of seven-card stud the other night, which you didn't see too often unless you were doing the dealing.

How, he wondered as he put a few things in an overnight case, could he ever write a simple sentence without support from a cigarette?

Smoking and writing well went together like smoking and writing nonsense.

It helped a person pass the time between capital letters.

Baseball players didn't smoke at the bat. Surgeons didn't smoke with somebody's guts in their hands. So John Grape sat down at his typewriter to see if he could string together a few words without being poisoned first.

Sheldon Hammond found him grinning at a sheet of paper.

"I hit a car," Sheldon Hammond said. "Over at the driving range. Sliced one. *Shoot*." He took a towel from around his shoulders and dabbed at his forehead. "Dented the fender of a Lincoln."

John Grape said, "This is a good day." He read what he had written, for the twentieth time.

"Do you know what a Lincoln fender costs?"

"A *very* good day."

"Eleven hundred dollars. She said she was going to sue me for mental anguish. *Ha*. Fat chance. Tell me how much mental anguish a person can suffer in *forty-five seconds*. I hit her fender. She goes off in a ditch, gets out, and starts the mental anguish baloney. It takes *weeks* to get mental anguish, everybody knows that. So all I'm out is the eleven hundred."

"Look at this."

John Grape handed his roommate what he had written.

Sheldon Hammond read: *This is the first sentence I have ever written without smoking.* Then he turned the paper over.

"This is it?"

John Grape frowned. "That's it," he said. "Went a lot better than I expected. What do you think?"

"Redundancy aside?"

"What redundancy?"

"*Ever.*"

"*Ever?*"

"*Ever* is like *very*."

108　　"I happen to like *very*," John Grape said, "very much."

"Back in the . . . third or fourth grade, I learned you shouldn't use *ever* when referring to something that hadn't happened. The simple use of a negative, like *I didn't*, suffices, see what I mean? *I didn't ever* is redundant."

John Grape scratched out *ever.*

Now his piece of writing read: *This is the first sentence I have written without smoking.*

"It's different," Sheldon Hammond said. "There's that."

Given the opportunity to redefine a human's role in the scheme of things, John Grape checked himself into the infirmary and asked for all the shots the law allowed.

He was determined to show all the experts a thing or two about will-power.

Confucius probably said it first, but Popeye said it the fastest: You are what you are.

The premise here is that given a certain genetic composition, your personality, your very *being*, is as predictable as the color of your eyes. This depressing point of view had been reinforced by the courts, with respect to divorce. The inability to do much about one's life, as it relates to an irate spouse, is called incompatibility. So it's a *law*, you can't change for the better.

In other words, people who profess to have improved themselves are fakers out to get something, like eternal life.

Of course, all this was easy for Popeye to say, because the man who drew *him* was a goddamn billionaire.

John Grape chose to think that you were what you were because you didn't need to be anything else. Or couldn't think of anything else to be. To prove a person could change for the better without having been threatened by a preacher or a doctor, he pushed down his jeans and showed a nurse his hind-end and told her to start sticking.

He wouldn't have wished his latest dreams on the world's most evil person.

First, he dreamed that four judges sat at the bench with their arms around each other.

"How do you find him?" the women asked, nodding toward where he sat securely bound.

"Insane," the foreman of the jury said.

Then Mort Goldberg said to a meeting of literary agents in the place where he worked, "Quick, somebody find me a writer. I've got one of the greatest ideas in the world." He hesitated for ten percent of a second. "Unfortunately, it killed the first guy who tried to write it."

Then John Grape's daughter was carrying a tray full of beers to several customers in a smoke-filled country bar. Then she was saying, "Say hello to your grandfather," as seven children sat crying in the back of a rusty pick-up truck.

An Internal Revenue agent said, "Mr. Grape, you can no longer deduct pencils and paper, to say nothing of travel expenses, gambling, or get-well expenses, because the statute of limitations has expired on your status as a novelist."

As John Grape dreamed, a doctor and a nurse stood at the foot of his bed in the infirmary.

"But your honor, it's *my* fucking house," John Grape yelled, thrashing around on sheets soaked with perspiration.

"Such language," the nurse said.

The doctor made sure the straps over John Grape's stomach were secure, then he looked at a chart and said, "He's off cigarettes, caffeine, and alcohol for the first time in . . . decades."

"Five thousand on the fucking Chiefs plus the four and a half points," John Grape said to somebody in a place far away.

"All we can do is sedate him."

"He *is* sedated," the nurse said.

The doctor looked at his watch. "Give him another shot in five minutes. If that doesn't hold him, give yourself one."

● ● ●

110   John Grape dreamed that he crept around behind his house and peeked in his den window.

"You may kiss the bride," a minister said.

A handsome male pulled Deloris to the floor and began tearing off her clothes.

"It's all right," Deloris said to the minister. "This is the second marriage for both of us."

John Grape dreamed that he fainted and rolled down the slight incline leading to his beloved creek, then floated away feet first.

"Let's hope *that* holds you," the nurse said, yanking the needle out of his arm.

She took some scissors out of a jacket pocket and cut off a couple or three inches of her curls.

John Grape had closed his teeth around the nurse's hair when she leaned down to give him a shot.

3

While John Grape was trying to cope with a numbing headache, a sour stomach, chills, fever, and depression as he entered his twenty-sixth hour of the good life, Deloris and forty-four of her closest friends sat on and among the rocks on the far side of the creek, listening to Brahms played by a string quartet from Boston.

The string quartet performed on a platform that had been constructed on some level ground just south of the house. The occasion was a prespring party. Waiters in formal gear—tails, black ties—moved about the hill, serving wine and snacks off silver trays.

Deloris and Bonnie sat halfway up the hill on a quilt and leaned against the trunk of a big pine tree. "He's three days late with the alimony," Deloris said.

Bonnie, who had been helping Deloris cast away her puppet strings and walk, wanted to say that she had told her so.

So she did.

Bonnie's ex-husband had been late with an alimony payment once.

She had him tracked—he was found selling paintings of Jesus, Elvis, John Wayne, and tigers that glowed in the dark to tourists with no taste, or a sense of humor, in Santa Fe—petitioned the court, and the ex-husband had to pay the private detective who brought him back, which was pretty funny in its own right.

"And he was never late again," Bonnie said.

The private investigator's name was Hunsacker. He specialized in runners, ex-spouses on the hoof.

Deloris had a sip of wine and said perhaps the money was in the mail.

"Yes, and the meek will inherit the earth," Bonnie said.

They listened to the quartet, no simple task because it was hard to concentrate with so many men sitting down below.

"He's trying to look up my dress again," Deloris said, bringing her ankles and knees together.

Bonnie said she saw him.

He was a banker named Hoskins, and he had been trying to look up Deloris's dress all afternoon, even while the string quartet, which didn't come cheaply, was playing.

During the course of the afternoon, Deloris had been hounded by a succession of saps, one of whom put his hand on her thigh, another of whom asked her to spend the weekend on his boat, which he would rush out to buy if she said yes. Deloris had started to wonder if they were all alike.

Bonnie, who had been divorced two years, said most of them were alike up to a point, unless they were gay, in which case there *was* no point.

She doubted that you could get to know one of them too well before sex.

Widowers were the exception. You couldn't go wrong with a nice widower.

They knew what was important in life—a touch, a smile, a ballet; and the average widower's mellowness made up for the fact that he might be a little on the feeble side.

Bonnie told Deloris to be patient, then offered to give her a hand with Hoskins, who really looked like a dummy with his head all twisted around backward. She did so by raising her cotton sundress off her knees and crossing her legs, left to right, slowly.

The banker's jaw slackened.

"That should get him through a long, hard night," Bonnie said.

Deloris asked about the private investigator's first name.

It was Marvin.

Bonnie said the skill with which he found deadbeats was unmatched; and, as important, he was homely.

"It's hard having to think about this," Deloris said.

"Remember what your therapist said. This is *business*. No other aspect
of it lives on."

Deloris nodded, then smiled. "You're right," she said. "It wasn't like a bad
marriage. It was like a bad debt."

4

John Grape, wearing a terrycloth robe, sat at his desk and wondered if he were competent enough to rejoin society. He would have to rejoin by means of a long- distance telephone call, because there was nothing very human or civilized in the immediate vicinity.

He had been released from the infirmary forty-five minutes earlier, and he felt lethargic. He had been out of touch for around seventy hours. He didn't remember much of what had happened at the infirmary, but he assumed that it hadn't been a lot of laughs over there; when they wheeled him out, one nurse crossed herself and another hid behind the curtains.

Band-Aids covered needle marks on both arms.

He guessed they had tranquilized him similarly to the way basketballs were filled with air—they had undoubtedly really poured it on.

As he was about to make a telephone call, Sheldon Hammond entered the room, joyfully as always, kissing a card on which his most recent golf score had been recorded.

John Grape put the receiver down and decided to see if he could visit on a reasonably intelligent level with his roommate; because if you could communicate with Sheldon without dissipating, you could make it anywhere.

"I *did* it," Sheldon Hammond said, pretending to swing a golf club.

Had there been a golf club in his hands, and had there been a ball teed

up in front of his feet, the television set off to the right wouldn't have stood
a chance.

Sheldon appeared to be swatting insects away from his face, or warding off evil spirits, instead of swinging a golf club properly.

"I broke a *hundred and five*."

"A hundred and five what, Sheldon, windows?"

Sheldon Hammond grinned. "Good to have you back, roomie, it's been pretty boring these last few days. I shot a hundred and *four*."

He stared off in space, remembering the last putt that went in to give him his best score ever, and perhaps kept him from shooting 109, since the last putt was launched from well off the eighteenth green and was traveling about thirty-five miles an hour when it smashed into the flag stick and accidentally fell in the hole.

"You okay?" he said.

John Grape shrugged and said it was too early to tell because the feeling had not returned to his body, although it was up past his ankles.

"Somebody said you had a rough couple of days."

"Who said that?"

"A nurse who resigned."

"Have I been making any sense at all?"

"Approximately as much as you ever did."

John Grape reached for the telephone.

He called Louis Archibald.

"I've been wondering about you," Archibald said. "Listen, I want to thank you for the work."

"Why is that, Archibald?"

"Well, I don't exactly get to eat lunch in The Four Seasons every year."

"*Eat?*" John Grape reminded Archibald that he had not been commissioned to investigate any chefs.

"You think a person can go in a place like that and hang around two hours by a plant?"

"Have you ever heard of waiting in the bar?"

"Four drinks and what I had, the duck salad, cost about the same."

"So what do you have besides a stomachache?"

116   "Thursdays, she's running in the city with that jogging club of hers, same as always. Run, eat, shop, the usual. The day before yesterday, here's something you might be interested in, she goes to dinner with some guy to a place called The Pines, it's six or seven miles from where you used to live."

"What guy?"

"Actually, he's probably a little old to be a guy, still. White hair, he's sixty he's a day, more like a duffer."

"What's his name?"

"I don't know."

"Nice work, Archibald," John Grape said.

"I need more time to collect names."

"Maybe it's her art teacher."

"I wouldn't be a bit surprised. Outside of dinner, there's nothing but a handshake."

"How much is a picture?"

"Of the white-haired gentleman?"

"No, of the assistant cook who does duck salad."

"Very funny. It depends. A hundred and five, usually."

"That is a goddamn insult to my remaining intelligence," John Grape said, having a bite of a carrot stick.

"We're talking about a discreet shot taken from inside a coat sleeve, a Japanese camera the size of a cigarette lighter."

"Draw him," John Grape said.

"Oh yeah, there's one more thing. Yesterday afternoon right after lunch, she gives some goofy school fifteen grand."

John Grape closed his eyes and said, "Please no."

"Let me get my notes. It's called Coventry Community College. It's what, twenty miles away. It's one brick building and one little white house. Not a leaf of ivy in sight. Very low profile. The fifteen grand goes for some women's study program. I think they're naming a room, maybe even a wing, after your ex-wife. If you ask me, the administrators at the school have the look of some people who have glommed onto a sure thing. The money is going to be used to fund, hang on, I wrote it down somewhere, they had a little ceremony in front of the rickety white house, here it is, the money is going to be used on a study of women in the postal service, how do you like those apples?"

A white pill helped John Grape digest them.

He told Louis Archibald to lay off the salad—hadn't he ever heard of a hamburger—and then hung up.

Later that night, Sheldon Hammond said, "So that's how you write a book."

John Grape stopped typing.

The new book was going surprisingly well. He had typed six whole pages without an assist from a cigarette.

The material seemed to be a little on the dry side; but what did he know for sure, he was only the writer.

"Stream of consciousness?"

"Not exactly."

John Grape turned off his typewriter.

"You don't just sit down and let it flow?"

"No, you think a long time, first."

"I was thinking about writing a book about my work. How do you like *Down in the Mouth* for a title?"

John Grape shrugged and said he wasn't skilled enough to offer advice beyond the absolute that writing was very difficult and could turn a person into another Pee Wee Herman if he wasn't very careful.

"Maybe I could take a couple of courses," Sheldon Hammond said.

John Grape shrugged again. Teaching writing was similar to selling tip sheets at a racetrack: Touting was much easier, and more financially rewarding, than screwing around down in the trenches yourself.

Writing is presented at most meccas of enlightenment as a field of study where hard and fast rules make things grow, just like over at the botany building. By pretending that this plus that equals success in the writing business, maybe nobody will know that only nuts write really well, consistently.

"The way you learn how to write is by reading," John Grape told his roommate, who then said putting together a book didn't look that hard, judging by some of the trash you saw in the stores.

118   John Grape opened his top desk drawer, took out a Gideon, and put his hand on it. "I swear to God Almighty and Jesus, writing is hard."

Sheldon Hammond said there was no reason to get mad.

"So what are you working on?" he asked.

"My experiences."

"You're kidding. *Here?*"

"Here, there. It's about being divorced, a lot of things. It's about turning your life around. I hope."

Sheldon Hammond sat up in bed and tossed a copy of *Golf Digest* aside. "*I'm* here. You're writing about *me?*"

He hadn't given it much thought. "When the time comes, probably."

"Now wait just a damn minute. You can't write about me. I'm a private citizen."

"You're part of my experiences here, Sheldon."

"Let me get this straight. You can invade a person's privacy just as long as you're writing a *book?*"

"The truth is its own excuse in this country, Sheldon, as far as I can tell. Relax, I won't use your name if you don't want me to."

"You going to use my *shirt?* My socks?"

He was pumpkin-colored, this day.

"If you wouldn't mind."

"I mind," Sheldon Hammond said, unbuttoning his shirt.

"It would sure help me capture the . . . spirit . . . of the place."

"We start from scratch, now that I know what's going on."

"Fine," John Grape said.

Sheldon Hammond went into the bathroom and changed clothes, returning in tan slacks and a cream-colored knit shirt.

John Grape asked him, "You playing fifty-four holes tomorrow?"

Sheldon Hammond sat on the edge of his desk and considered his answer carefully. "Golf is not the most important thing in the world," he said after a minute. "Golf is good exercise for the joints."

"Does this mean that we can sleep until dawn for a change?"

Sheldon shrugged. After a bit, he said, "You're not making a note what I said about exercise."

"I can remember it."

Sheldon Hammond would not speak again for nearly thirteen hours, when he would say, finally, "There is no substitute for regular exercise and proper nutrition."

5

Marvin Hunsacker, who could find anybody anywhere anytime, had studied criminal justice at college and was all set to become the police chief of one of the world's great cities. He was a very bright young man.

He had been recruited by most of the better police departments and signed on with Philadelphia after editing the entrance exam he also aced. Most future police officers worked four hours on the exam. The average score was 76. Besides answering all 125 questions correctly, Marvin Hunsacker caught and fixed 19 grammar mistakes on the test it took him only 45 minutes to complete.

It was obvious that Marvin Hunsacker had a head on his shoulders.

Keeping it there turned out to be more difficult than he had foreseen. Three weeks after he had been graduated from the police academy which, after earning a masters degree in criminal justice, was like revisiting the tenth grade, he walked in on the armed robbery of a pawn shop.

What transpired was degrading.

The villain robbing the pawn shop turned and pointed a pistol at Marvin, who said, "Don't do anything you'd be sorry for later."

The criminal complied by pulling the trigger of his gun; he'd be sorry later only if he gave up.

The bullet struck the frame of the pawn shop door, no more than ten inches from Marvin Hunsacker's left eyeball, and caused him to rethink his decision to work in the public sector—once his knees quit shaking and the owner of the pawn shop had leaned over his counter and clubbed the robber into submission with a wrench.

To get anywhere in the police business, you had to serve some street time down with all the maulers.

Granted, people who had earned perfect test scores were taken off the front lines quicker than the kids who became police officers by correctly guessing the answers to questions like:

Miranda was:

(a) A woman who wore hats made of food.

(b) A man who didn't understand his rights.

(c) All of the above.

(d) None of the above.

(e) Some of the above.

The correct answers were any except (d).

Despite the fact that people like Hunsacker were not required to dwell endlessly in the gutter, the time passed very slowly with your gizzard at risk.

Another aspect of the law enforcement business that concerned Marvin Hunsacker was the lack of motivation at the entry level. A number of people he had gone through the academy with had decided to become police officers because they couldn't think of anything to do—saying, it beat the army because you didn't have to salute.

So after three months of bobbing and weaving his way through what amounted to a convention of rogues—Marvin Hunsacker's beat was the downtown area where the victims were usually criminals, too—he quit being a policeman and spent four years with an agency in Chicago that specialized in the recovery of stolen treasures like art and jewelry.

And now, according to *New York* magazine, *People,* and one of those cage liners you buy at the check-out stands at grocery stores, he was in a class by himself when it came to finding people intent on lying low.

If Marvin Hunsacker couldn't find somebody, there was always a very good reason for it. Or a very bad reason for it. They were dead.

He was batting around .750 with people who had come to violent ends. With the living, he was 41 for 41.

122   He charged two hundred dollars an hour for his services, on top of expenses; and he didn't travel coach or sleep cheap. But, he explained to Deloris Worth as they sipped espresso on the redwood deck behind her house, fees paid to an investigator pursuant to the apprehension of a criminal were frequently held sacred by the court: As her friend Miss Carter (Bonnie) had said, anybody attempting to shirk a legal obligation was responsible for resolving all encumbrances encountered thereafter.

"Can he write it off his taxes?" Deloris wondered.

"My fees?"

Deloris nodded.

"No, crime is not tax deductible."

"Good," Deloris said, filling Marvin Hunsacker's cup.

He took down all the pertinent information, most of it the usual: Money—late. Whereabouts—unknown.

Tough call, deciding when to start looking for somebody. Still . . . Deloris Worth's ex-husband was only two weeks late with the alimony; and generally, Marvin Hunsacker was not hired until the money was months late, *years*, even.

But on the other hand, simple oversights and problems with the mail were usually resolved within days by honorable people.

Miss Worth certainly knew the subject in question better than anybody, so Marvin Hunsacker said he'd rely on her intuition about when to proceed.

Marvin Hunsacker took with him a list of John Grape's friends and associates, in case push and shove came to jump and run.

Marvin Hunsacker took one look at a picture of the big guy—he found an old photo in a box in the attic—smiled, and said he'd be easier to find than some buildings.

6

Warren Godfrey, the staff psychiatrist at Sunrise, returned from his reference library with five books, and dust all over his suit.

One of the books was at least six inches thick. He had carried the reference material from his library to his office on a small dolly.

"When was that thing written?" John Grape asked of the largest book, which was frayed around the edges.

"Nineteen forty-seven."

"Not exactly the last word."

"Some things never change, John."

The name of the volume was *Human Behavior*.

"You never know," John Grape said about the inevitability of certain things.

Judging by the cut of Warren Godfrey's clothes, and the fine Swiss timepiece on his left wrist, serving as the staff psychiatrist at a health factory was a decent enough way in which to glide through life. Most of the people who spent time at Sunrise had the common decency to be psychotic on their own time—one of the reasons why nobody flipped out here was because special counseling cost extra—so Warren Godfrey's role in the scheme of things was to show up at the no-smoking and no-drinking classes and tell everybody they could do it if they really wanted to.

Which could get a little boring.

124   "As difficult as it might be to believe," he said, lining the books in a row on his desk, "sometimes you miss the raw nuttiness of the street."

"Cracking up is a poor man's disease?" John Grape said, wishing that Warren Godfrey would turn the pages faster. At $125 an hour for extra counseling, a person couldn't afford to get *too* well here.

"When it comes to certain manifestations like robbery, yes." The staff psychiatrist took a new notebook from his desk to use on John Grape's most recent urge—the desire to quite cursing like a linebacker whenever he thought about Deloris. "Now John, I have a few questions before we start on the books here. I don't want you to feel burdened. We have, in a relatively brief time, quit smoking, drinking, and gambling."

"Strike before the tranquilizer wears off, that's my motto. Before the money runs out. Don't forget eating. I've also quit that."

"How much weight have you lost?"

"Thirty-eight ounces."

Warren Godfrey did something with his face that resembled a smile. John Grape said it sounded better than *a few pounds*.

"You don't feel overwhelmed by all you're trying to accomplish?"

"Warren, it's you or golf."

Warren Godfrey worked through lunch in order to present John Grape with the following bit of advice: Think before you speak.

And this prescription was only an educated guess.

He had gone through nearly forty-five pounds of research material without finding a case study about somebody who wanted to stop swearing.

"Somehow, you seem to have more in common with born-again Christians than any other group I've come across," he said, frowning at a number of texts still open on his desk. "Most sacrifices of this nature are usually religiously motivated."

"You look hard enough, you could probably find two or three atheists with principles," John Grape said.

"But you simply want to quit swearing . . ."

"For the hell of it."

Warren Godfrey made a note.

7

Days and people and vegetables came and went. He was usually too sore to turn the pages of his calendar, which measured time day by day.

They had him doing all sorts of stupid strenuous things, like pulling oars while sitting anchored to the floor, touching his ankles, and that s— stuff.

Sheldon Hammond, who hadn't said fifty words after he learned that John Grape was writing a book that might include him and his clothes, went back to Dallas. "I love my family and my work," he said as he left.

John Grape signed up for another two weeks.

Rather than force anybody else to sit around in a three-piece suit reading James Joyce, John Grape moved into a single room, which cost an extra $150 a week. He was accepted for another session without a single gasp. He was pained by the expensiveness of the place. Spending thousands while writing on the come made him queasy. Yet he worked on his book after dinner each night.

He did nineteen pages about how people shouldn't be made rich simply because they had *married* somebody; moreover, he wondered in print about the rent money. Say a person lives free eighteen years. That's 216 months of rent-free living—216 months times a rent of a measly $400 is more than $85,000.

So why isn't rent money subtracted from what a lesbian says a man owes an ex-wife?

Much of what John Grape wrote was a little on the venomous side, so he toned it down as best he was able. But he made the point that you shouldn't take a person's house.

He also began a study of the Episcopalians and their church. Deloris was a devout one of those. Pretty gutsy people, the Episcopalians, particularly during the Revolutionary War, when the church of England cut off their supply lines to heaven and left them dangling, pawns without a bishop.

The Bible read a little choppy, though.

It could have used a good editor.

Whenever he thought about a cigarette or a beer or a bet, he'd do push-ups and sit-ups.

And there was always this: If things didn't work out to his satisfaction, he could always start having fun again.

The morning he lost his tenth pound, Clark put a gold star on his forehead.

He remained calm and thought before he spoke. He had never done either of those before and was anxious to see if there was a future in it. He had also decided not to worry about things over which he had no control.

The telephone was ringing as he returned from being baked in a steam room.

It was Archibald. They talked about Deloris's social life, then the detective excused himself from his telephone to accept delivery of the morning mail. He expressed concern because John Grape's check for services rendered to the tune of $770 was not yet there.

"Now where were we?" Archibald said.

"In the limousine."

"Right. Listen. You sound funny."

"What makes you say that?"

"I don't know. You're quieter."

"Good."

"Whatever," Archibald, who had called collect, said. "The limousine is silver. They take it from the Met in the city, that's the Metropolitan Opera House, where they watch a ballet that lasts six days, to a restaurant called Derek's, you ever hear of it?"

"No."

"It's pretty new, I think. She's all over him."

John Grape took a towel from around his shoulders and said, "Explain yourself, Archibald."

"She's got his arm."

"That's not all over him."

"Maybe you're right. She's in this black dress cut down to her ribs. You wear a dress like that, you could be standing a foot away and you're still all over somebody."

John Grape had a bite of celery. "Who is he?"

"G-u-y V-i-l-l-e-r-e-t. The first name is not pronounced the way it looks. It rhymes with flea. He's not from this country. He used to be a right-winger for the Rangers, led the league in a couple of scoring categories, if you get my drift. Six feet three, around two ten, eyes blue, muscles all over muscles."

"You're telling me she goes out with a *hockey player?*"

"A former player, he's a coach now. Anyway, there's a bar in Derek's, it connects with the main dining room, I've got a perfect view of their table. The whole place has an art deco theme, everything is overstuffed except, may I add, the drinks. They're in a half circle of a booth, sitting *very* close together, having some champagne, laughing. Dinner is routine. It's getting very chummy by this time. Then, right before the dessert, this guy gets laughing so hard, something must have come loose, he takes his *teeth* out, can you believe it?"

"Good," John Grape said.

"These hockey players must have about three teeth of their own. He takes the false teeth out, puts them in a saucer, it's a wonder the head waiter didn't call the police, a fancy place like that. Once the man puts his teeth on the table, the evening pretty much goes to hell."

"What else?"

"Well, she basically gets up and leaves, can't say as I blamed her, the inside of somebody's mouth next to your purse. He follows her out front."

"His teeth are back in by this time?"

"Right. He puts them in walking through all the tables. On the sidewalk out front, he puffs up and says she's about to miss out on the thrill of a life-

128   time, which we all assume is him in, you know, bed. She says you're all alike, you're pissants, gets in the limousine, and takes off."

John Grape wiped his brow with the bottom of his sweatshirt and asked Archibald to do him a big favor next time: Start at the *end* of the story.

He hung up and took his pulse.

It was, strangely enough, normal.

8

He called home to straighten out a couple of things.

Deloris said, "Hello," after one ring.

"You're probably wondering where some money is."

He had gotten the unlisted number from his daughter, whose grade in English was all the way up to an F-plus; on a more somber note, she was dating a guy who had met Castro.

"You owe me one thousand, five hundred dollars, plus fifteen days of interest," Deloris said without emotion. "Otherwise you don't exist."

Keep it up, John Grape thought.

"This is business."

"I *owe* you nothing."

"That's a matter of opinion. Yours, and everybody else's. How'd you get this number?"

He had a bite of apple and thought before he spoke.

"You're calling long distance, I can hear the static."

"I would like to apologize," John Grape said. "Can we please start this conversation again."

"Yes, thank you. Where is the money you owe me?"

"I owe you nothing."

Deloris dropped the receiver. John Grape heard it bounce off his kitchen floor a few times.

"Hello," he said. "Hello. I would like to apologize again."

130   "Yes, what, I'm here," somebody said after a few seconds.

"Who are you?"

"Buck."

"What are you doing in my house?"

"I am celebrating. And this is not *your* house."

"What are you celebrating, Buck?"

"A bust."

"So you're a cop."

"My *bronze*, you ass."

"My mistake."

"Deloris has asked that I speak with you about money."

"Tell her I need an extension. Tell her times are bad. Tell her I need a month."

"She says no."

"Tell her she has no choice in the matter."

"She says she does."

"Tell her that if she does not agree to an extension, I will never pay her another penny."

"She says that if the money isn't here by the day after tomorrow, she'll put some big *dogs* on you."

"Get out of my house," John Grape said.

There was some more banging.

The next person to come onto the line was named Arnie.

He was the new gardener.

John Grape hung up, secure in the knowledge that the big dogs would never look at Sunrise.

9

arvin Hunsacker pinned a map of the world to a wall of his office, which was all leather and wood, wrote *Grape* across the top of the map with a black Magic Marker, and said to the newest member of his firm, a young man named Tuttle, "This person owes alimony."

Tuttle, ever the eager learner, nodded and made a note. "Funny name, Grape."

Tuttle had been a policeman in Albany for even less time than Hunsacker. Two weeks; then a drug dealer came at him with a hatchet.

"John Grape. He was, and for all we know still may be, a writer. One decent book that was evidently blind luck. A number of stinkers meanwhile. He has made it clear that he does not intend to pay the money that is due for a considerable period of time. His ex-wife has hired us to find him."

"Got it," Tuttle said.

"Grape is gone."

"Where?" Tuttle asked.

Marvin Hunsacker looked at his assistant, poured himself some decaf, and said that that was what they had been hired to find out. "He could be anywhere in the world. So how do we find him, without cooperation from any law enforcement agency?"

Tuttle frowned at the map.

132   "Maybe he's here," Marvin Hunsacker said, tapping the end of a ruler at Alaska. "Or here." He touched South America.

"First of all," Tuttle said, "we ask around. Friends and business associates."

Marvin Hunsacker sighed. "We say to his best friend we're looking for your pal so we can squeeze some alimony out of him?"

Tuttle squinted at the map again.

"Enemies," he said. "We ask them."

"Have you any idea what your enemies are doing?"

Tuttle shook his head, a signal which seemed to mean no.

"This is much different than police work," Marvin Hunsacker said. "People do not come into this office and confess. They seldom leave trails of crimes to follow. From this instant on, I want you to use your mind, not your extensive memory of police procedure in Albany or cheap detective novels."

"All right."

"Thank you very much."

Tuttle crossed his legs and alternated his attention from the map of the world to a personality profile of the subject, provided by the ex-wife.

Presently, Tuttle put his pen beside his notebook and said, "We'll never find him."

10

Three young men stood in the middle of the shallow end of the indoor swimming pool, holding John Grape by his chest, stomach, and legs so he wouldn't drown. Wolfgang Zimmering stood next to a cameraman at the side of the pool. They were putting together a promotional videotape of the good life at Sunrise that would be sent to hundreds of travel agents.

"Ready?" Wolfgang Zimmering said.

"Almost," Mark, who was in charge of the indoor pool, said. "Deep breath now, John."

"O," John Grape said, spitting out some water, "kay."

"Flexible movements, not stiff and rigid. Loose and free."

John Grape nodded.

Mark said, "Here we go."

"We're rolling." Wolfgang Zimmering touched the cameraman on the shoulder.

The three swimming instructors let go of John Grape.

"Blay," he said into the water.

"Don't *talk*," Mark said. "Move your arms."

John Grape flailed at the water.

"Don't fight it," Mark said. "Close your mouth. Good *heavens*."

"What's going on down there?" Wolfgang Zimmering asked. "I thought you said he was improving."

134

"Phlub," John Grape replied.

"*Damn,*" Mark said. "Evidently, he peaked when he floated a little this morning."

John Grape took a deep breath and paddled and kicked for all he was worth, but he was sinking, rear end first. As his backside sank, his chest and head came up and out of the water. Then his top half moved on over backward until he was once again horizontal, parallel to the bottom of the pool but face-up. He looked like something that was being basted on a rotisserie.

Soon, the whole of John Grape went under in five feet of water.

He drifted to the bottom of the pool head-first, got his feet under him, stood, rubbed his eyes, spat out some water, and said, "I sank again."

"Clear the pool," Wolfgang Zimmering said. "Get Godfrey. Mark, this film goes in your résumé."

"Are you afraid of water, John?" Warren Godfrey asked.

They stood by the shallow end.

"That's right," John Grape said.

"Why are you afraid of the water?"

"Because I can't swim."

Warren Godfrey smiled understandingly. "Is there anything in your past that might make you feel that way?"

"Yes, I couldn't swim when I was a kid, either."

"What did you fear most about the water?"

"Its depth."

"John, have you considered whether it might be to your best advantage to avoid being in the water, rather than attempt to learn to swim?"

"Somebody I need to get to know swims like an eel."

"Okay. But I can't tell you that there's nothing to be afraid of. This isn't like other phobias. The object of this fear can, in fact, kill you."

"What *can* you say?"

"Kick your feet harder."

They held him on his back.

They held him on his stomach.

They held his hands while he kicked his feet.
They held his feet while he moved his arms.
They floated him back and forth across the shallow end.
They showed him how to open his eyes under water.
They showed him how to breathe in gulps.
Each time they let go of him, he sank.

"Let's hope the Red Cross doesn't hear about this," Mark said.

"You know," another of the swimming instructors said, "I think the man actually has a physical problem. There's something wrong with his equilibrium."

"The doctor said there wasn't anything wrong with his inner ear," Mark said. "Except that his inner ear is a little wet."

"Go ahead, whisper, *laugh*," John Grape told them.

He stood on the diving board over fifteen feet of deep trouble.

"Nobody's laughing," Mark said.

"I'll show you."

"That's the spirit."

"And there he goes again," Mark said.

John Grape ran down the diving board, roaring. He jumped feet first into the deep end and began kicking, pounding, and twisting around near the surface.

"What do you think?" Mark said.

"Actually, he might be doing better," one of the instructors said, looking at the second hand of his watch.

Waves splashed onto the tile by their feet.

John Grape executed an involuntary somersault about three feet under water.

"Party's over," one of the instructors said. "Who's turn is it?"

"Mine, I'll get him," Mark said, diving toward John Grape, who stood on the bottom of the swimming pool with his hands on his hips, too mad to breathe, should the opportunity present itself sometime in the near future.

11

Marvin Hunsacker mailed John Grape a package.

The package was slightly larger than a shoe box and contained a few pairs of cheap sweat socks. Interwoven into the toe of one sock was a small electronic device that gave off a signal over distances ranging up to a half a mile. The gizmo cost $450, and Marvin Hunsacker made a mental note to himself to set aside two minutes at some later date and think of a way to get it back.

He mailed the package to John Grape, in care of his last known address, the Shadybrook Apartments. He had checked with the manager and had learned that she was not keeping any mail for the fat guy named Grape. Even people trying to disappear love their mail. Who knew, maybe they'd win some jackpot sweepstakes, and then they wouldn't have to be gone anymore. Writers might get royalty checks. Mail had to go somewhere.

Marvin Hunsacker followed John Grape's mail.

Actually, assistant Tuttle followed it most of the way.

After Marvin Hunsacker mailed the sweat socks and the electronic gadget, Tuttle sat behind the post office wondering what would happen if the box were put in the belly of an airplane bound for . . . Spain.

Tuttle couldn't climb into the cargo compartment of a jet going to Europe.

Following the package could get expensive. And cold.

And you wouldn't think anybody trying to disappear would have mail
delivered to his doorstep.

Tuttle's instructions were to follow the beep on the screen until the package went somewhere meaningful, and then call the office.

It was an absolute wonder the world held together while things got delivered through the mail.

Bills? They were never misplaced, mishandled, or late. But packages— they must move gifts around inside post offices with their noses.

Marvin Hunsacker mailed the package at a quarter after noon one Tuesday.

Nothing happened until dark; but Tuttle had to stay in his car all night on the off chance the graveyard shift was more energetic than those they replaced.

Such was not the case.

Nothing happened Tuesday night, so Tuttle slept in the car and got a stiff neck.

He sat a half block from the back exit of the small branch post office with a little gun-thing that resembled a microphone pointed at the gate all the mail vehicles drove through.

Nothing happened Wednesday or Wednesday night.

Tuttle slept fitfully and got a stiff back.

If somebody didn't kick the package outside, and soon, he was concerned his joints might lock him into the permanent shape of an automobile seat.

Thursday afternoon, at half past two, as Tuttle was wondering what else he might enjoy doing for a living, the package finally left the branch post office and was driven directly to a coffee shop where it sat in the back while the civil servant took a forty-four minute break.

The Communists were infiltrating the postal service: it was the only answer.

Tuttle called Hunsacker with the news that the package was being moved, however slowly, and said his legs were going numb. He was told to stay with it. The package went to a smaller branch office twenty or

138   thirty miles down the road; Tuttle was so tired by this time, he wasn't sure what state he was in.

God help me, he thought, when the truck left the little post office without the package—there go two more days and nights.

But somebody new must have been in charge of the tiny post office because the socks were sent packing in an hour and a half.

Tuttle was jolted awake, and followed the box until it stopped again.

Marvin Hunsacker joined him in the parking lot of a strip shopping center four or five miles from where John Grape used to live.

"It went there," Tuttle said, pointing to an office next to a barber shop. He tried to rub some circulation into his legs.

"It's still there?"

"Thank the Lord."

Marvin Hunsacker nodded.

Painted on the glass door of the office was JAMES MELLOW. Below that was INVESTMENT COUNSELOR.

Hunsacker removed from his inside suit coat pocket a list of John Grape's friends.

One was Jimmy Mellow.

"The man is a bookmaker," Marvin Hunsacker said.

"All this for nothing," Tuttle said, bending left and right at the waist.

"Please continue with that line of reasoning."

Tuttle stopped stretching. "Some friend is keeping his mail."

Marvin Hunsacker put the list of John Grape's friends away.

"And who's to say," Tuttle said, "the friend knows where he is."

"Exactly."

"So we know nothing, except who's keeping his mail."

"Exactly *wrong*. We almost know where he is."

"You're telling me he's *inside* there?"

"No."

"You're telling me the bookie knows where he's gone?"

"No."

"But *we* know?"

"*We'll* know as soon as I tell you."

"*You* know."

"Almost. Before long, Tuttle, I will be the only person in the world to know where he is."

"That's not possible."

"Care to make a gentleman's bet?"

"I'd care to very much."

"Five hundred dollars."

Marvin Hunsacker extended his hand.

Tuttle frowned at it.

"Gentlemen do not bet . . . *beers*."

12

They projected images of John Grape onto a big screen in the auditorium.

The first slide was of him walking around the oval track with his stomach hanging out of a rubber sweatsuit.

On slide two, he was smoking a Camel out by the front gate.

Slide three: He was on an Exercycle, holding his right side, his face purple, seeming to call out in pain.

"This place have a *dungeon*?" somebody in the audience asked.

Slide four: He did a sit-up, his face just pink, here.

Slide five: He was in the dining room, frowning at some green and orange things on his plate.

Slide six: He was smiling a little as he was being weighed.

Slides seven through ten: He jumped into a swimming pool. And sank. Three men jumped in after him. And dragged him out.

"Get a horse," somebody in the crowd said.

Slide eleven: He did a push-up, with his nose beating his stomach to the floor.

"Who's that?" somebody wondered.

Twelve: He jogged around the track—you could tell he was moving at a faster clip than a walk because on this slide, both of his feet were off the ground at the same time.

Thirteen: He pulled on the oars anchored to the floor of the exercise room.

Fourteen: He toasted the camera with some carrot juice.

Fifteen: He trotted across the desert with a huge orange sun in the background.

"I would like to use that shot on our brochure next year," Wolfgang Zimmering whispered.

John Grape said maybe, since it was a long shot and he was unrecognizable. "For a price, for top modeling dollar."

Sixteen: He jumped into the indoor pool again.

Seventeen: He remained on the surface.

Eighteen: He pulled himself out of the water, having just willed himself across the width of the pool.

Nineteen: The three swimming instructors awarded him a medal.

"Please meet John Grape," Wolfgang Zimmering said, turning on the lights.

"So anyway," John Grape said from a podium in front of a class for fatties, most of whom had arrived this morning, "I'd rather do a sit-up than give a speech." He glanced at some notes. "Which shows how much I hate speeches."

Several slobs applauded politely.

"So anyway, not all that long ago, I was smoking three packs of Camels."

"A week?" somebody wondered.

"A day. Sometimes an hour. And I was pretty, uh, big. And—oh yeah, drunk. Let's see, I've lost twenty-four and a half pounds and . . . "

He had a sip of grapefruit juice.

". . . I can sort of run a half mile. It's not much, but, uh . . ."

"How do you feel?" somebody asked.

"Well, not bad. Different. When you . . . give up things like smoking and alcohol . . ." He had another sip of juice. ". . . and gambling and what have you . . . you have to fill that free time with something. And that can be a *lot* of free time. So you . . . this is a little hard to explain . . . you fill your time with new interests . . . you keep moving . . . you think healthier."

"Do you feel *good?*"

"Well, it's hard to find a frame of reference . . . it's hard to remember

142   twenty years ago . . . I don't feel bad." He put his notes in his pockets. "So anyway, you can do it. Actually, I feel great."

Eighteen fatties tried to spring to their feet, grunted their way toward their feet instead, and gave him sort of a standing ovation.

13

Clark handed John Grape a computerized exercise program for the next couple of months—it could be updated through the mail at the end of that time for a nominal fee.

He got his diet for the same period of time from Rita.

She kissed him on the cheek.

Clark shook his hand.

Then Wolfgang Zimmering handed John Grape an envelope

"A collection of your inspirational sayings?"

"No, it's your bill."

The balance due was $5,120.

"Come back and see us," Skipper said, opening the front gate. "Let us know what you're . . . *down* to."

John Grape and Wolfgang Zimmering walked to the curb to wait for the station wagon.

"Five thousand, one hundred and twenty dollars," John Grape said, staring at the receipt. "I planned to spend less than half that here." He had paid his bill with traveler's checks. At the moment, he had around $27,000 to his name.

Not too bad, if you ran a small whale blubber shop in Alaska, and your wife had a good job.

Very bad, if you were not earning money.

"As you can plainly see, we gave you ten percent off the second and third weeks. Normally, unless one applies for the extra time before hand, the discounts do not apply."

"And you cannot put a price tag on health."

"I was just preparing to say that."

The station wagon for the airport came around the corner.

"I have something important to say to you." Wolfgang Zimmering put his hands on John Grape's shoulders. "Listen carefully."

"As opposed to what, out here?"

"If you ever smoke *one* cigarette, if you ever take *one* drink, if you ever fail to exercise or maintain good nutrition, if you *ever* misuse yourself, then my friend, you have . . . wasted a considerable amount of money."

There was a common denominator all former wrecks could relate to.

Wolfgang Zimmering lifted John Grape's right hand, then slapped it.

A high five from a man with little emotion and no sense of humor; it was the supreme compliment.

John Grape was the first in line at a ticket counter in the Phoenix airport.

The ticket agent had asked, three times, "Can I help you?"

"Come on," a man behind him said. "Let's go."

John Grape turned to discover a red-faced man puffing on a filtered cigarette—a walking public service announcement for estate planning.

"I don't have all day here," the man said impatiently.

"You're probably closer to the truth than you know," John Grape said, blinking at the smoke. "You probably have all day today, tomorrow, the day after. But next month, next *year* . . ." John Grape waved at the cigarette smoke. "I seriously doubt you've got that."

Then he heard himself talking about the hazards of secondary smoke, about how inhaling fumes from somebody else's cigarette had been proved dangerous.

"*He's* screwing around up there, *he's* holding up things, he's lecturing *me*?"

The man looked around for support.

John Grape said that he had a constitutional right to be healthy.

"It's okay to cause a person to be late, *that's* healthy?"

"Either you put the cigarette out, or I will."

"What a fucking place, airports," the man said, grinding out the cigarette under the heel of his right shoe.

"And please watch your language."

"Thank you," a woman three back said.

John Grape returned his attention to the Departure board behind the ticket agent.

He thought briefly about changing his plans.

Seattle—get a job in a sardine factory. Be a lumberjack.

Omaha—the beef business. Get a route selling jerky.

Houston—sell used cars. Or old oil wells.

It didn't sound like there was anything close to a best seller in the lot.

"Los Angeles on the four o'clock flight, one way," John Grape said to the ticket agent.

"*Figures*," the man behind him said.

14

"ello," Marvin Hunsacker said to the gentleman working the first window at the post office. "How's it going today?"

"Fair."

"Well, things will look up, you mark my words."

"You a psychic?"

"Almost."

Marvin Hunsacker slid a yellow card across the counter.

"I'd like to turn in this Change of Address card," he said.

"You just did it," the postal employee said. "Wait a minute, is this name *right*?"

"It's Grape," Marvin Hunsacker said. "John."

"What kind of name is that?"

"French."

"You're all set."

Marvin Hunsacker joined Tuttle by a wall next to some Wanted posters.

He had just redirected John Grape's mail from Jimmy Mellow's place of business to his own front door.

"Dazzling," Tuttle said. "It's *low*. But it's breathtaking."

"I'll take the five hundred dollars out of your monthly check."

"Five hundred dollars *is* my check. But you still haven't found him yet."

"You can buy your way out of this mess for . . . four hundred dollars."

"It's done."

They shook hands.

"Let your mind work for you," Marvin Hunsacker said as they headed for the door. "If you let it lead, you will cover shorter distances."

"We should try a Change of Address card with somebody like Oral Roberts," Tuttle said.

That was the spirit, Marvin Hunsacker told him.

15

The reason The Palms was not as popular with the fish-egg-and-bottled-water set as some of the other residence hotels in the greater Los Angeles area was that not one celebrity had ever overdosed there.

"I don't want to be morbid about the whole thing," Combs, the live-in manager, said, "but it's the truth. Some places, they stop just short of putting A FAMOUS MOVIE STAR DIED HERE on the marquee. Pretty sickening, isn't it."

"Pretty sickening," John Grape agreed.

This was the fourth residence hotel he had looked at since he had arrived in Los Angeles six hours ago, and he was about ready to check into a linen closet, just to keep from driving around lost anymore.

He had been careening around town in a nineteen-seventy-four Ford that he had leased from an operation called Rent Some Bolts.

The car rented for $9.95 a day. This one listed badly to the left.

"The closest we ever came was a ventriloquist," Combs said.

He stopped to pick up a cigarette butt from the garden area in the courtyard. "Gentleman by the name of . . . Batten, Bracken, something like that. Britton, that's it, Sid Britton. Very big with the toddlers. It was on a weekend, a Saturday somewhere around 1979, Britton drinks a pint of rum, has a pill sandwich, his blood pressure drops to about twenty over five. One of the housekeepers finds him, we rush him to the emergency room, there's our claim to fame. That palm tree is a hundred and two years old."

They stopped to admire the tree that was the focal point of the open-air courtyard, around which all the so-called *suites* had been built.

"There's not a rat in that tree. You've heard of maps of the stars' homes?"

John Grape nodded.

"Maps of where the stars are buried?"

"Yes."

"Well, now there's a guy putting out a map of where the stars *died,* you know, the ones who got it in wrecks, suites in residence hotels. What's this world coming to."

John Grape said he didn't know; he was only passing through.

"You stop that," Combs said, kicking a pebble off the sidewalk. "I got too many depressed people living here already. You get ten percent off the second week."

John Grape nodded some more.

"Cash, a credit card, what?"

"Probably a little of everything."

The telephone in the office rang. Combs handed John Grape the keys to a few of the vacant suites and told him to make himself at home and kindly get the description of any maintenance worker who threw bugs from the rock garden into the swimming pool.

The average suite at The Palms had a combination living-dining room full of wood furniture that squeaked; a bedroom with a sitting area behind a closet door; a tiny bathroom with a shower the size of an old-fashioned phone booth; and a kitchen with fixtures destined for a museum depicting early pioneer life in southern California.

The courtyard area was the big palm, three thin little palms, a rock garden (the first such garden John Grape had ever seen where the rocks appeared to be sickly), a waterfall that was busted and dry, and a square swimming pool that was wet, or at least dampish. The pool was only five feet deep and was host to many dozens of black bugs.

"They're not fooling anybody," Combs said, returning from his call. He frowned at the maintenance workers who were shaking their heads at the

150   pool. "They'd rather scoop bugs out of the water than pull weeds. The god-damn bugs in the water there, they can't even *swim*." Combs made a sour face. "You're not fooling anybody," he said to one of the maintenance workers. "You're telling me all those bugs drop from the *sky*?"

The worker wiggled his fingers to simulate a black bug crawling from the rock garden to the pool.

"They're bringing the bugs from home in a jar," Combs said. He turned his attention from the courtyard to the suites. "We used to be tastefully decadent, which is very big." He handed John Grape a registration card. "Then some guy from one of the rating services got bit by a wasp in his room and took his *tastefully* back."

"I thought you said each unit had a bathtub."

"I said *tublike*."

John Grape frowned.

"With the showers, the door opens around a foot off the floor. Put a rag in the drain, have a seat, the water builds up ten, eleven inches. *Tublike*."

For $270 a week, who could quibble.

John Grape started in Suite 14, which was on the ground floor, by a soda machine. But that stay didn't last long.

Upon entering Suite 14, he noticed somebody walking around upstairs; he *saw* somebody walking around. The upper and lower floors seemed to have been separated with several layers of reinforced chicken wire—they sagged a little when somebody took a step.

So John Grape moved to Suite 26, which was in a second-floor corner.

Shortly after he stretched out on the bed for a nap, he heard swearing. Thinking that somebody had come for his watch and his wallet, he stumbled out of bed and prepared to defend himself, noticing after a bit that he had been awakened by a conversation that had taken place in a car stopped at the intersection just below his bedroom window.

The intersection, governed by a spotlight, was twenty yards from his pillow.

The quietest spot in Suite 26 was the sofa in the living room, so John Grape slept there.

But it turned out that Suite 26 cost $295 a week, not the previously quoted cheaper rate, and there was no discount for the second week.

"Why?" John Grape asked when Combs arrived with an updated rate card.

"I forgot to tell you that Sid Britton, the man of a thousand hands, almost bought it right here," Combs said, pointing to a spot in front of the sofa.

John Grape shaved off his beard the first night he was in Los Angeles, and barely recognized himself.

No one else did, either.

16

John Grape stood on the poor side of Wilshire Boulevard, the Neiman-Marcus side, where a person could still shop for a shirt without having called for a reservation, and wondered why he used to like Beverly Hills so much. He had been well off when he was here last—when his movie starring Redford had premiered—that had to have been it.

Rich, you could fall in love with a panhandle.

Now, he felt very much out of place.

It was as though he had returned to the scene of a fraud.

Despite the fact that the tourists had cluttered up the sidewalks so much, and a considerable number of wealthy natives had begun shopping in Asia, the most important natural resource in this part of town still seemed to be divorcées.

Women with tan-white wedding-ring fingers were everywhere. They dressed to shop for dresses. They used the sidewalks in front of the stores like runways at beauty contests; they weren't browsing—they were checking out their reflections.

If what you bought to wear was worth more than what you were wearing, then it was obvious you were only *pretending* to be rich.

Before crossing Wilshire Boulevard into Platinumcardland, John Grape reminded himself not to drink the water over there; because it had been aged in a bottle and cost money.

• • •

He was twenty minutes early for his appointment with Dr. Rose, who was one of the finest plastic surgeons in Beverly Hills and therefore the world, and that gave him time for a glass of grapefruit juice with six seconds to spare.

He stopped at a small café and attempted a purchase from a waiter whose grasp of English didn't extend far beyond *Hi*. He was finally able to get a glass of juice, for which he was charged $3.10, by drawing an apple on a napkin.

Places like this should be required to put signs, *English Spoken Badly Here*, in the window.

There was no sign in front of Dr. Rose's office.

The outside of the building was painted light blue. The glass door was darkly tinted, and two display windows were full of crystal. For a second or two, John Grape thought that he had taken a wrong turn and was about to enter an art gallery. But the address over the door matched the one on the brochure he had received while he was hanging tough out in the desert.

The air around Dr. Rose's office seemed to give off a sweet odor. Every morning at three, somebody must hose off the sidewalks with Gray Flannel.

Presently, he saw the shrewdness of it all. Since there was no sign out front, John Grape didn't have to wait until nobody was around before he ducked inside.

The receptionist's name was Monique, and her only flaw was a thick French accent that had John Grape frowning shortly after he presented himself at the front desk. Monique shook a finger at him, then she stood and pushed his forehead up to get rid of the wrinkles he had made with the frown. Frowning was evidently against the rules.

Monique handed John Grape a few forms and nodded at the chairs, one of which was occupied by a woman who had a Band-Aid across her nose.

Original art hung on the walls of the waiting room. The chairs were soft leather.

Browsing material included picture books autographed by the photographers.

"Does this place have a cover charge?" John Grape asked Monique.

She did what she did best, which was shrug.

John Grape thought about checking out operations in a middle-class neighborhood; but he decided that when you were messing around with something as important as your face, you couldn't let somebody fresh out of carving school get his or her feet wet at your expense. So he filled out the forms and the questionnaire.

Question 6 was: *Who is your favorite singer?*

He should have brought a tape recorder.

There was no way he was going to be able to remember all that was amusing or even terrifying when it came time to bring his notes up to date.

After the forms, an assistant named Jackie introduced herself and led John Grape though a corridor lined with before-after photographs of plug-uglies who had been turned into productive members of high society by a few flicks of Dr. Rose's talented right wrist.

Jackie wore a cashmere sweater and a short black leather skirt—not exactly the standard Nurse Jane costume.

She led John Grape to an examination room where the answer to question 6—Frank Sinatra—was singing softly from somewhere.

There was no examination table. There was an examination chair, which appeared to have once been part of a zebra.

Dr. Harry Rose sat at an antique desk by the door. He seemed to be short and he definitely had curly hair.

He wore a silk smock and was reading a travel brochure.

John Grape had called from Arizona to express interest in The Works.

All procedures were priced á la carte, however, with no discount based on volume.

Dr. Rose circled John Grape a few times as though inspecting something about to be put up for bid at auction, then pulled up a stool for a closer look at the areas beneath the eyes and jaw.

John Grape said, "What happens next, you call your Dad?"

"I am *the* Dr. Rose."

"He's only forty-two," Jackie said.

"Same here."

"Then you got here just in time," Jackie said, feeling John Grape's slightly rubbery neck.

They talked it over. Whenever Dr. Rose described something like how flesh was removed from near the jugular vein, Jackie would cross her legs and suddenly the prospect of being skinned didn't seem so menacing anymore.

She was in charge of morale.

"I was unsightly once," she said.

"Where?" John Grape wondered, looking her up and down.

"Nashville."

John Grape couldn't wait—said he had to write that down on the spot. He told Dr. Rose and Jackie that he was going to write a book that touched upon his experiences here, thinking that the possibility of being exposed in print would cause everybody to bear down—carefully.

"Well, then," Dr. Rose said, pushing his glasses to the top of his head, "if anything goes wrong, it might be to everybody's best advantage if you didn't come out of the anesthesia."

John Grape looked from a group of figures that totaled $11,400 to some pictures of people who had had the bags removed from under their eyes.

"See how much younger they look," Jackie said.

John Grape made the point that one of the reasons why they looked younger was because in the Before pictures, they wore rags and frowned, whereas in the After shots, they wore sequins and tuxedos, and they laughed.

"You also need to have your spirits lifted," Jackie said.

"I thought it was eleven-four including the nose."

"Excluding."

"So how much for a nose?"

Jackie thumbed through some pages in a notebook. "Yours would be approximately thirty-nine hundred dollars."

John Grape moaned slightly and brought the bottom line up to $15,300.

"You get yourself all fixed up," Jackie said, showing him snapshots of people who had recently given up their chins for Lent, "and I'd go out with you in a second."

"You like buses?"

Jackie said she had no idea.

While they waited for Dr. Rose to return from taking the bandages off a bust enlargement, Jackie fiddled around with a calculator and spread the cost of John Grape's nose work—there was a bump that had to go—over twenty years. She could sense that otherwise he was about to keep the old nose.

He could have a nose that went straight for around fifty-four cents a day.

He volunteered to pay it out that way and started to write Jackie a check for $3.78 for the first week.

She put her calculator away.

When Dr. Rose got back, they discussed pain and healing and scheduling problems and they walked to the reception area.

John Grape had to decide what work he wanted done before the close of business the day after tomorrow because Dr. Rose had only one morning open during the next three weeks, then there was a convention.

"Fort Worth?"

"Holland," Dr. Rose said.

Jackie gave John Grape brochures that explained such things as how long various scars lasted. A picture of a smiling mummy was on the front of one pamphlet. Jackie compared the pain from her nose realignment to a minor sinus headache.

Dr. Rose had several routine questions that he was obligated to ask before any surgical procedure could be performed.

The first question was: "Are you a criminal?"

John Grape said, "No."

"Are you planning to become one?"

John Grape scratched his chin.

"God, he's *thinking* about it," Jackie said.

"Only to finance the nose."

"Fine," Dr. Rose said, extending his hand.

17

arvin Hunsacker was pouring himself coffee by his secretary's desk when the mail arrived on Monday.

"I see you've got yourself a new assistant," the mailman
said.

"Sorry?"

"Grape, John."

"Oh. Yes."

"They come and go, don't they."

Marvin Hunsacker smiled.

"This is a very demanding business," he said.

"No kidding?"

"All the new investigators go through a trial period. Coffee?"

"Black. It looks easy on television."

"Television lies."

"Why?"

"Because most of what we do is think. That can be very difficult to dra-
matize."

"You ever been shot?"

"Not even *at*, since I quit the police."

"Loose blondes for clients?"

"Let's see." Marvin Hunsacker sat on the edge of his desk and squinted
at the ceiling.

158   "If you have to think about it, you probably haven't," the mailman said.
"I don't doubt you're right."
"So what is it you *do*, anyway?"
"I find things. People and things."
"And what happens if somebody doesn't want to come back?"
"I only find them," Marvin Hunsacker said, puckering up. "I don't *touch* them."

John Grape's mail was:

A third notice from a department store.
A brochure advertising X-rated magazines and movies.
A fourth notice from a department store.
A tip sheet that predicted the winners of various horse races at selected tracks in the northeast.
A letter from a gasoline credit card company that said his account had been turned over to a collection agency.

"Nothing?" Tuttle said.
"Yet."
Tuttle stood in the doorway of Marvin Hunsacker's office, as he did each morning after the mailman arrived.
Marvin Hunsacker slid John Grape's mail across the desk and told Tuttle to remove this forwarding address from the envelopes, reseal everything, and see that it was delivered to Mr. Mellow's office.
"So maybe nothing will ever come that will tell us where he is. Maybe I'll be getting my four hundred dollars back."
"Tuttle?"
"Sir."
"Something will come."
Tuttle shrugged.
"Tuttle?"
"Sir."
"How's our mind?"
"It's coming right along, sir."
"You're thinking."
"Virtually nonstop."

"See this glass of water?"

Tuttle nodded at what was in front of Marvin Hunsacker.

"Tell me, Tuttle, is it half full or half empty."

Tuttle took a step toward the desk.

Marvin Hunsacker held up his right hand.

"We will assume for the sake of this conversation that the level of water is precisely the same distance from the top and the bottom, that it is *exactly* half something."

Tuttle frowned.

"I'm *not* trying to find out if you're an optimist or a pessimist, Tuttle. This glass *is* for a provable fact, half full or half empty. So you have a fifty-fifty chance of maintaining your employment with this firm."

"*Full,*" Tuttle said.

"No, I'm sorry, but you're wrong, Marvin Hunsacker said, taking a sip of what was left in the glass. "It was originally full. Then I drank half of what was in it, which makes it half *empty*. Had I been filling the glass, then it would have been, of course, half full."

"Please don't fire me," Tuttle said.

18

ecause of all the traffic, there were not enough hours in the day to get it done in Los Angeles. The city had run out of time since John Grape was there last. It came as no great surprise.

People living in southern California think 50 is cold and 85 is hot; the weather has been attracting perfect strangers for as long as anybody can remember.

Los Angeles tries to keep the traffic on the freeways moving with a unique split shift: Common laborers hit the road before 8 A.M., then upper management arrives with the top down at around 10. Even so, it was hard to get there from here on time without following along in the wake of some siren.

Because of congestion on the freeways, everything is pushed farther back into the night. Soon, they'll start singing the anthem between the first and second quarters at the Laker games. The Dodgers and Angels will have eighth-inning stretches.

Already, the Daily Double out at Santa Anita involves picking winners of the second and third races, not the first two, which is the way it works at tracks located in places that have some time left.

At the nice hotels, a maid is liable to turn the covers of your bed down with you in them; they put the mints on the pillows at around midnight, while you're supposed to be at dinner.

● ● ●

John Grape was late for his voice lesson, which made him late for his appointment at the Fothergill Institute of Hair Replacement, which meant that he would probably have to cancel his dance lesson or appointment with the dentist, just to get back on schedule.

The voice work was going well. He wasn't bad at sounding different.

Lauren Bacall used to have a squeaky little voice—so the story went. She lowered it by screaming on purpose. If she could do that to become a star, so could John Grape.

He took voice lessons from a man named Marcel Tutman, who taught actors and actresses how to assume accents for upcoming jobs on the stage and screen. John Grape told Tutman that he could use a nice new low drawl for a role in a play.

Marcel Tutman himself was late for John Grape's third voice lesson. He had been called out on an emergency—to teach Sylvester Stallone that afternoon to speak like an Irish nobleman for a role in a film that was scheduled to start principal photography inside a month. The film about the good life in Ireland was being rushed through because there had been trouble at the studios about the proposed production of *Rocky Junior: The Kid Takes Over* and *Rambo VII: The War on Poverty*.

So John Grape sat around with marbles under his tongue, reciting names from the telephone book.

He'd study with a ventriloquist, if that became necessary.

Forty-five minutes into the lesson, Marcel Tutman called his office with the news that he would be occupied the remainder of the evening. After only twenty-nine hours of concentrating intensely, Sly Stallone had started to sound like an Irish setter, which was a step in the right direction.

John Grape would receive a refund for this lesson. Good. It was the answer to the horseplayer's prayer: Please let me break even today; I could use the money.

There were, he learned, five basic positions in ballet.

These positions concerned the proper placement of the feet and arms.

One must be able to assume the five basic positions before he is permitted to go through more complicated gyrations, like *pliés*, at the *barre*.

The *barre* is a piece of pipe you hang on to so you won't come unwound

162   at an inopportune time. A *plié* is where you turn your knees out and crouch while standing flatfooted.

It sounds simple. Then things in your thigh start crackling.

Even the most stupefyingly complex leaps and spins branch out from the five basic positions, one of which was about to cause John Grape's hamstrings to pop like bad violin wire.

As far as he could remember, the position he was having trouble maintaining was number four—the one where you put one foot directly in front of the other. Then you were supposed to turn your feet out so your toes pointed due right and left. Furthermore, you were not permitted to wave your arms in order to keep your balance.

John Grape had to practice this position with his aching back against a wall.

It hadn't taken him long to discover the secret of ballet. The secret was to make the impossible appear routine.

The man who taught John Grape ballet had a name with twelve or thirteen letters in it, starting with *D* and ending with *ski*.

He was sixty-four. Even so, he could still present a very nice *battement*. This is where a person jumps straight up repeatedly—*boing, boing, boing*—and moves one foot around the other and then back to its original position while in the air.

The man whose name began with *D* gave ballet lessons in a house minus the inside walls, just off Santa Monica Boulevard. He addressed John Grape as "My courageous fellow." He had never given lessons to a forty-two-year-old man who knew absolutely nothing about ballet.

John Grape, in the beginner's class reserved for people older than thirty, was getting pretty good at pretending there were bluebirds in his fingertips. When you conjured up such a vision, your hands could seem graceful even if they were only resting at your sides.

But he had not yet mastered the technique whereby a person could assume one of the five basic positions without wincing; so most of the time, he waddled around the studio like a man with both feet asleep.

One of the students in John Grape's class was named Cindy, a woman who didn't know her own strength. While spinning, she had the strength of a horse on a merry-go-round.

Toward the end of John Grape's fifth ballet lesson, Cindy kicked him in the right thigh, came on around, and whacked him on the back of his head with her left forearm. He fell, whereupon Cindy fell on top of him, driving him to the floor with her right shoulder buried in his stomach.

After flashes of light he saw Cindy standing over him, pointing a meaty finger his way. She was saying, "You could have *killed* me."

How? John Grape wondered, rubbing the back of his neck; he hadn't brought his elephant gun to class.

"He pulled me *over*."

"That is not so," said a sprig of a thing named Perry, the only other male in the beginner's class, "you did a *fouette*."

"You're a liar," Cindy said.

A *fouette* is where somebody spins around on one foot, with the other foot leading the way. It should never be attempted in a beginner's class in mixed company. During a *fouette*, the outstretched foot and leg lead a dancer in circles the way a big, heavy steel ball leads an Olympic hammer thrower in circles—it clears a path.

Perry knelt beside John Grape and offered his condolences.

Cindy said that John Grape should wear a bell, like a cow.

John Grape closed his eyes as wet cloths were applied to his neck, and attempted to reconstruct the series of events that had led to his being tackled at the line of scrimmage for no gain.

Oh, yes, Cindy had asked for John Grape's assistance while she practiced a few *pirouettes*.

A *pirouette* happens when a male loans a female the first finger of his hand so she can spin beneath it. The female uses a partner's finger as a base of support. Only, Cindy must have mistaken John Grape's finger for a brass ring—she tried to twist it off.

He stayed around to watch a videotape of a classic ballet.

In fact, he sat with ice packs on his right thigh and neck, and over his solar plexus.

164   "Spunk is important," his instructor said, surprised that he had chosen to stay and watch the tape rather than call a chiropractor.

Classic ballets were shown every Wednesday evening. This was *Giselle*.

When a woman on the screen did a few *pirouettes* beneath some poor fellow's finger, John Grape cringed. He looked across the room at Cindy, then nodded at the television monitor to call her attention to the way the male dancer had emerged unscathed. Cindy gave him the finger.

19

arvin Hunsacker called The Palms and asked to speak with John Grape.

"He's not here, he's swimming," Combs said.

Marvin Hunsacker didn't hear a word of the answer because an airplane was flying over The Palms, which was two miles from LAX and on the approach path when the Santa Ana winds were blowing.

"What?" Marvin Hunsacker said.

"What?" Combs said.

"What?"

"What?"

When the engine noise subsided, Combs said, "Talk fast, I hear another one coming."

"May I speak with John Grape please?"

"He's not here, he's swimming."

"No, I said, Grape, G-r-a-p-e."

"He's s-w-i-m-m-i-n-g."

"Well . . . could you get him."

"If you'll pay the mileage."

"I don't understand."

"He's not swimming here. He's swimming in the ocean."

"Oh," Marvin Hunsacker said. "Oh."

"You want to leave a . . ."

166   The roaring started again.

"No," Marvin Hunsacker said. "I'll call back."

"That's *one* way to do it," Tuttle said, looking over Hunsacker's shoulder at the mail that had come for John Grape. The most revealing piece of mail was an American Express bill, with an airline ticket from Las Vegas to Los Angeles and a receipt from The Palms included in the charges. "Asking for him by name. Hoping that doesn't send him packing."

Marvin Hunsacker got up and moved to the map with *Grape* written at the top and drew a black line from the northeast to Las Vegas, and then on to southern California. He circled Los Angeles four or five times and told Tuttle to have a seat.

"Tell me what you would have done," Marvin Hunsacker said, capping the black Magic Marker.

"Well, I would have either asked for a John, or I would have asked for somebody with a similar last name, like maybe, I don't know *Grade*. I would have hoped to confirm that he was staying there without letting anybody know whom I was actually looking for."

"Very good," Marvin Hunsacker said.

"Thank you."

Tuttle smiled.

"But not great. Please tell me why I didn't do that?"

"Tell you why you asked for him by name?"

"Yes."

"Here we go again," Tuttle said. He went to the window and looked outside. Working here was harder than solving the Cryptogram in the newspaper. "Since he was registered there in his own name . . . let's see . . . he obviously wasn't concerned about somebody finding him in that place . . . uh, if he was registered in his own name, then he was probably going around town using his own name . . . sure, he'd use his own name so he could charge things . . . then a call asking for him specifically . . . that wouldn't automatically flush him."

"Basically," Marvin Hunsacker said.

"There's *more*?"

Marvin Hunsacker smiled. Tuttle wondered why he hadn't chosen a simpler line of work, like busting secret codes for the government.

"Had he not been registered as John Grape, then I would have known he was there under an assumed name."

"Because of the American Express receipt."

Marvin Hunsacker winked.

"All right. Tell me this. What if he had come on the line? What would you have said?"

"Be my guest."

Tuttle looked out the window again before saying, "Well, the hell with it, this is giving me a headache, I have no idea."

"Exactly. I would have hung up."

Tuttle was told to reserve Marvin Hunsacker a first class seat on a comfortable flight to Los Angeles—one that left around noon—and a suite at the Beverly Hills Hotel.

"Good old American Express," Marvin Hunsacker said, handing John Grape's mail to Tuttle. "Nobody gets bills out faster."

20

John? John Grape thought, walking through an underground parking garage at Century City.

That was almost something—ironic, probably.

Jerry?

Butch?

Eric?

Art?

Gus?

Butch?

Gus?

John Grape walked faster and took the stairs leading out of the garage two at a time.

Century City is a neighborhood full of tall buildings and people who appeared to have been graduated from college within the month. As John Grape walked between buildings, he decided that he would bring his daughter here before she signed up with the WACs. Most suits worn by the young businessmen had to have cost at least $350.

He was here for a name.

John Grape was very bad about names. If he couldn't think of a name for a character he was writing about immediately, he'd agonize over it for weeks and then go with something like *Lance*. And he was certainly not going to be any Lance.

He needed a great name to pass along to a one-eyed man Combs, The Palms manager, knew.

The one-eyed man was in the business of manufacturing quality identification.

John Grape explained to Mickey Horowitz, who was a senior vice president at an advertising agency called Creative Marketing, that sometimes a writer could get too close to a story. Sometimes you wasted a lot of time brooding when you should have been writing. Sometimes a fresh point of view could work wonders.

Mickey Horowitz nodded a mile a minute.

The title Senior Vice-president must have been something a person inherited, like Duke or Duchess, because there was no way Mickey Horowitz had been around long enough anywhere to earn it.

John Grape guessed his age to be twenty-six or twenty-seven. He wore light-colored clothing and red suspenders.

They sat at a glass table, which made John Grape feel uncomfortable because his shoes were scuffed.

"What I'm trying to say," he said, tucking his feet under his chair, "is that I'd like to buy a great name for a character in a book I'm writing."

Mickey Horowitz said *that* was a little unusual.

But there was nothing to worry about.

He closed his eyes and concentrated hard for a moment, then pressed a button on an intercom and requested the company of an associate named Ricardo, who could name anything.

Ricardo wore black high-topped tennis shoes with an expensive-looking linen suit.

During the last few months, he had come up with great names for streets, apartment complexes, a motorcycle, and a professional wrestler born Louis Hornbeck.

"Tell us what you know about pro wrestling," Ricardo said to John Grape, who answered, "Not much, outside of the fact that those guys don't hit what they're aiming at very often."

Ricardo smiled and said, "There used to be good and bad. But professional wrestling has grown so much, a guy has to be a specific kind of good or bad. And, of course, his wrestling name has to reflect the best or worst qualities." Ricardo took off his jacket and rolled up his sleeves. "And let me tell you, the great names are long gone. Our Louis Hornbeck had a very pronounced forehead, that was our starting point."

"He's no scholar," Mickey Horowitz said.

Ricardo nodded and smiled. "You take one look at Louis, he's a bad guy, there's no doubt. Only what kind of bad, how bad?"

"Ricardo decided on the worst."

"I'm looking for a name for somebody who takes advantage of the weak, the poor, the ignorant, the infirm. So Louis Hornbeck becomes Lou 'White Trash' Beck."

Ricardo took a newspaper clipping from a briefcase and slid it across the glass table to John Grape.

The headline was: LAWSUITS EXPECTED TO FOLLOW MELEE.

Ricardo said that Lou's new name had made him even meaner than he had been before, which was plenty mean. "All colors despise him. Last week in the Cotton Bowl in Dallas, we draw twenty-nine thousand. On the way to the ring, Lou steals some popcorn from this little girl, it's unbelievable. Then during the featured match, we're going against a guy named Joe America, Lou puts him out cold with an illegal sleep hold, throws an *old lady* out of her wheelchair on the first row, takes the wheelchair into the ring, and runs over his paralyzed opponent five or six times, stomps the wheelchair into smithereens."

"It made the CBS Evening News," Mickey Horowitz said. "So as you can see, you've come to the right place."

John Grape told them that he wanted a great name for a male in his early to mid-forties—somebody who would star in an adventure story wherein wit and guile would be more in character than violence.

Somebody charming, confident, adaptable, fairly rugged, and calm.

Ricardo said it would be no problem—the name would be ready in five to ten days and would cost only eight hundred dollars.

arvin Hunsacker tapped Combs on the shoulder and asked for a few seconds of his time.

Combs was preparing to climb a ladder and affix a mirror to the trunk of a palm tree so that he could see what the slothful maintenance workers were up to, or, more literally, *weren't* up to, from the front desk.

"They're throwing blacks bugs into the pool here," Combs said, nodding at a maintenance worker who was dipping out insects from the shallow end. "What's that smell?"

Marvin Hunsacker looked around.

Combs said it was *soap*.

"It's me, then," Marvin Hunsacker said.

"*Hey.*"

Combs waved the mirror at a maintenance worker. Then he pointed at the office, "Boom, boom, *boom*," he said, pointing from the office to the mirror to the pool. "*Gotcha.*"

The maintenance worker shrugged and held up a net full of bugs.

"Is John Grape around?" Marvin Hunsacker asked.

"No," Combs said. "You a friend of his? I didn't think John had any. He's a very private person. Runs and reads, it's about all he does."

"*Runs?*"

"Runs."

"John . . . jogs?"

"No, he runs."

"Is he going to be back soon?"

"I doubt it."

"He hasn't . . . moved?"

"We respect a person's privacy here."

"Mr. . . ."

"Combs."

"I'm only in town this afternoon. I simply wanted to say hello."

"Well, he could probably use a friend."

Marvin Hunsacker wondered why.

"He's in the hospital," Combs said.

Marvin Hunsacker twirled the two keys to his rented Cadillac.

"Came as quite a surprise to me, too," Combs said. "He looked all right."

"He wasn't injured?"

"Not so far as I could tell. He stopped by the office last night and paid for his suite for a couple of more weeks, said he was going to get a couple of things fixed. Seemed pretty happy about it."

"Which hospital?"

"I wrote it down inside."

Combs had Marvin Hunsacker hold the mirror at various angles until they found one that enabled him to see the entire swimming pool from the front desk.

Then he picked some flowers from the garden, put them in a Dr. Pepper bottle, and asked Marvin Hunsacker to pass along his sympathies or congratulations—whatever was required over at the hospital.

John Grape shared a hospital room with a man named Corker, who was in to have some cartilage removed from his left knee and some ligaments reattached to the proper bones.

Corker had injured his knee two weeks ago when he attempted to kick a golf ball out of some heavy rough and onto a fairway.

"It's hard for a cheater to sue anybody," he said, grinning.

Corker was very concerned about John Grape's well-being. He looked at his watch and told Marvin Hunsacker that they wheeled John Grape off to

surgery two hours and fifteen minutes ago, and that he had heard nothing
in the meanwhile.

"He couldn't think of anybody to notify in case anything went wrong
down there," Corker said, "so he listed me."

According to John Grape's roommate, he had been accompanied to surgery by a voodoo man and the opening act at the MGM Grand.

Corker was concerned most about Martin Fothergill, who, along with his
brother Horace, owned and operated the Hair Institute, a one-story building on Sunset Boulevard next to a joint where the featured attraction
appeared bottomless while standing on her head.

"People who play with knives shouldn't be allowed to have *goatees*,"
Corker told Marvin Hunsacker.

Martin Fothergill was tall and skinny and reminded Corker of a mad sci-
entist out of a fifties horror movie—one of those black-and-whites where
some evil doctor stirred things in a vat with oars.

"And," Corker said, "the fucker is *bald*. What does that tell you about his
famous hair-replacement technique."

Corker had asked John Grape if he checked Fothergill's papers; anymore, you could get a degree of some type by answering a question like:
Who was not buried in Grant's Tomb?

"John's getting that." Corker said, nodding at a brochure on a bedside
table.

The hairstyle on the cover of the brochure was called the Monte Carlo,
which was a replacement procedure that involved the taking of hair from
the nape of one's neck, where it never stopped growing, and its subsequent
implantation to areas where the hair was thin or receding.

"It's supposed to make a person look like Michael Douglas from the temples up," Corker said. "Look at the price. It sure as hell won't make you
look like Michael Douglas from the *billfold* up."

The Monte Carlo cost $3,100.

"*Unless* you don't come out of surgery," Corker said. "I had them pencil
that in on John's surgery form. They kill him, all bets are off. And that's
what they're doing to his face."

"They?"

Marvin Hunsacker sat down on the edge of John Grape's bed.

174   "A short doctor with curly hair, he's wearing a Hawaiian shirt that's got to glow in the dark. There's an assistant wearing size four slacks over a size eight butt; she's a former Miss Nude Universe unless I miss my guess."

Mavin Hunsacker stared at a big circle that represented John Grape's face.

There was a big X over the nose.

There were small X's beneath the eyes.

There were wavy lines along the jaw.

There was a check mark just below the chin.

Two attendants wheeled John Grape into his room an hour later.

He had bandages all over his face, head, and neck. A trickle of blood ran down his cheek.

"Goddamn, what happened?" Corker said. "You drop him down a flight of stairs?"

"Who's . . . this?" Marvin Hunsacker wondered.

"It's John," Corker said.

"Where's . . . the rest of him?" Marvin Hunsacker frowned at the patient's flat stomach.

"Probably in some garbage can down in surgery," Corker guessed.

The attendants lifted John Grape onto his bed.

They said he was doing fine and that he'd sleep for some while, probably through the afternoon and night.

Marvin Hunsacker returned to his hotel and strode briskly into the bar for a drink of straight wine.

22

arvin Hunsacker leaned over the bed and said, "Hello there, my friend."

John Grape opened his eyes and wondered who that was. It hurt to wonder. The only thing that didn't hurt was sleep. But he hurt so much when he woke up, sleeping almost wasn't worth the effort.

The top of his head hurt most of all.

It felt like he had a bad strawberry up there, the kind you got as a kid when you tripped and skidded across some asphalt on your knees. It felt like the top of his head was *oozing* something.

His physicians had said a certain amount of pain was to be expected.

But they had not done the pain justice.

The only thing John Grape could compare the pain to was an abscessed tooth; it felt like he had an abscessed head.

"This is," John Grape said to the person standing over him, "Room Four Twenty-One."

"Yes, I know," Marvin Hunsacker said.

Some aid for the friendless, John Grape guessed; an angel of mercy sent to cheer up a visitor in a strange land.

"So how do you feel?"

"Like a million," John Grape said. "Yen."

His whole head was encased in bandages, save for eyes, nose, and mouth openings.

"My name is Marvin Hunsacker," Marvin Hunsacker said, looking over his shoulder at Corker, who was asleep. "And I was up until eleven-thirty last night, trying to think of the most painless way to say this. I never like to pick on a man when he's down."

"What'd they do, put in red hair by mistake?"

"No."

"What is it, then?"

Marvin Hunsacker cleared his throat.

"Mr. Grape," he said, "I'm here for your ex-wife's alimony."

John Grape closed his eyes and lay perfectly still for a minute.

Then he pushed a button on a wall.

"Nurse's station," somebody said.

"Bring me a handful of pills, please," John Grape told the woman.

Marvin Hunsacker said, "Can I ask you a question?"

John Grape sighed.

"What are you *doing*?"

"Why in the world didn't you come a couple of days ago?" John Grape said, shoving himself a little more upright in bed. "Before they took knives to me. While I had a few dollars left."

"I refereed a polo match a couple of days ago."

John Grape told Marvin Hunsacker to pull up a chair; then, since he couldn't think of anything better, he told Marvin Hunsacker what he was doing. After that, he told him what motion picture studios paid for the rights to original stories. Sometimes, motion picture studios paid as much as a million dollars for original material. Marvin Hunsacker gasped.

Corker woke up.

Marvin Hunsacker wondered if there was a place where two people could speak privately.

"There's a patio down the hall."

"You feel up to a ride?"

John Grape nodded.

"Tell me how you found me."

Marvin Hunsacker told him.

They stared at each other admiringly.

The private investigator pushed John Grape's wheelchair past the television room toward an elevator that led to a sundeck.

"So you had my mail forwarded to your house."

"To my office."

"That's a great way to find out a few things about a person."

"Thank you."

"You should be very proud."

"That's high praise, coming from a person of your . . . *capabilities*."

"You do what you have to do," John Grape said.

"How much are you running?"

"Only about a mile a day, Marvin. Anyway, it was like I was kicked out because I had a heart attack." He glanced up and over his shoulder and got dizzy. "Do you see what I'm saying?"

"Not entirely, no," Marvin Hunsacker said as he followed a bright yellow line on the floor.

"Drinking, gambling, working, all compulsion is a sickness."

"Interesting analogy."

Marvin Hunsacker slid John Grape into an empty elevator.

"Did I tell you I'm being baptized a week from Thursday?"

"Congratulations."

"New eyes, contacts. Teeth. Four on the bottom have to go. I'm having the rest bonded, painted white."

"Doesn't surprise me."

He pushed John Grape to a fountain on the sundeck, sat on a short brick wall, and crossed his legs.

"I like you," Marvin Hunsacker said. "Perhaps I like you more than I normally would because—well, my wife and I are having some difficulty at home."

"Kiss it good-bye."

"Kiss what good-bye?"

"Your home."

"Never."

John Grape stretched. "I'm glad she didn't send some muscle."

"Some muscle would never have found you."

They smiled at each other.

"I've thought about investing in show business from time to time," Marvin Hunsacker said.

"A person can never have too much money."

The detective stared off into space. "May I come to the point?"

"Paying you off is my only hope."

"You're fortunate Cynthia and I aren't getting on."

"I'm fortunate you're married. Nobody gets on. At least they don't think they do. I'll pay you five percent of what I make if you'll go away."

"That's absurd," Marvin Hunsacker said.

"It could come to more than fifty thousand dollars."

"Only if you get very lucky."

"Marvin, I feel weak, so please listen. This is worth something, whatever it is. It's worth good money if it has to be turned into a novel. As nonfiction, it has unlimited potential. It's like some . . . *presence* has taken over this body. I'm a different person. I am in the process of accepting Jesus Christ as my savior. There's nothing left of what I was. Ask her psychiatrist. Some hypnotist killed me off. Did you see *Tootsie*?"

"Certainly."

"Then please give me a break."

"Heavens," Marvin Hunsacker said. He rubbed his eyes. "Tell me how the book is going."

"Very well. For the first time in my life, I miss being away from the type-writer. But I could use some money. After paying for all this, I'll be down five or six thousand, maybe less."

"After you pay the alimony you owe?"

"No, I forgot about that," John Grape said.

"In the event you're . . . unable to go home?"

"Because you tell her what's going on?"

Marvin Hunsacker shrugged. "Or if she recognizes you."

"It's a novel."

More patients were wheeled to spots near the fountain, so he pushed John Grape further.

"I'm going to need twenty percent of what you make off this."

"Ten, Marvin."

"If Miss Worth finds out I didn't accurately report what's going on out here, I could find myself in a great deal of trouble."

"That's nonsense and you know it. Tell her you found me before I had all this done."

"It's time for Mr. Grape to return to his room," a nurse said.

"Let me," Marvin Hunsacker told her.

Corker had been taken to surgery to have his knee fixed, so they had the room to themselves.

"Why are you getting divorced?" John Grape asked.

"It's nowhere near that stage," Marvin Hunsacker replied.

"Children?"

"Three."

"You're a heartbeat from a life of squalor."

"Fifteen percent of everything, novel or nonfiction, the paperback sales, overseas rights, cable television, licenses for dolls or T-shirts, all of it."

"Deal."

"Payable in cash."

"I'll see to it."

John Grape closed his eyes.

"I'm going to have to have the alimony that's due," Marvin Hunsacker said.

"There are some traveler's checks taped to the bottom of the medicine cabinet at that place where I'm staying. The front door key is inside my jacket in the closet."

"I found you in . . . Montana."

"Fine."

"Working on some novel."

"I'll dedicate this book to you."

"If you do, I'll sue you," Marvin Hunsacker said.

23

John Grape left the hospital four days before his doctors wanted him to; it was either premature evacuation or declare bankruptcy, in which case nobody would have taken the stitches out.

A night at The Palms cost $295 less than a night in the hospital, and the service was much better.

Combs hired an olive-complected woman named Chimi to keep John Grape's suite tidy during his period of recovery, and bring him vegetable and fruit plates from a diner across the way. The first days he was out of the hospital, he was only able to write in three hour-and-a-half spurts—while the pain pills were working.

A week after he had been back at The Palms, he ran in a very crooked line along the beach.

He went to get his name one Friday afternoon.

Mickey Horowitz said they were just about ready to turn his account over to a collection agency. John Grape, face and head still bandaged, said he had been in an accident. They took him to a big conference room where an easel stood covered at the head of a table.

"This is what makes our work so rewarding," Horowitz said. "Seeing a client's face at the moment of discovery."

Ricardo yanked a piece of velvet from over the easel.

John Grape stared at it:

AMOS

HUNTER

It was printed that way, vertically, in huge black block letters.

Mickey Horowitz smiled.

Ricardo smiled.

John Grape got up and went to the front of the room for a closer look.

Something seemed to be missing, like: Starring in *Porgy & Bess*.

"So what do you think?" Mickey Horowitz said.

"It sounds like he should be hammering steel," John Grape said over his shoulder.

Amos Hunter.

Amos?

"The Hunter is not bad."

"They don't come any more adventurous," Ricardo said proudly

"But Amos. Don't you think it's a little . . . *earthy?*"

"No, it's very American," Ricardo said.

"Ricardo has a sailboat to name this afternoon," Horowitz said, ending the presentation.

John Grape got to keep the card on which the name had been printed, but not the piece of velvet.

He cut corners until he dreamed one night that he was being buried underneath an avalanche of cafeteria meatloaf; so he treated himself to some decent food at a place called Montague's.

As is well known, a considerable percentage of waiters and waitresses in southern California are out-of-work actors and actresses. Most should be out of work.

John Grape had the misfortune to draw a promising comic for a waiter; the man had evidently promised his parents he would be a comedian even if it took the rest of his life. It would probably take the fellow until his *next* life to come up with an original opening for his act.

John Grape wished he had gotten an actor, because you could only be so dramatic over sole.

His comic did hilarious things like refill the water glass when some evap-

182 orated, make pads of butter disappear in a napkin, and replace silverware that hadn't been touched.

He had to be stopped so John Grape could eat in peace.

Over starters, John Grape had called for his waiter, who was twelve inches away, and asked if he could have another napkin.

"I knew we should have never put our logo on those things," the waiter said. "Would you consider stealing an ashtray instead?"

"You don't understand," John Grape said.

He motioned for the waiter to lean down, to look under the tabletop.

"There's some soup in my fly," he said.

The waiter sulked throughout the main course, but finished strong.

"Check," John Grape said.

"*Mate*," the waiter replied, handing over the bill.

Besides being side-splitting, he was also right.

The meal, without alcohol or dessert, cost eighty-eight dollars.

His bandages were changed every third or fourth day. They got smaller and smaller. Everybody said he was coming along.

One afternoon as he left Dr. Rose's office, a nice looking woman with red hair said, "Hello there."

When John Grape realized that he had been spoken to by an attractive woman, he turned around and said, "Sorry. Hi. You're very beautiful."

The woman said she took exercise class Monday, Wednesday, and Friday at this time, down the street.

"Why?" John Grape said.

The woman blew him a kiss and said she hoped she'd see him around.

The afternoon he returned to The Palms wearing only six small Band-Aids, Combs said that John Grape looked like his own son. A couple of days later, he said, "Now, you look a little like George Hamilton."

John Grape hoped it was only a phase.

He paid bills, started shopping around for a cheap airplane ticket, and sent along a deposit for a nice room back home while he still had the money.

arvin Hunsacker put a stack of hundred-dollar bills on the coffee table in front of Deloris Worth, and said, "This also includes next month's alimony."

"No interest?"

"I don't think anything can be gained by backing him into a corner."

"There's satisfaction."

Marvin Hunsacker shrugged.

"Where'd you find him?"

"Out in Montana."

"*Montana.*"

"A little place called Moose something or other. Moose Head. It's not much more than an intersection. A general store, a tavern."

"That's odd."

Marvin Hunsacker thought of how odd and tried not to blush, and had a sip of coffee.

"He's not what you would call an outdoor person."

"He was indoors when I saw him. A little cabin. Very rustic."

"What's he doing in Moose Butt, Montana?"

"Moose Head. Writing, I believe."

"That's a good one."

"I'm sorry?"

"He can't write a lick."

184   "I thought," Marvin Hunsacker said, wiping a drop of coffee from the table, "he was a writer."

"Euphemistically speaking."

Marvin Hunsacker smiled.

"He *types*."

"Oh."

"*Garbage*."

"I see," the investigator said as he fought to suppress a hot flash.

"How'd you find him?"

"Through a friend."

"You made him aware of the consequences if he's late again?"

"Firmly. I'm certain there won't be a problem." He sipped the coffee, not tasting it, burning his tongue. "He did have that one nice book, didn't he?"

"He had the one great idea. I helped him fix it."

"Well, maybe he'll come around someday."

"Never, Marvin. He'll never have another sane thought. He'll spend the rest of his life trying to write books that don't make sense."

"That would be a shame," Marvin Hunsacker said, finishing his coffee and ending all sensation in his mouth. "In terms of keeping the money flowing."

"What'd he look like, anyway?"

"Oh," he said, handing Deloris the bill for his services, "about the same."

25

He went to the racetrack, Santa Anita, which was out by the mountains, one Saturday afternoon.

He bought a *Racing Form* and handicapped all the races and watched without betting as the horses he liked finished seventh, tenth, fourth, sixth, third, seventh again, ninth, ninth once more, and fifth.

He thought that was pretty funny.

He closed out his account with Archibald, who was heartsick over losing such easy work. He worked putting fliers on the windows of cars parked at Dodger Stadium. He traded his $9.95 car for one that cost $6.65 a day, checked out of The Palms, and began sleeping in the back seat in a KOA campground just outside town on the road to San Diego.

He ran, attended church services regularly, worked on his book in long hand, and waited, hoping he would heal completely before he went broke.

PART THREE

1

John Grape felt like Methuselah, just before the end.

Methuselah had passed away after a brief illness at the age of 969.

As the cab driver brought him up to date on the state of things in New York, beginning with the Yankees, John Grape could only nod. The driver's name was Sam Totino.

"The Yankees got a guy playing shortstop hitting one ninety-five," he said. Clearly, Sam loved to talk. Everybody who operated heavy machinery early in the morning loved to talk, it seemed. Talking undoubtedly kept them awake. "Stevie Wonder could hit one ninety-five, swinging at sounds. Course, Stevie would be a liability in the field with most teams. But the Yankees could use him in right. They got a guy out there, needs a garbage can lid to stop the routine grounders."

John Grape stretched. He didn't want to seem rude. He wanted to sit quietly and try to think of where his next meal would come from.

He had $1,256.76 to his name.

He tried not to worry about things over which he had no control.

As if in answer, his stomach growled.

The airplane he had recently wobbled off had left Los Angeles at 11 P.M. He had saved ninety-five dollars forsaking frills like sleep. The attendants, who had been banished to this run until they each lost forty pounds, couldn't contain themselves in the tiny aisles and repeatedly banged into his armrest with their hips. He hadn't slept since Kansas, when the pilot came on the intercom—he liked to talk, too—and called everybody's attention to Wichita just off the left wing. At three in the morning Wichita bore a striking resemblance to the Mojave Desert. When John Grape leaned over and glanced out of his window at Kansas, he couldn't have sworn with any certainty whether the airplane was flying right side up; the few lights could have been stars.

By the time he came up with something reasonably intelligent to say about the fact that baseball players were frequently paid ungodly sums of money to catch flies—he was going to say it was a shame—Sam Totino had turned his attention to the state of things over at the park.

Every few weeks the mounted police would ride lengthwise through the park, making a lot of noise. Then thirty minutes later, foot soldiers would move through the area, turning over rocks and rooting around in the bushes, collecting narcotics.

The presence of mind-altering drugs in hollowed-out tree trunks explained why a squirrel was run over in the park every forty-five seconds. Those poor little things couldn't think straight, Sam Totino said.

The highlight of the ride in from Kennedy was when Sam Totino moved smartly through what had seconds before been a terrible traffic jam caused by a taxi that had experienced engine failure in the middle of an intersection.

"You might duck down a little," Sam Totino said over his shoulder as he turned on a switch under the left side of the dashboard. "Just to be on the safe side. Sometimes they throw things."

The switch was connected to a siren up by the motor.

When Sam Totino turned on his siren, vehicles that had been motionless began clearing a path. A panel truck pulled right, into the service entrance of an apartment building. A limo went left, over a curb and onto a sidewalk.

"What's amazing in this day and age of general contempt for the law," Sam Totino said, rolling steadily toward the intersection, "is the respect the average citizen still has for a siren. Very comforting."

He had bought his siren from a mail-order house in Maine. It cost $130 and was not to be used to simulate a police car, fire truck, or ambulance.

Evidently a lot of people used sirens to keep predators out of chicken houses, because that was what the cab driver had written on the order form beside *Reason for Purchase.*

As he pulled around a Federal Express truck which, when it had inched its way right, seemed to have nicked a Loading Zone sign, he pushed the button under the dash all the way down and produced a series of high-pitched blasts that caused a few pedestrians to flatten themselves against the fronts of buildings.

The driver of the stalled cab, holding the small of his back with his left hand, put his shoulder to the door frame and shoved his vehicle out of the intersection.

It was clear sailing the rest of the way to The Royale, which was one of Sam Totino's all-time favorite hotels because so many skinny, pale women stayed there.

"It would be like a dog with a good bone," he said, stopping near the main entrance. "You'd think."

John Grape opened his eyes.

Once his ears had stopped ringing, he had dozed off. The cab ride to Manhattan was more fatiguing than the three-thousand-mile plane flight from LA.

He had slept for about a minute and fifteen seconds.

"Where are we?" he said.

"Your hotel."

"Please wait for me."

Sam Totino glanced into his rear-view mirror. He had heard *that* one before. The last time he heard it, his fare went into the front entrance of a hotel, out the back, then undoubtedly to a bar to celebrate the free ride.

"Tell you what," he said. "Let's bring everything up to date. But I won't reset the meter and stick you for the surcharge on the front end."

"How about a percentage of my movie?"

"What?" The cabbie said.

"Never mind."

John Grape passed four ten-dollar bills forward and winced.

"Luggage?" the doorman said through the front passenger window.

Sam Totino shrugged and said, "He wants me to wait."

"But this is an unloading zone."

John Grape unloaded five more dollars and sighed.

"Tell me about pale, skinny women," Sam Totino said to the doorman.

"They're bad for business. They eat like birds and tip chicken feed."

The person in charge of the front desk at The Royale was Maurice.

Dust didn't stand a chance here. The area around Maurice, most of which was marble and old wood, was spotless. *Maurice* was spotless. John Grape guessed that during breaks, Maurice took off his pants before sitting down, to keep from becoming mussed.

"*Good* morning," Maurice said. "Do you have a reservation?"

John Grape yawned and looked at a RESERVATIONS sign hanging over Maurice's space. Then he glanced to his left at a window reserved for checking out. He blinked a few times and wondered if he should have gone there.

Maurice reached under the counter and got a Kleenex.

John Grape accepted the tissue, then stared at it.

"I thought you had something in your eye, sir."

"No." John Grape quit blinking and handed the Kleenex back. Maurice dropped it in a trash can. "I'm just tired, that's all. I haven't had a good night's sleep in some while."

"We'll take care of that. Name, please."

"My name is Grape."

"Have a mint, sir," Maurice slid a tray of red and white striped things forward.

John Grape should have left Los Angeles at noon, there was no doubt about it. Or he should have sold his clothes and bought a first-class ticket. He had underestimated the value of rest. Before he could request that they please begin again, Maurice had turned around and was typing on a computer.

"All is as it should be," he said over his shoulder.

He returned to the marble counter with a registration card and a silver pen. He officially welcomed John Grape to The Royale.

"I'd like to cancel my reservation," John Grape said, sliding the silver pen back. He tried to make this exchange less awkward with a smile, but it didn't work.

Maurice, who had been at The Royale six years, and who had never so much as sucked in his breath when somebody with a strange name like Grape checked in, and who had been a finalist in the Employee of the Year contest a record five times, licked his lips and touched his tie, which didn't need touching, and wondered if somebody from the night shift might be trying to have some fun at his expense.

"*Sir?*" he said.

"I'd like to cancel my reservation," John Grape said, softer this time.

Maurice glanced at the reservation confirmation, which had been made almost a month ago. It had been accompanied by a deposit, so this was no joke.

He folded his hands on the counter.

"I see," he lied.

A beautifully dressed, thin, pale woman who was checking out just left.

John Grape leaned over the marble counter and nodded for Maurice to join him there for a more private conversation.

"It's about my deposit," he said. "I'd like it. I *need* it."

Maurice snapped back to his previous upright and more dignified position.

"You see," John Grape said, leaning farther and farther over the counter, "I've had some wearing financial times lately. I was hoping to stay here, right up until the last minute, but . . ."

"*Please* don't climb onto the counter."

"This is just a little embarrassing, discussing personal matters with a stranger."

Maurice was again up for Employee of the Year. The person who won last time, a waiter named Roland who worked in the restaurant, had put out a burning tablecloth without spilling a drop of wine; so maybe reacting calmly in times of great peril counted for more than making sure that some of the richest and most powerful people in the world had the best accommodations and service of their lives, as hard as *that* might be to believe.

And certainly, canceling a reservation made by somebody you could reach out and *touch* had to count for something.

194 Maurice started to make a note on the registration confirmation, but couldn't think of the proper phraseology because cancellations were always telephoned in, and the people in the back took care of this part.

He fiddled some more with his tie and asked, "Where do you wish the deposit sent?"

John Grape started to lean over the counter again.

"*Stop* that," Maurice said.

"I want cash."

Maurice had a red and white mint.

"Cash is the whole point." John Grape looked at Maurice's nametag. "Maurice. To be honest, I could stand some money right now."

"It has to be processed."

"But it's *my* two fifty."

John Grape and Maurice frowned at each other.

After a few seconds, Maurice raised the reservation confirmation from the counter to his eye-level—he wasn't *about* to let this drifter out of his sight—and said that John Grape was *not* due $250. "Reservations canceled *minutes* before the scheduled check-in time do not qualify for the full refund. They're pro-rated downward. Steeply."

He put some numbers together in his head and guessed that the refund would be in the neighborhood of $120; and he said one twenty as though it were something you put in a bum's cup.

"Where do you want the refund sent, once it's processed?"

"You'll be the first to know."

"Stamp," Maurice said sullenly.

"You mean, for the envelope with my money?"

Maurice nodded, about one inch.

"Take it out of the one twenty I have coming."

Finally, there was something to make a halfway decent note about.

"I still plan to stay here one day," John Grape said, looking around the lobby, the theme of which seemed to be understated elegance. "There's one more thing, Maurice. It's about my *mail*."

Maurice started this round of leaning.

"I left this as a forwarding address. You know, back when I was planning to be here a while. Back before things . . . soured. A bill for some clothes

I charged, one or two credit card statements, that's all that should show up. So I was wondering if you might hold my correspondence until I can get settled in somewhere."

"Stop this *immediately*," Maurice hissed.

"But one of those bills won't be forwarded to a Grape."

"Out," Maurice said.

"One of the bills will be sent to . . . another name. Hunter."

"Away from my counter."

"I know this might sound a little complicated so early in the morning."

"Out of my lobby."

"It's like a pseudonym. Would you like to see a driver's license or two?"

"Away from the sidewalk, as well."

"Maurice . . ."

"*Forever.*"

"What about my mail?"

"I will personally," Maurice said, raising his right hand as though he were being sworn in to testify at a murder trial, "put every piece of it into a *sewer.*"

"I'd appreciate it if you wouldn't put the one twenty I have coming in the sewer."

"One hundred and nineteen dollars and . . . *seventy-five cents.*"

"Whatever."

Maurice hit a silver bell.

"He said, "Back."

Instead of Front.

As in: Toss this one into the alley.

"You *what?*" Sam Totino said as he yanked his vehicle to the nearest curb and stopped in front of a deli.

"I'd like to see something in the sixty-dollar range," John Grape said.

Sam Totino removed his ball cap and shook out some hair. "You haven't been in town in a while, am I right?"

John Grape nodded.

"Let me tell you a little something about the hotel and motel business here." Sam Totino turned around. "This is not a place like Cincinnati,

196   where there's great, there's very good, there's fine, there's swell, there's
not bad at all, right down to horseshit. Here in Manhattan, there's perfect,
there's disgusting, there's a park bench."

"Tell you what," John Grape said, looking at some figures relating to his
net worth. "I can probably go up to sixty-five a day for the room."

"I hate to be the one to break the news to you," Sam Totino said, replacing his ball cap, "but the places that charge sixty- five for the day also
charge sixty-five for the *night*."

"Do the best you can. I'm on a strict budget."

Sam Totino said the last budget-minded person who had come to
Manhattan was Barry Goldwater, and look what happened to him.

The Moran, located four blocks from Times Square as the crowbar flew,
had seen better days, weeks, months, years, decades, and quite probably
even centuries.

It was a brick building of many stories. Most of the stories were obviously
of the hard-luck variety. As for the structure itself, there were ten floors. A
few bricks were missing in front. The wind, or vandals, had ripped most of
the awning off its pipes.

As Sam Totino stopped his cab at the front entrance, the doorman,
whose face was a line drawing of a bloodhound's—wrinkles were
everywhere—shuffled forward and asked what they were looking for.

"I'm a son of a bitch, he thinks we're after directions," Sam Totino said
over his shoulder to John Grape, who had scooted to a window and was
looking up at The Moran. To the doorman, whose name was Arthur, Sam
Totino said, "Your guests don't usually arrive on wheels, do they granddad? They hit the door running, isn't that it, looking for a hideout?"

Arthur said, "Huh?"

John Grape thought The Moran seemed fine.

"You planning on sleeping on a ledge?" Sam Totino shook his head and
said it wouldn't be a bad idea to look around inside before John Grape had
a few close friends over for a housewarming. As he searched through the
glove compartment for a pocket knife with which to defend himself as he
unloaded luggage—Arthur weighed around 130, and a two-suiter would

probably drive him to his knees—a police car approached from the rear
and stopped beside the taxi.

"Motor trouble?" the cop riding shotgun asked.

"Did I tell you?" Sam Totino looked in the rear-view mirror. "Nobody
stops at one of these places to *lodge*."

He told the cop that the motor was fine.

"Say," the driver of the police car said, "you see a guy run by here a couple of minutes ago? Baggy sweater. Jeans. Tennis shoes."

"Thick glasses," the officer by the window said.

"What'd he do?" John Grape asked them.

"He's been cooking things he shouldn't," the cop riding shotgun said.

San Totino began rolling up his window as fast as he could.

"Like pets."

As they walked through the lobby, which gave off an odor of mustiness,
Arthur said there had been a Murdock working at The Moran for forty-nine
years.

He had tried to lift a suitcase, had failed, and now served as an advance
scout.

Sam Totino carried one bag, John Grape hauled the other.

"My father worked here before me," Arthur said, stepping over an old
man's legs. This frail guest was sitting in a ragged chair, his body splitting
what was left of the fabric.

"Let's hope the hell he's *asleep*," Sam Totino said of the man whose legs
they had stepped over.

"I haven't missed a day of work in twenty-seven years, isn't that something?"

"You deserve the Congressional Medal of Honor," Sam Totino said.
"This place got a registration desk?"

"Course, I live in the basement, so it's pretty easy to keep the streak
going, drag yourself upstairs, put in an hour or two, even if you've got a
fever."

Arthur made a left by the water fountain, which had gone dry in the
drought of 1937.

"This place is full of the Murdock tradition, that's my point."

"You're probably wondering what this conversation is all about," Sam
Totino said, waving at what he hoped was cigarette or cigar, not carpet or
wood smoke. "He thinks you're *buying* this building. He wants to keep his
job, what there is of it."

"Why would he think that?"

"You came in a cab, you're not drunk, you're wearing socks, you don't
have a gun."

The desk clerk was watching a baseball game on a small black-and-
white television set.

"Do you have any vacancies?"

"For what?" the desk clerk said without taking his eyes off the screen.

Room 402 was at the back of the building.

Arthur knocked before entering.

He nodded at the bathroom, then told John Grape what he was supposed
to do in case of fire. In case of fire, even if the overhead sprinkler accidentally worked, you were supposed to open the window and yell the Spanish
word for fire, whatever it was, probably something like *fiero*, at the apartment building across the alley.

Room 402 had a bed, a table, a lamp, and a desk.

"If rooms could talk," Sam Totino said, looking around, "this one would
be arrested for outraging public decency."

This was the first time he had seen bars over *fourth floor* hotel windows.

Arthur told John Grape to watch for punks in the apartment building
across the way; sometimes they tried to steal things with long poles.

"You mean the firemen over there?" Sam Totino said.

Before he rejoined the safer traffic outside, Sam Totino showed John
Grape how to save money. The way you did that was by wrapping ten one-
dollar bills inside the most expensive piece of clothing you had, which in
John Grape's case was a sport coat containing a little silk. You tucked the
coat with the money inside between the mattress and box spring—it was
the first place they looked. When the thief yanked out the sport coat, the
ten dollars in ones would fly all over the place. He, or she—the criminal—
would toss the clothing aside and run with the loose cash.

And presto—you just saved some good money.

"They'd take ten dollars wrapped inside a Persian rug, toss the rug in the garbage," Sam Totino said. "The nice thing about thieves that frequent a place like this is that they're very stupid."

John Grape tipped Sam Totino ten dollars for the ride, the help with the luggage, and the suggestion about preserving the most valuable part of his wardrobe.

Before stretching out to rest, at some risk, he called Maurice at The Royale with the happy news that he had an address where the deposit could be sent.

"I'm pleased for you," Maurice said coolly.

"Send it to Amos Hunter at The Moran."

John Grape could tell by the silence that Maurice was no longer pleased.

"The Moran . . . in which city?"

"This one."

"Heaven forbid," Maurice said. His tone became softer—pity, John Grape guessed. "Who is Amos Hunter?"

"I am."

"*Sir.* We cannot send the refund to a name other than what's on our records."

"Sorry." John Grape said he should have thought of that.

"Are you in a . . . room?"

"Four-zero-two."

"And you're registered there as . . ."

"Amos Hunter."

"I suppose we could address the envelope to *Occupant, Room four zero two*, once it's processed."

"Go ahead and send it to Grape. I'll talk to the desk clerk."

"I'd like to be one of the flies on the wall," Maurice said.

2

John Grape had thought the whole thing over one more time and had almost decided to step onto the jogging path in Central Park where Deloris and her fast friends from an athletic club ran twice a week and say:

"Hi. Guess what, it's me. You were right about everything and I was wrong. I did this all for you. Let's go have something to drink that has one calorie."

You'd think a person would have to be impressed with somebody who had spent thirty-odd thousand dollars setting up a Diet Coke date. All of John Grape's improvements would prove he had changed for the better, simply to make Deloris happy. The fact of the matter was that he was nervous and far too frightened to attempt to be somebody else. Being caught impersonating a normal human being for personal profit would hurt. Forever. Admitting guilt was just the ticket. Over a diet drink and an unsalted cracker, they could begin conspiring to defraud a publisher and major motion picture studio out of millions of dollars. They would *pretend* Deloris hadn't recognized him. She could help him finish his book. It would be fun, dreaming up things that might have happened had she not known it was him.

Given Deloris's fondness for millions of dollars, John Grape was confident that their new relationship would last until death, or fat, did them part.

So he stepped from behind a large boulder as Deloris and a dozen or so members of her athletic club approached. He glanced at his ex-wife's face, stared at her legs, which were easy to find thanks to some scant jogging shorts, and then he smiled and thought:

So this is love.

Deloris ran toward him from a distance of about a hundred yards.

John Grape watched her through some small binoculars.

Love, he learned standing there, was a 50–50 proposition, a perfect balance of physical and mental desires. He wanted to take Deloris to the ballet, then rip off her dress and have sex on a deserted stairwell during the intermission. When the desires to share brains and sex were equally important, well, all a guy could do was grin.

John Grape had sure *thought* he hated Deloris.

But he was wrong.

He had planned to fake the part about changing because he loved her, which in itself would have been revenge enough for having been flushed from his house.

Being truthful would be a whole lot easier.

The feeling of complete and total joy that he experienced as Deloris's perfect breasts came bouncing his way froze him; and he stood grinning and gawking as she ran onward.

She was on the far side of the sidewalk.

Two men ran between her and John Grape.

He couldn't make his "Hi, it's me, I did it all for you" announcement in mixed company.

A private moment was called for.

Also, Deloris didn't like men who grinned and gawked.

John Grape quit it and stood frowning as Deloris ran by without looking his way.

To the best of his recollection, she had never run this swiftly before. It was as though Deloris and the people from her athletic club were running down a steep hill.

Overcome with the need to hold Deloris close as soon as possible, John Grape stepped onto the sidewalk and began running as fast as he could within the space of twenty-five yards, which was not too smart because it caused a cramp in his right thigh. Had he stopped to rub his leg, Deloris and

202   her friends would have been on the other side of Central Park having lunch by the time he had worked out the cramp. So he put his thigh out of his mind and thought about making up some ground by moving left through an open space; but a person limping through a soccer game would not make the kind of favorable first impression he had in mind.

People serious about their running stayed off uneven surfaces whenever possible.

John Grape had no choice but to run faster.

Making a comeback on a jogging trail was more difficult than he had imagined.

He forgot to take the binoculars from around his neck and they bounced from his chest to his forehead. He had to break the strap and throw the binoculars into a bush.

It took him several minutes running full-out to get close enough to Deloris to notice that her hair was not tucked under her ball cap. She had cut her hair short, which figured, the way he liked it long.

When he was within twenty-five yards of the group, Deloris slowed down and let a runner from her club pull even. It was a man. He whispered something into Deloris's ear. She laughed. The man sped up. Deloris reached out with her right hand and pinched the guy's backside.

Well . . . she was, after all, single.

She didn't know somebody was back there a few dozen yards, loving her.

While John Grape was admiring the backs of his ex-wife's thighs and wondering what ever happened to shorts that came down to your legs, Deloris straightened her right sock—and John Grape found himself virtually on top of the shockingly beautiful woman who had a white shack at a minor university named for her.

He opened his mouth to say "Guess what?"

Or "Guess who?"

But his tongue stuck to the roof of his mouth.

He tried to lick his lips.

Before John Grape could get his tongue going, Deloris glanced up and to the right as she picked up speed.

John Grape looked into her eyes and saw them narrow.

Their feet hit the sidewalk together.

He smiled.

Deloris frowned and said, "You're supposed to pass on the *left*, not the *right*."

He could *see* the illustration that showed on which side you were supposed to pass. *The Runner's Bible*. Chapter Two. The Rules of Etiquette. Rule 1: *Always* pass on the left.

It would be difficult to discuss the thrill of running after you had disgraced yourself by passing on the wrong side, so John Grape went straight where the sidewalk dipped down and to the left.

He ran straight across some dirt.

Off a curb.

Into a street that cut across the park, and was open to car traffic.

The first thing he ran into was the path of a taxi moving left to right.

The driver jerked his vehicle toward the curb, leaned out of his window, and threw coffee at John Grape, Styrofoam cup and all.

Fortunately, the coffee was heavy on the cream and not too hot.

But some of it got by John Grape's arms and in his eyes.

Concerned that a Thermos and more cabs might follow, he cut sharply to his right and almost ran under a horse pulling a carriage.

The carriage driver yanked hard on the reins, causing the horse to rear onto its hind legs.

Two elderly tourists were in the back.

When the horse's feet came down, the carriage shot forward.

The elderly man's head banged against something hard.

His wife's purse fell onto the street and she slipped to her hands and knees trying to grab it.

The carriage driver looked over his shoulder at the elderly man holding his neck, and then at the elderly woman holding her ribs, and correctly guessed that there went his tip.

A young man feeding pigeons from a park bench ran into the street and scooped up the purse without breaking stride.

204   The carriage driver lashed out with his whip at John Grape, catching him twice on the neck and once on the back.

It was, John Grape thought, a good thing Deloris had been running in the other direction during all this.

Not wanting to be whipped anymore, he ran behind the carriage, dodged a couple of bicycles, hopped the far curb, and wove his way around people on blankets while heading in the direction of the thickest trees.

John Grape sat on a park bench and wondered why he hadn't said "Hi, it's me."

Granted, they had only been next to each other a couple of seconds. His tongue had been stuck, and it had been all he could do to stay upright.

But couldn't he have given her a sign to let her know he had learned his lessons well and was back to make amends?

When she had looked into his eyes, she hadn't known who he was, of that he was certain.

So she had been proved wrong about his ability to change. Was that confirmation of a big job beautifully done what had kept him quiet?

Oh well, he decided an hour later—the reason behind his silence was no longer a factor.

And actually, keeping quiet was the only way he'd ever get Deloris and his stuff back, and achieve immortality as an author.

Nobody could ever live with the guilt this truth would bring.

Deloris would be too humiliated to take him back, knowing how badly she had misjudged his character. And he would be forever ashamed of not having changed sooner.

John Grape hadn't a prayer.

So Amos Hunter got up, stretched his tight muscles, and jogged a mile.

As he moved gracefully through the park, he arranged important matters neatly in his mind: If Deloris recognized him now that he had deceived her for a few seconds, she'd come after him with a knife. So all he would have to do was strangle her first.

Complicated, stuff, love.

3

"So I'm sitting around the corner at Joseph's having the trout," Mort Goldberg said, "and this thin, healthy stranger walks up to my table."

"You're having the trout fried or you're having the trout broiled?" Julius Tannenbaum asked.

"Fried."

"You should have it broiled, it's easier on the arteries."

"So anyway, I know right away this thin person is no waiter because he speaks English."

Julius Tannenbaum smiled.

"He says, out of nowhere, John Grape has a message for me. I say something like how the hell is old John, anyway. And he leans down kisses me on the face, right on the side of the mouth."

"Sounds to me like it was a regular waiter after all," Julius Tannenbaum said.

Mort Goldberg looked over a few notes he had made to himself after having been kissed on the side of the mouth in Joseph's by John Grape.

"He almost got badly injured over in the park," he said, "running around like some teenager. He had a point, trying to meet her spontaneously, doing something she likes. But there's a limit."

"I am amazed," Julius Tannenbaum said. "A man of my age, I never thought it would happen again."

"*You're* amazed. Try being kissed by somebody who came back from the dead."

They sat in Julius Tannenbaum's office, the walls of which were covered with jackets of books that had been big sellers. A few of the jackets were starting to suffer the ravages of time; a few were cracking around the edges.

Julius Tannenbaum was the president of the literary agency where Mort Goldberg worked. He was seventy-four. He poured himself some water. He loved water because it cleansed the system. He drank a glass of water about every ten minutes.

That seemed a lot of water. Mort Goldberg wondered exactly how much water that was. It had to be around a swimming pool of water a year.

"Mort?"

"Yes, Julius."

"You're going to have to excuse me a minute. I have to go to the bathroom. But keep talking. I'll leave the door open."

Julius Tannenbaum had installed a private bathroom in what used to be a closet.

"And you're telling me she didn't recognize him?" he said, running water in the sink.

"He's a different person, Julius, top to bottom, and inside out as well. God would have a hard time recognizing John. He's very calm and composed. It's actually a little goddamn creepy."

"Amazing. Mort, can you hear me?"

"Sure, Julius."

"Did I ever tell you about the biggest book I turned down?"

He had; hundreds of times.

"The spy book?"

"No, Mort, *not* the spy book."

Julius Tannenbaum returned to his desk and poured himself another glass of water. "Piss on the spy book."

No kidding, Mort Goldberg thought.

"The book I'm talking about makes the spy book pale. I have only told three people this story, Mort, and they've all passed on."

"Don't put a hex on me, Julius."

Julius Tannenbaum had several big swallows of water. "I'm in the literature business three short months, I pass on *Gone with the Wind*, what do you think of that?"

Mort Goldberg grabbed the arms of his chair so he wouldn't fall out.

Julius Tannenbaum lowered his head and said, "Those pissants in that mansion. Who in their right mind could have guessed all that goddamn whining and burning would turn out interesting. You write that story now, it sells nineteen copies, there's not even anybody naked from the waist up."

Mort Goldberg suddenly remembered how to talk and said it happened to everybody. "Last week, I passed on representing a guy who wrote a book about a few hairy things that ate some little kids. And I heard an hour ago, it sold for a few bucks."

"Well, for the love of Christ, that's an absolute *disgrace*."

Mort Goldberg frowned and wondered what was.

"Turning down something that devours children."

Mort Goldberg, who was only trying to make the man for whom he worked feel better about passing on the second greatest story ever told, rubbed his eyes.

"*Goddamn it*, Mort, I don't ever want a chewed-up kid to pass through this office untouched again."

"I apologize from the bottom of my heart."

Julius swirled some water in his glass. "You should be ashamed, letting a thriller go."

"It was more like an adventure. I'm grieved about it, though."

"You should be. Still, nobody will put *He Passed on 'Gone with the Wind'* on your tombstone."

"They won't yours either, Julius."

"Only because I will be cremated and everybody who knows is dead. Can you *believe* anybody cared about a bunch of drippy goddamn southerners batting their eyes for seven hours?"

"No, Julius. It's like a cult classic. Nobody can predict one of those. *Wind* is so terrible, you can't quit watching, like a car wreck. Anyway, put it out of your mind, they'll remember you for this one, for John's book."

"That would be nice." Julius Tannenbaum had some more water. "It would be extremely pleasant to get a good night's sleep this century. Tell me what you have in mind for this, Morton."

"The film rights first, the book second. A private investigator the woman put on John found out about this, so he's in for fifteen percent."

"Tell me what he's written."

Mort Goldberg opened a cardboard box containing most of John Grape's work-in-progress. "He's produced quite a few scenes, some notes, it's all pretty up to date."

"So how is it?"

"It's not all what you would call perfect. He did some of it in longhand, sleeping in the back seat of a car out in Los Angeles."

"What would you call it?"

"A little disjointed, a little unruly, there's a lot of raw energy flying around that needs to be harnessed."

"So in other words, what he's written is putrid."

"It's his first shot at nonfiction, Julius, that's all. The early stuff is fine. The man has been living under a lot of pressure. We can always hire somebody to tie it all together, to fix the continuity. Remember what we always say."

"What is that?"

"You can't fuck up a good idea, Julius."

"I remember. It's a shame we can't use that on our stationery. Film first, book second."

"Yes."

"I tend to agree, Mort. So tell me this, the idea's so good, why weren't you in California ten minutes ago?"

"A couple of things, Julius. The closer he gets to having his house back, the more we're going to get for the story. Also, I wanted to talk to you about money."

"You know our motto, Mort. Get All You Can."

"Not that kind. John needs some money right away. It's why he brought the story to me now instead of later. I'm very concerned about him. He's up, he's in good spirits. But he's got some crazy damn idea in his head about loving her, which is a little frightening, Julius. You know what they say about love. It can bankrupt a person. There's no way of telling how long his good mood is going to last, staying over at The Moran."

"I thought they condemned that place."

"It looks like they tried. You should see his room, it's a cave with bats. I need to get him out of there. Nobody can think straight with people shining flashlights into your eyes from the building across the alley. I think we need to give him some money and take it out of what we sell the film rights for."

"Giving a person money before we sell something, this is against all we stand for."

"He can't take the woman to The Moran for cocktails, Julius. We make him a loan. This story is the best collateral I've ever seen."

Julius Tannenbaum tapped his fingers together.

"Somehow, giving money away rubs me the wrong way," he said, unnecessarily.

"I just don't want him going anywhere else with this story. Loaning him a few dollars, it's a nice gesture."

"How much money?"

"I was thinking five thousand should hold him until I can get something on paper out in California."

"You believe in your heart of hearts that this is a better story than Scarlet and Rhett, those assholes?"

Mort Goldberg guaranteed it.

4

ohn Grape stood with his hands in his pockets, staring up at something that had more in common with a bolt of lightning than anything else he could think of.

The odd thing was, this lightning seemed to go up.

A jagged line five inches thick extended from the lower right-hand corner of the canvas to the upper left-hand corner, pausing in the middle to swallow something the size of a softball.

To the left of this painting was a mass of red shaped like a baseball diamond or a snow cone; and to the right of the jagged line was a big green dot that covered all but the four corners of an otherwise undamaged canvas.

Of the lot, John Grape liked the dot best. No matter where you moved around the room, the big dot seemed to be staring directly at you.

This was the Wiseman Gallery, a small, cluttered place owned by a man who seemed scaled to size—Wiseman was about five five.

"The contrast is very notable," he said.

John Grape nodded and wondered exactly which contrast the gallery owner was referring to—the contrast between all three paintings, the contrast between the frames and the canvas, or the frames and the wall; or the contrast between the asking price and sanity.

Surely, he couldn't have been talking about the *color* contrasts of each painting, since white was the background on all three, and white pretty much contrasted with everything.

Anyway, John Grape, who had no place in his life for sarcasm, kept nodding and said, "Tell me about the artist."

"She's *alive*," Wiseman said.

"So I gathered," John Grape said, smiling at the price tag on the dot. "Otherwise, this would cost more."

"I mean, *vibrant*."

John Grape stepped back. "You don't have anything of hers that's larger?"

"Not at the moment."

"That's a shame."

Wiseman blinked so his eyes wouldn't start spinning cherries. "Miss Worth works out of her home. She might have some more expansive pieces there. Perhaps I could call for a viewing."

John Grape looked at the date on his watch and said he wasn't sure how long he would be in town, this trip. "Her home . . ."

"It's not an hour's drive away."

John Grape turned back to the dot. It cost $1,000. That made the frame worth around $985.

When he looked over his shoulder to ask if the artist did commission work, Wiseman was sitting at his desk with a telephone to his ear, tapping a pencil on a blotter. He was saying, ". . . so the same cut applies to everything sold from your studio." He covered the phone and said to John Grape, "How is tomorrow noon at her studio?"

What studio? John Grape wondered. "I'm sorry?"

"Miss Worth can see you at noon tomorrow."

John Grape nodded.

"Your name please."

"Hunter."

Wiseman passed that information along, hung up, and wrote the studio address on the back of a business card. "You'll love the drive. Very scenic, and Miss Worth has a *fabulous* place."

"Might I ask a rude question?"

"Day or night."

212   "The price of this work . . ." John Grape touched the bottom of the large green dot. "Surely that can't include the frame."

"Just barely," Wiseman said with a smile.

5

hen he checked out of The Moran, he felt as though he had just landed after a rough flight, and he thought about kissing the sidewalk out front, but decided to blow it a kiss instead.

He began the checking-out process the minute the five thousand from Mort Goldberg arrived, but he wasn't in the clear for well onto an hour because upon returning from the Wiseman Gallery, it was discovered that there was a man sleeping in his bed.

He couldn't check out *around* the person sleeping in his bed because his sport coat with the ten one-dollar bills wrapped inside was between the mattress and the box spring. And, there was no telling how anybody bold enough to sleep in your bed would react after being rudely awakened.

So the desk clerk had to go to Room 402 to see what was up.

But first, the desk clerk had to be found.

He was in the basement, looking for the maintenance engineer, a man named Holcomb who, as it turned out, was the one who had gone to sleep in John Grape's bed.

Holcomb was supposed to be inspecting air conditioners and was pretty embarrassed about the whole thing. He explained that his unconsciousness was due to a dizzy spell. That he had taken his shoes off and pulled the covers up to his chin as he fainted was, John Grape thought, an accomplishment.

6

"Hi there," he said to Maurice, who was working at his computer behind the marble counter.

"Well," Maurice said as he looked over his shoulder. "I see some good came of the deposit. That's an attractive shirt." He turned off the computer and went to where John Grape stood grinning.

"Thanks," John Grape said. "What deposit?"

"*Your* deposit. From *here*."

"I didn't get any deposit."

"Yes you did."

"I was just going to ask you to apply it to my current bill."

"*What* current bill?"

"I'd like to see something in a nice suite."

"*Hush*."

Maurice stepped back to compose himself. Eventually, he spoke: "I sent your deposit to that horrible place yesterday morning."

"I didn't get it."

"I *sent* it."

"I thought you said it would take a while."

"I rushed it through personally. I was trying to do you a *favor*."

"Just cancel the payment on the deposit and apply it to this bill."

"Who *are* you?"

"My name is Hunter."

"You cannot apply a refund to one name to an account of another
name."

"Why?"

"It's *evil*," Maurice said.

"Calm down, I'll go over there and get the check and cash it. Now could I please get a little service."

John Grape picked up a brochure full of color pictures of the different suites that Maurice slid his way. "So as you can see," he said, "things have taken a turn for the better."

Maurice looked at his watch. He would go off duty in eight minutes. It was a long time to stall, but it probably beat the alternative—slapping a prospective guest.

"I don't quite understand," John Grape said, looking at a picture of a suite that was available on the twelfth floor.

"Is there a problem?" asked a man standing at the cashier's window. He, his nameplate said, was the assistant manager.

"No, Maurice is doing a perfect job," John Grape said.

Being perfect was evidently par for the course because the assistant manager didn't so much as smile.

"Now, the suite on the sixth floor costs three . . ."

"Ninety," Maurice said.

"But the suite on the higher floor, on twelve, is only three fifty."

Maurice nodded.

"Why is that?"

"The suite on six has a fireplace."

"Oh. The fireplace works?"

"No."

"So it's decorative?"

"Yes."

"So the extra forty is for the ambiance."

"To a degree."

"I think I'll take the suite up on twelve. I'm no ambiance chaser."

John Grape grinned and picked up a silver pen. Maurice slid a registration card forward. John Grape practiced his new Hunter signature a few times on the brochure advertising the suites.

216   "Let me explain something to you," Maurice said once John Grape had finished monkeying around with the registration card. "You are a guest of this hotel as of this moment, not when you enter your suite. So if you run out of funds in the elevator, you *owe* us."

John Grape smiled.

Maurice leaned across the counter and took the silver pen from the guest's shirt pocket.

7

The chauffeur's name was Charley, and he was enjoying himself immensely in the middle of all the nature.

Most chauffeuring work these days entailed the driving of substance abusers around town.

Anymore, people went in together on limos the way they shared condominiums at ski resorts; a half a dozen yahoos could combine their finances and act rich for not much more than the price of a cab.

Charley enjoyed driving for the ordinary rich—people who carried their valuables in billfolds, not Baggies—people who tipped in currency, not powders.

This spin through the Connecticut countryside was definitely more like it—no traffic, no noise. And Charley certainly deserved a breather because the night before last, he had driven six Herbalife junkies—three couples—around until 2 A.M. These people were in town for a convention and they spent five hours telling Charley how much money they made selling Herbalife products, which were some things that were supposed to help you lose weight while maintaining proper nutrition.

Charley had seen less enthusiastic holy rollers. He was afraid that the Herbalife people were going to strap him down, stick a funnel in his mouth, and pour a couple or three malts made out of seed down his throat.

They tipped him a sampler case of Herbalife products, for crying out loud. Charley thought about mixing some of the powder in with his Frosted

Flakes, but decided to wait until all the results had come back from the lab; he was concerned that prolonged use might turn a person into a complete and total jackass.

"You go over the hill and make a left," John Grape said from the back seat of the limousine.

"There's nothing to it," Charley said. "You see the compartment to your right? My card is in there. Take a few. Ask for me by name next time. I specialize in nature drives. Birds love me."

Charley went up the hill in question and pointed out a woodpecker halfway up a pine tree to the right of the road.

John Grape realized for the first time that he was a different person when he saw the large silver object in his front yard. You eat differently, you exercise, you study new things—it makes you calmer, for openers.

The silver piece of metal in John Grape's front yard appeared to have fallen off an airplane.

Before, he would have tried to rip it off its base.

Now, he simply said, "Go."

"Where?" Charley wondered. He verified that the address given as a destination matched some numbers painted on the curb. "We're here."

"Drive to the corner."

John Grape turned and looked out the rear window at the silver thing in his front yard.

It was ten feet tall, easily, probably closer to twenty.

It could have been anything from a banana to a boomerang.

It looked more like a quarter moon than anything else.

It sat on the spot where John Grape's mimosa had been.

"First and foremost, it's art," the mail carrier said, leaning against the right front fender of the limousine.

He had just come from delivering mail to a house several hundred yards south of the silver object in question.

Charley had parked the limo behind the mail carrier's small motorized vehicle, which was the size of a golf cart. He remained behind the wheel of the limousine, reading a paperback western.

John Grape stood next to the mail carrier.

He attempted to place his mind in the middle of a calm sea.

"But there for a while, it was anybody's guess what it was," the mail carrier said. "A lot of people thought it was going to be a satellite dish. Me, myself, I thought it was a device aimed at establishing contact with our friends from outer space."

The mail carrier smiled at his joke.

John Grape frowned toward the north.

"But it's art, no doubt about it. The guy who did it confirmed it. You an art lover?"

John Grape nodded.

"You thinking about getting yourself one of those?"

John Grape kept nodding.

"Bring your checkbook. Somebody said it cost fifteen big ones."

John Grape put his fingers to his temples and pushed, hoping to alleviate some of the pressure that had started to build there. "Who did it?"

"Somebody from Hungary, Rumania, Czechoslovakia, one of those countries. There was a big block party the day they unveiled it. The people from across the street raised all sorts of hell, claimed it violated the building code. When the sun's in the west, it's like a laser beam, the way it reflects into those poor people's living room. But I'll tell you one thing, you wouldn't have seen me delivering the mail without a club this time last year." The mail carrier looked up and down the street. "*Dogs*. German shepherds. Danes. Cujo wouldn't have lasted ten minutes on this run. But now, you could deliver the mail with hamburger meat in your pocket. You see the movie *Two Thousand and One*?"

John Grape nodded.

"Remember the silver thing that started all the monkeys hopping around?"

John Grape remembered.

"*Dog hell*, that's what the artist captured with his piece of sculpture. There hasn't been so much as a cocker acting up since the day that thing arrived." The mail carrier laughed.

John Grape asked, "Was it easy to get up?"

"Once they got the tree out."

"The tree."

"Roots like this." The mail carrier made a circle with his hands to show that a few of the roots had been six or seven inches in diameter. "Mimosa. Nice one, too."

"Did they dig it up?"

"Partially."

The mail carrier made a buzzing sound and pretended to move a chain-saw back and forth in front of him.

John Grape thanked the mail carrier for his time and then crawled into the back of the limousine on all fours.

Now he loved and hated her, simultaneously.

He had forgotten about the dog and was just able to get his left arm in front of his face to keep from being bitten.

The Scottie was in a bush, or had been.

John Grape had walked around to the south side of the house to see if a few of his shrubs were still there, and if they were, to see how they were doing.

They were doing fine. Except for the bush with the dog in it.

When John Grape knelt to see what had caused that bush to lose a few limbs near its bottom, the Scottie came airborne out of the foliage to repay a few old debts, like the times it had been thrown into the creek.

John Grape fell over backward and got a lot of dust on his suit, but managed to get a hand around the dog's mouth before it started barking.

Since he was the only person the Scottie had ever found disfavor with, he had to do something; so he came running, holding the dog by the back of the neck with his right hand, and its mouth shut with his left hand, toward the limousine parked at the curb.

"Quick," John Grape said. "Hit the trunk button."

Charley put down his paperback western.

All four of the dog's legs were in motion.

"*Hurry,*" John Grape said.

"What's the problem?"

"I want to put this dog in the trunk for a while."

"What *for?*"

"I guess they never forget a smell."

"That's a bad reason. You're not putting a dog in my trunk. It's cruelty to animals."

"I haven't got time for this," John Grape said, glancing over his shoulder at the front door. He drew back the Scottie and flung it into the limousine through the driver's door.

Charley ducked.

The dog landed on the far side of the front seat, found its feet, and began growling.

"Easy boy." Charley held out his hand. The Scottie sniffed it and got quiet.

"When I come out, don't worry about opening the door," John Grape said. "Even if a woman is with me. I'll get it. Just keep the limousine between the dog and me. Cover its eyes if you have to."

"Usually, I just drive," Charley said.

John Grape's writing room, which had been a made-over garage to the right of the house, was now a painting studio—the curtains were open and you could see smears of paint all over the place, even on some of the canvases resting on easels.

The front trim of the house, once a bark-colored natural brown, was lime.

The lined curtains in the living room had been replaced with something frilly. Because the living room faced west, the sun would soon cause the flimsy curtains to disintegrate.

There was new furniture in the living room. This furniture was contemporary and sharply angled. Two chairs resembled cubes. This living room looked like a waiting room in a dentist's office. As John Grape stared slack-jawed at a glass-and-chrome table that would have been more useful in surgery, an Oriental housekeeper opened the front door.

The last he heard, Oriental housekeepers didn't come cheap.

He started to say hello, but once he caught sight of the interior of his house, he forgot what he was going to say. He didn't recognize the front hallway.

"You here to see some art?" said the Oriental housekeeper.

John Grape closed his mouth and nodded.

The housekeeper stepped out of the doorway.

The front hall, which took you past the living room and on into the den, had been painted bright yellow; but it didn't really matter what it had been painted because it was covered with . . . well, art. Paintings extended from the floor to the ceiling and were all sizes, even round. "Sixty-one on left wall," the housekeeper said. "Forty-two on right, many more in studio."

She led John Grape into the den, which had been paneled with oak the last time he had seen it.

This was no longer the case. The paneling was gone. The walls had been stripped bare. The beige carpet had been ripped up and rolled into a huge cylinder and moved near the fireplace. The built-in bookcases were built-out, gone.

"Tea?" the housekeeper said.

John Grape licked his lips and nodded.

His corduroy chair, the leather chair—had vanished without a trace.

He leaned against a wall.

The nervousness he had experienced on the way in was gone, as was a little of the love.

The curtains that had covered the sliding glass doors leading to the red-wood deck out back had been removed and were wadded into a ball next to the carpet, and a sheet was pinned to the curtain rods.

A red-haired woman sat in a folding chair in the middle of this devastation. She sat hunched over, staring at two large books that lay open at her feet, wearing a bright purple cape that extended from her neck to the floor.

John Grape remembered to breathe and looked past the woman in the cape at a cubicle that had been stuck on the redwood deck. The cubicle blocked the magnificent view of the rocky hillside on the other side of the creek.

A nuclear reactor at the base of the Grand Tetons would have not been more out of place.

John Grape turned an ear toward the east and listened.

He heard water.

At least his creek was still there.

The housekeeper handed him a cup and nodded to a folding chair that was leaning against a wall and said that Miss Worth would be here shortly.

John Grape pointed at what was on the redwood deck and said, "What's that?"

"Hard to say," the housekeeper said. "I mean, hard to *pronounce*." She moved her lips several times, practicing. "Tan-ning . . . *module*."

John Grape had a sip from his cup.

The housekeeper handed him a tea bag.

"I thought it was a little weak," he said.

The red-haired woman sitting in the middle of what had been his den was named Dahlia. No first, or perhaps last, name—just Dahlia.

She was an interior decorator, and she was here to pull some color from somewhere—maybe some cream from the ceiling, some silver from the kitchen sink, or some tan from the wing of a sparrow sitting on a tree limb out back—and transform the den from a drab and dreary and lethargic room full of ghastly memories into something with a little verve. She said.

Dahlia tossed John Grape a business card.

He said it was nice to meet her.

There appeared to be no structural damage to the den, that was the thing to remember.

Every few seconds, Dahlia would rise from her chair and walk to a wall and hold a color sample against it. Sometimes she felt a wall with her fingertips, as though it were a Ouija board.

Suddenly, she turned to face the kitchen and said, "It works. You never know until you've seen it in different moods."

John Grape, who had never seen a chocolate-colored kitchen, sipped his tea.

"Every kitchen within twenty miles is green or yellow. Bright. Airy. Boring. *Bright* is what they teach in all the correspondence schools. This kitchen will have an air of permanence. The earth tones say—I'll be here long after you're gone, friend."

John Grape said that particular shade of brown blended nicely with a tree trunk outside the kitchen window.

"Thank you," Dahlia said.

Then she carried some samples to the largest den wall. "I'm thinking about two things here. Tell me your first impression."

The first sample was black.

"It's different," John Grape said, wondering how much it would cost to restore order here—ten thousand dollars surely.

"This is my other idea," Dahlia said, digging around in a big bag for more samples.

One was green.

One was silver.

John Grape thought they were fine together.

"These won't *mix*." Dahlia looked at the ceiling. "I'm talking about *different walls*, here."

John Grape sloshed a little tea on his slacks.

"Pastel for the day, silver at night. The new walls would slide over the original. Up or down." Dahlia looked up and down. "Given the way the roof slants so gradually, the best way to handle it is probably to build the walls sliding down."

Dahlia looked at her watch, then started packing away her samples.

"Into the *earth*?" John Grape said, dabbing at his slacks with a napkin.

"What we're talking about here is two looks within the same twenty four-hour period."

"It might be easier and less expensive to buy another house and go over there at night," John Grape said.

Dahlia was busy walking around the room and dictating her most recent colorful thoughts into a tape recorder.

And then she was gone, leaving in her wake nothing but a bad chill.

John Grape jumped when Deloris stepped out of the tanning module.

Then he looked at the rubble around him and quickly relaxed.

Deloris closed the door to the cubicle on the deck, squinted up at the sun, and touched her toes a few times.

She wore a black one-piece bathing suit that fit about like Saran Wrap would; it fit very snugly.

She took a towel from around her shoulders, tied it to her waist, and did a few stretching exercises, bringing each foot up behind her and to a point near the back of her head. She walked up the ramp leading from the deck to the house, pausing twice to kick a few pine needles over the side. She opened the back door, took an apple from a basket on a folding chair, then looked at the man who had come to see some big art.

She looked at him a long time.

"*You're* Mr. Hunter?"

Writing was once again a priority in John Grape's life. Discovering that your house had been gutted this way was a story that had to be told. So he stood, smiled, nodded, then took a step forward.

It was simple: If she recognized him, he'd put his hands around her neck and squeeze.

"Didn't I see you in the park the other day? In the city?"

"Yes," John Grape said, lowly and slowly.

"Not again," Deloris said. "Your voice. It's almost . . . familiar."

She closed her eyes.

John Grape took a step nearer his ex-wife's lovely neck.

"Please excuse me." Deloris tried a deep breath. Still with her eyes closed, she said, "When something reminds me of . . . an unpleasant part of my life, I'm supposed to relax completely and think pleasant thoughts." She shook her arms and hands. "For about three months, *everybody* sounded like . . . a person who no longer exists."

I *did* it, John Grape thought. Rather, I'm doing it. I'm cheating you out of my money.

"Anyway," Deloris said, opening her eyes, "you're the one who runs on dirt."

"Only when I'm late for an appointment."

"Now wait." Deloris had a bite of an apple. "I don't like to be followed."

John Grape, his new deep voice seeming to originate in the pit of his stomach, said he didn't blame her.

"Then would you please explain how you got here. How you found me."

"The name of the gallery where your work is on display was on the back of your sweatshirt. The other day in the park. So I went there and enjoyed what I saw."

"Oh." Deloris looked at her watch. "Well, you're early."

"Please forgive me, I was simply anxious to see more of your work."

"Forgive a *compliment?*"

"I'd like for you to have this." John Grape took a small package from

226   inside his suit coat and put it on the folding chair the interior decorator had used. "It's for the inconvenience."

"What inconvenience?"

"The interruption."

"I was only in the *tanning module*."

"I appreciate your time."

Deloris glanced at the gift. "I'd like to get something straight. What *exactly* are you here to see?" She pulled up the front of her bathing suit.

"A large self-portrait would be nice," John Grape said, showing her his new teeth.

Deloris had another bite of apple. John Grape could see that she was wondering if that was just another in a long series of lines. So he said, "It's the truth."

"It's your voice, again."

"I've had a cold."

"It's my fault. I thought I was overimagining things."

Deloris shook herself like a wet dog—relaxing some more, John Grape guessed.

"Maybe I should call my therapist," she said. "This is the first time I've been alone with a man in this God-awful room. A *monster* used to lurk here." Then she shrugged and opened what John Grape had put on the folding chair. "I'm back to the present," she said. "For *good*."

John Grape's smile indicated that he was extremely pleased.

The gift was a two-month's supply of vitamins manufactured in England and designed especially for people who ran regularly.

Deloris shook a few tablets into her hand. "I wish you hadn't done this."

"Why?"

Deloris shrugged. "It seems like the right thing to say."

"It's not."

"Well. Thanks for the vitamins."

"Not that you're crying out for them."

Deloris pulled the swimming suit down on the bottom.

"You haven't told me your first name," she said.

"It's Amos."

Deloris said, *"What?"* Then she blushed.

"You don't like it?'

"I'm sorry. It's not that. I just thought it would be, I don't know, something simpler."

"So did I," said John Grape.

Deloris apologized for having gasped at his first name and said she'd change clothes and show him the studio.

John Grape went to wash his hands. He walked toward the bathroom, which had been off the back hallway, realizing after a few steps that this was not a particularly wise thing to do. He wouldn't know where the bathroom was. So he turned right and looked up at the wall that had been keeping the interior decorator up nights.

"Have you thought about a mural here?" he said. "Painting it yourself?"

Deloris said she'd never tried anything *that* large

"All you'd have to do is use a bigger brush."

He turned to find Deloris smiling. "The restroom?"

"You were headed in the right direction. Second door on the left."

John Grape entered the bathroom, recoiled at the orange wallpaper, then soaked his face in a sink full of cold water.

They stood in the studio, looking at large paintings, several of which were surprisingly recognizable as people who had arms and legs and hands and everything.

John Grape's mahogany desk had been shoved into a corner and was being used as a bench on which to store and mix paint.

The desk, which had cost $1,100, was now pink, green, blue, black, and orange.

Deloris had changed into a baggy sweatshirt and tight jeans.

They stood under a new skylight.

John Grape stepped back for a better look at an oil painting of people who had wires hooked to their extremities.

"*Copellia*," he said. *Copellia* was a ballet about puppets that came to life. It was one of his favorites, he told her.

Deloris, who had not met many men who *had* favorite ballets, cocked her head one way, then the other.

228 "But the second act is a little long. The scene where Frantz has too much to drink goes on forever."

Deloris thought: *Say* something.

"But the *pas de deux* in the wedding scene is worth the wait," John Grape said as he turned his attention to a painting of Swanhilda who, as everybody knew, was the female lead in *Copellia.* "Did you know *Paganini* opens tomorrow night?"

Paganini was the story of a brilliant violinist who sold his soul to the devil, haunting music courtesy of Rachmaninoff.

"It hasn't been done in this country since . . ." John Grape turned to face Deloris, who had never discussed ballet with a male younger than sixty five. ". . . 1946, I believe."

"Yeah, right," Deloris said.

John Grape smiled and lifted the painting of Swanhilda off the wall and said he'd take it; he'd contact Wiseman at the gallery and make the proper arrangements.

Deloris finally thought of something to say: "Don't you even want to know what it costs?"

John Grape leaned Swanhilda against a wall and studied her at great length.

"No," he said.

"I'm divorced, too," Deloris said. "Thank *God.*"

"You seem to be doing fine."

They were back in what was left of the den, nibbling like rabbits on cold cauliflower bits.

"Fortunately, he's dead," Deloris said.

John Grape swallowed a piece of cauliflower whole.

"I wish I could take all the credit," Deloris said.

"For *killing* him?"

Deloris nodded. "For killing the memory of him. He's still alive. Maybe. Who knows. Or cares. But I had help getting that marriage out of my system."

"I met your decorator," John Grape said, looking around.

"I meant therapy."

"Oh."

"Hypnosis. You know what? When the therapist and I killed him off, it was *great fun*."

Deloris smiled and asked John Grape what he thought about therapy.

"I love it," he said.

"So you're in the investment business."

"Yes."

"Sounds interesting."

"Sometimes."

"I know nothing of it."

This came as no surprise to John Grape.

"Do you live in this part of the country?"

"I have places east and west. I'm staying at The Royale this time."

"I can't place the accent."

"Santa Fe."

"I didn't know there was a *New Mexico* accent."

"There were probably only eight or nine of us born there, back before it got trendy. I'm a small part Navaho."

"Now about this painting you want." Swanhilda sat propped against the fireplace. "I'd feel a lot better pricing it *before* you bought it. Mr. Wiseman likes my work more than most people. What would you say about . . . seven hundred?"

"In that case, I'll take a few more."

"Will you please *stop*."

Never, John Grape thought.

"Seven hundred is more than fair," he said.

"Well . . . thanks."

"Five-thirty?"

"I don't understand."

"*Paganini*. Tonight. Tomorrow. I'll send a car, we'll eat afterward. You pick the spot."

"I guess I forgot to mention something," Deloris said. She stood and walked to the sliding glass doors and wiped a smudge off. "Some people I've been out with in the meanwhile . . . well, it's all very depressing. So I've taken a vow of abstinence from men for one year."

230   John Grape dropped some cauliflower, but caught it before it hit the floor.

"Ending . . . when?'

Deloris, her back still to him, said, "Eleven months. I'm sure you'll understand."

"Yes, well, fine," John Grape said.

Deloris showed him to the door, and left him on the front porch when the telephone rang in the kitchen.

He wondered what this would look like as the last scene in a movie. Some actor would be standing on a porch with his hands on hips, hyperventilating, as the closing credits rolled across the screen. A film with such an ending would probably be relegated to the drive-in circuit, if it got made at all.

"What are you doing?" John Grape asked a man leaning on a shovel off to his right.

"I'm getting ready to dig up this little fir here. From the living room, it blocks the view of the piece of sculpture."

"Why don't you leave the fir alone."

"I'm the *gardener*."

"Why don't you go pull weeds out by the curb."

"Are you with the Sierra Club?"

"No."

"Then get off the property."

"Excuse me," Deloris said from the front door.

John Grape was getting in the back seat of the limousine.

Charley stood by the curb with the dog in his arms. The Scottie was asleep.

"You forgot this." Deloris held up the painting of Swanhilda.

"Get it," John Grape told Charley.

The dog seemed to growl in its sleep.

"Thanks again for stopping by," Deloris said, waving.

"Right. Sure thing."

Charley went to the front door and traded the dog for the painting.

They sat parked near the entrance to the turnpike.

John Grape had two road maps across his lap.

"You buy that?" Charley asked about the painting next to John Grape.

"Yes."

"What is it?"

"A scene from a ballet."

"Oh," Charley said. "You, uh, like that sort of thing?"

"That's right," John Grape said, shifting the maps around. "Do you have a problem with it?"

"Not me. Whatever keeps a person going, that's what I say."

"Are you booked later today?"

"Nope."

"Make a right."

"But the city is left," Charley said.

Katie lay at college, smoking and drinking.

She was stretched out on the patio of her sorority house, listening to music from four or five portable stereos and trying to squeeze all she could from the late spring sun.

It was finals week.

It was also partly cloudy and cool, 70 degrees, according to somebody on one of the radios. But the patio behind the sorority house looked like the sundeck on a boat pulling out of Saint-Tropez; girls in bikinis were crammed onto the patio like winos in a public shelter on a rainy night. Four girls had climbed onto the roof over the back door in order to be closer to the sun, skin cancer be damned.

"*Hello,*" John Grape said from a fence down a little hill from the patio.

"Jennifer," Angelica said.

"What," Jennifer said.

"What," Jennifer said.

"What," Jennifer said.

The latter lay by a beer cooler.

"I think there's some guy waving at you," Angelica said.

Jennifer said she saw him. "That's no guy, it's a man."

"I think he's waving at Jennifer," another Jennifer said.

They were *everywhere*. This was the Year of the Jennifer. Four of them were members of this sorority. Fortunately, one was engaged, and gone a lot. The Jennifer in the pink bikini—the young woman who had been stretched out by the beer cooler—was the sorority president. She stood and looked at the man by the fence, who was waving both arms over his head. She touched her chest and said, "Me?"

John Grape shook his head no.

Jennifer pointed to Jennifer and then Jennifer.

John Grape pointed to his left.

Jennifer in pink walked that way, stepping over bodies. When she came to Katie, John Grape nodded.

"Katie," she said, "I think somebody wants to see you."

"I think he's cute," Angelica said.

"He's old enough to be your uncle," Jennifer in pink said.

"I have an uncle younger than I am, for your information."

Jennifer in pink frowned. "Your *grandmother* had a son after your *mother had you*?"

"Something like that," Angelica said.

"You and your kid-uncle ought to play the state fairs," Jennifer said. "Be careful, Katie, he could be weird."

Angelica said that if he was, help him over the fence.

Katie wore a green bikini. She had a Budweiser in her right hand. A cigarette hung from the right side of her mouth. She scraped some grass off her foot on the fence. She flipped an ash off the end of her cigarette with her tongue.

"What's the problem?" she said.

"Why aren't you in class?" John Grape asked her.

"Who are you, the truant officer?"

"No, I'm your father," John Grape said.

Katie took a long drag off her cigarette, rolled her eyes, then had a sip of Bud.

"When did it happen, *last night*?"

"When did what happen?"

"When did my mother . . . *marry you?*"

"I've had a long day," John Grape said, rubbing the back of his neck. "I'm not your *step-father*."

Katie took a step away from the fence.

"I'm your . . ."

Katie dropped her cigarette and beer, and screamed.

Eight young men were playing touch football on a field near where Charley sat in his limousine, wondering why he got all the scrambled eggs. Other drivers took widows to their stockbrokers. Charley got the destruction derbies.

When Katie screamed, the eight young men who had been playing touch football abandoned their game and ran toward all the yelling.

When Katie screamed a second time, Jennifer in pink, the sorority president, reached into her purse and got a canister of Mace and began running at the fence as fast as her tiny bikini top would permit.

Charley tossed his western aside. He had a perfect view of the parties converging on John Grape from opposite directions.

Jennifer was the first to arrive at the fence.

She began spraying Mace too soon and almost ran into some of it.

She ducked and kept spraying.

John Grape said, "Wait, I'm . . ." and was instantly covered by a cloud of Mace, some of which blew onto the first fellow to arrive from the touch football game.

His name was Doug.

He clawed at his eyes and ran head-long into the fence.

"Doug, I can't tell you how sorry I am," Jennifer said later, once the air had cleared. "You were tremendous."

He bled from the temple and was carted off to the infirmary.

Charley helped John Grape, whose eyes were puffed shut, into a booth and said he was going to look for a place to wash the limousine, which had picked up some dust and Mace by the intramural field. If you turned in a vehicle that started people coughing, they'd dock you.

234   John Grape said the one thing missing in his life was a friend; he asked that Charley please stay with him.

During the ride from the sorority, Katie rode up front while John Grape explained things to the best of his ability.

Charley almost hit a parked car.

Katie said she was going to be sick.

John Grape said all he was trying to do was get by.

"Where are we?" he asked as he sat on some plastic. Because of what was in the air—smoke, music, and grease—he assumed he had not been taken to the library.

"Some bar," Charley said. "That could use a hosing."

"Katie?"

John Grape had a damp towel over his eyes. When he tried to see, he experienced a great deal of pain, and tears ran down his cheeks.

"What's the problem?" a waiter said. "A little too much hot sauce on the Fajitas?"

"Outside of the fact that you cannot hear yourself think, there's no problem," Charley said.

"Not many people come here to think." The waiter wandered off.

"Is she here?" John Grape asked.

Charley told him, "Yes."

"What's she doing?"

"Frowning."

They sat quietly until the waiter delivered their order.

Then John Grape said, "This is what I get for becoming a better person. A better father."

Charley shook his head and said this was one for the books. What books, he had no idea. The law books, probably. He was certain that he was going to be called away from a day's work to be a witness.

John Grape felt around the table for his glass of soda with a twist.

"Katie, I haven't had a drink of alcohol in months."

She said, "This is *deceitful.*"

"Charley?"

"I'm still here. Unfortunately."

"Turning your life around is deceitful."

"I'll bear that in mind."

"Calling every week, writing, it means nothing. What are these?" John Grape touched a bowl of nuts.

"Nuts," Charley said.

"In the skin or out?"

"In."

John Grape scraped the skin off four peanuts and ate them. "You have to count every calorie."

"Sounds fun," Charley said.

Katie hit the table with her right palm and said, "You should have *told* me."

"What do you call *this*?"

"*Warned* me."

"Charley, do you have any children?" John Grape leaned back and rested his head on the edge of the booth so he wouldn't have to hold the towel over his eyes.

"A couple, yeah, ten and fourteen."

"Girls?"

"The fourteen."

"I don't envy you the next decade."

"Let me get this straight," Katie said, lighting a cigarette.

John Grape noticed the smoke close by—people with Mace in their eyes quickly develop other senses—and said she should stop that.

"The only reason you're here is because you want me to tell mother to start *dating* again?"

"Lord," Charley said, "are you in deep."

"I can swim like crazy, though."

"You're here to make money off a *book*?"

"You don't think I have some money *coming*? *Back*."

"You think mother will *enjoy* this book?"

"I think when the time comes, we'll both realize we made some mistakes and get on with life."

"Damn all this," Charley said.

"I'm trying to unite a family here," John Grape said. "In a way. Katie, you owe me one."

"For *what?*"

"For having you."

"Now she's leaving," Charley said.

John Grape guessed he wanted to check out of The Royale. Save money. He couldn't stay in a suite eleven months.

His eyes still stung, but he could see fuzzy outlines without squinting.

"You missed check-out time," Maurice said, "by *seven hours.*"

Then he put the tips of his fingers on his right hand to his mouth as though he were about to be ill.

John Grape's eyes were *scarlet.*

Maurice went to the slots covered with room numbers and handed John Grape a message that had come in a couple of minutes ago.

John Grape handed the slip of paper to Charley and asked what was on it.

"It says call Deloris Worth."

John Grape felt his way along a wall toward a pay phone.

Charley stepped up to the marble counter and said that he was not entirely pleased with Maurice's tone. "There's no way anybody could understand what that man has been through today. Kindly don't pucker up at him again."

Charley dialed for him and Deloris answered after one ring.

John Grape said it was Amos Hunter.

"Do you have a middle name?" Deloris asked.

"No, why don't you think of one for me."

"Maybe I will. Listen, I've been thinking about your invitation to *Paganini.*"

"I'm happy about that."

"Do you know that one man I went out with took his teeth from his mouth at dinner. At a party, men sitting on both sides of me had a hand on each of my thighs."

"They must have been either married or stupid."

"And there's another problem."

"What?"

"You always seem to say the right thing."

John Grape smiled.

"I have one very important question to ask you," Deloris said.

John Grape told her to go right ahead.

"What do you *want* from me?"

"Nothing. I want *for* you to go to the ballet with me."

"I accept the invitation if it's still open for tomorrow night."

"I was going to give the tickets away if you couldn't go."

"You have two for Saturday night?"

"Yes."

"Then we won't need mine in the orchestra."

John Grape sighed so loudly, Deloris said, "What?"

"Nothing, I'll send a car at five-thirty, how's that?"

"Fine. I hope."

"We'll eat afterward. You pick the spot."

John Grape felt his way back to the front desk, grinning all the way.

"Feeling better?" Charley said.

"We have a date tomorrow night."

"You and your . . ."

"Katie must have talked her into it."

John Grape reserved Charley's limousine for tomorrow afternoon and asked about ballet tickets.

As far as Charley could remember, the going scalper's rate for an opening weekend performance was in the neighborhood of two hundred dollars per orchestra seat.

"This ballet hasn't been done since 1946."

"Is that good or bad?" Charley wondered.

"Good for the scalpers."

Charley said he'd start asking around.

"I'd like to check back in," John Grape said to Maurice.

"He's got a fresh basket of fruit coming," Charley said.

"Let's go over this one more time so it's fresh in my mind," the assistant manager said to Maurice.

238   "Fine with me," Maurice said.

Returning to nature sounded like fun. Get some khaki clothing, start a natural food farm in Wyoming or Idaho. Enough starch.

"You checked him out *here*." The assistant manager tapped his pen on a credit card receipt. "For tomorrow. And you checked him back in here. Today. Beginning tomorrow."

"I believe so," Maurice said.

"Simultaneously?"

"Virtually. Well, not exactly. There was a period of a few minutes, he was on the telephone, when he was neither here nor there."

"Out-in. Today, for tomorrow?"

"I guess."

The assistant manager looked at the computer behind them.

"It was flashing *Fault.*

"You did all this in the computer before the gentleman signed the receipts?"

"He's no gentleman." Maurice's bottom lip began to quiver.

The assistant manager scooped up all the evidence and said, "Come to my office."

8

"*ort,*" Jerry Friedman said.

"*Jerry,*" Mort Goldberg said.

They shook hands and thumped each other on the back in a conference room at Horizon Pictures, a film company that occupied three floors of a glass building not far from the Hollywood Hills—three, four miles, who could tell for sure, there were so many fumes in the air today.

Jerry Friedman was the president of Horizon Pictures.

He was thirty-five years old and had worked in the development departments of a couple of the old-line studios for a total of six years; at which point it had dawned on him that he knew as much as anybody in the business, which was not that big a deal, because all anybody else knew was that kids, sex, blood, and guts sold tickets. Jerry Friedman had started Horizon one yacht, a Rolls, and a house that belonged to Jean Harlow ago—three, four years before, something like that, who could tell?

He had the reputation of one who was not afraid to take a chance if the right script came along—upon occasion, he was willing to throw caution to the wind and make a film featuring *adults,* sex, blood, and guts.

He reminded Mort Goldberg of a hummingbird; he could seem busy while standing perfectly still.

"So Mort," he said, pulling a chair away from a table that could comfortably seat the Dodgers, "how have you been?"

240

"Fair, Jerry," Mort Goldberg said, putting his briefcase by the table you could have bowled a line on. "I had a terrible flight in."

"I'm sorry to hear that."

"It's the cheap fares, they attract people used to traveling by boxcar. I'm next to this guy *clipping his fingernails* for five hundred miles. *Flossing his teeth* in public."

"You like fresh fruit?"

"To look at."

"To eat?"

"I'm a pizza man."

Jerry Friedman pushed a button on an intercom and ordered a few fried things to eat.

"And I'm in the business twenty-eight years and they're still giving me diet books."

Jerry Friedman smiled.

"Jerry, I heard you had a little bad luck on the film where some guy was supposed to come back from the dead."

"A little, yes."

"I heard the actor playing the one who was supposed to come back from the dead actually up and passed away on you."

"Yes."

"Well, did he?"

"What, Mort?"

"Come back from the dead?"

"No."

"You talk about a bad break."

"Life goes on, Mort."

"What's the new one I read about last week?"

"The Newton film."

"That's the one. You're absolutely positive Wayne Newton can act?"

"Beyond reproach."

"The man can sing *Swanee* in his sleep, I'll give him that."

Jerry Friedman looked at his watch. "What have you got for me, Mort?"

"I have the last original idea on earth."

"You've got a caper?"

"In a way." Mort Goldberg opened his briefcase and took out a small sheaf of John Grape's material. "The parting of the Red Sea is a caper, this is a caper. What I've got for you operates on a number of levels. Love, hate, revenge, intrigue, it's all here."

"Mort, in . . . thirteen minutes, I have a development meeting on the Newton film."

"I'd call in sick . . . sicker."

"Just so you'll know."

"Jerry, do me a big favor."

"Anything, Mort."

"Please don't fuck with me."

"Nobody is doing that."

"Play games with the people selling you scripts about the joys of puberty, the teen slop, not me."

"The meeting will last four hours, Mort. You want to make yourself comfortable, fine."

"Four hours from now I plan to be making myself comfortable in the nearest branch of the Bank of America."

"What do you have for me, Mort?"

"Jerry, I've got a guy who gets divorced, obliterated from every perspective. Financially. Emotionally. Then he comes back to remarry his wife for his house and his money *without the woman knowing it's him.*"

Jerry Friedman blinked.

Once.

Mort Goldberg smiled and said, "You're on the wrong side of the camera, you're a hell of an actor. When I first heard about it, I almost pulled a table full of food on top of me. The guy I'm telling you about, he gets a new face, new hair, he loses forty-some pounds, and that's only the *beginning.*"

"Mort?"

"Jerry?"

"I want you to remember what I'm known for."

"What's that?"

"Truthfulness."

"I don't know how it could have slipped my mind."

"Give me a second."

242

"Well, *maybe*." Mort Goldberg looked at *his* watch.

Jerry Friedman closed his eyes, put his feet on the edge of the table, and leaned back. After a minute or so, he opened his eyes and said, "Mort, off the top of my head, it seems . . . *thinnish*."

"My advice is to dig deeper than the top of your head."

"A little Mary Tyler *Mooreish*."

"Jerry, now I know exactly what a whore feels like, with the exception being that I haven't been paid."

Jerry Friedman went to the window and looked out at the muck caused by all the cars going ten miles an hour on the various freeways.

"Now don't get me wrong, Mort," he said. "I don't *mind* this idea of yours."

Mort Goldberg had some chips and dip that had just arrived. "I'm glad you agree that this is no ordinary caper, that's a very important stereotype to get out of the way. As I was saying, many levels. That's one of the fun things about handling a story that doesn't remind you of anything else. The last time I checked, incomparable equals priceless."

Jerry Friedman returned to the table, sat on it, and said, "Mort, let's not waste each other's valuable time."

"What am I doing, magic tricks?"

Mort Goldberg twiddled his thumbs.

"Here's what I think, honest to God. I like the idea. It's different. It's a little diamond in the rough."

"The author will appreciate your vote of confidence."

"Here's what I *don't* like."

Mort Goldberg shook a couple of peanuts in his right hand as though they were dice. He rolled them onto the table. "Craps. Maybe this table is dead. Maybe I need to find a new game."

"Is this the kind of treatment I get for being honest? Mort, I'm concerned your idea is too . . . *cartoonish*."

"Don't start that goddamn *ish* stuff with me again, Jerry."

"It's like a fantasy. It's like something from Kipling. Modern fantasies are very hard to package, though, Mort, particularly in a self-contained full-length feature film."

"You're trying to tell me this would have made a juicy *Love Boat*?"

"Since you brought the subject up, basically, yes."

"Oh, Jerry." Mort Goldberg shook his head. "You've been trying to screw people out of money for so long, you can't see the flowers for the manure. We're drifting apart. He *isn't* making this up."

"*Who* isn't?"

"It's not fiction."

"*What's* not?"

"He's *doing* it."

Jerry Friedman didn't know whether to smile or frown, so he did both, several times.

"Stunned silence, Jerry, that's our license to rob."

A few laps around the big table later, Jerry Friedman said for approximately the tenth time, "He's *doing* it?"

Mort Goldberg sat there eating and nodding.

"And she didn't recognize him?"

"Nope."

"So . . . what are they . . . doing?"

"Oh, the usual with people stuck on each other, dating, billing and cooing, that kind of thing."

Jerry Friedman, who hadn't eaten any red meat in three years, had two quick-fried steak fingers. He sat down and stacked his fists on the conference table, rested his chin on top of his right hand, and stared at the pages and tapes Mort Goldberg had brought with him. "You're telling me this is a nonfiction motion picture?"

"I'd love to kick this around over squid, Jerry, but we need some money, fast. The author, he's *out*. The woman, she has this *rich* tooth."

"I'm going to need a little *time*, Mort."

"Sorry, Jerry, we're fresh out."

"I need to talk to some people. I need to *think*." Jerry Friedman smiled. "They pay me a great deal of money to think, Mort."

"Well, you're screwing them blind today, Jerry."

"I have to see some people."

"Don't worry about me."

244   Jerry Friedman pushed a button on his intercom and said, "Cancel this afternoon."

Mort Goldberg folded his hands on the table in front of him.

Jerry Friedman turned over a few index cards to make sure he hadn't forgotten anything important, said, "Oh yeah, he took fifteen ballet lessons," then he leaned back in his chair and stretched.

Howie Kite stood suddenly and said, "*Holy shit.*"

Leo Marks, who had been leaning back in his chair with his cowboy boots propped against the edge of the desk in Jerry Friedman's office, squared himself on the floor and said, "Young man, I want you to listen very carefully to what I have to say. Just about every motion picture I've seen in the last half a dozen years, which I will grant you isn't that many because my stomach isn't what it used to be, contained the phrase you just used. I cannot begin to tell you just how offensive I find that phrase, not because it's so juvenile, which it certainly is, Howard, but more than that, it's so goddamn *uncreative,* do you see what I'm saying? Anytime a character is faced with an unexpected situation, you can see one of those *Holy shits* coming a block away. What this says to me, Howard, is that somebody is incompetent. It tells me the writer and the director are unwilling to work with the language in order to come up with anything original. So I would appreciate it very much if you would never use *Holy shit* in my presence, Howard, thank you in advance from the bottom of my tired old heart."

Howie looked out of the corner of his eye at Jerry Friedman, who frowned.

Leo Marks took off his ball cap and ran a hand through his white hair. "I like the story," he said. "It's a man's story, for a change."

Leo Marks was sixty-eight. He was a director of considerable skills, the last time anybody had looked. He had made three or four movies with John Wayne, a couple with Lee Marvin, and several with Jack Palance before sitting out the last eleven years because of the motion picture industry's propensity to focus on the trials and tribulations of teenagers, sex maniacs, visitors from outer space, and various and other sundry freaks of nature too boring for words—or pictures. So rather than compromise his

standards, the first being No Masturbation Scenes, Leo Marks had been bid-
ing his time at a horse ranch up in the hills until something of quality came
along.

There were those in the business who thought the passing of the old-
fashioned western and the old-fashioned detective story had doomed Leo
to the Celebrity Roast Circuit. But he didn't give a good goddamn about
what anybody thought.

Howie Kite didn't like the story about a guy who wanted his stuff back.

"I'd cut off a finger to write it," he said.

He *loved* it.

Howie Kite was thirty.

He was one of the hottest screenwriters around, having authored most
recently a film called *Beer Bust*, which to date had grossed $19 million
more than *The Bible*.

Beer Bust was the story of how five college juniors cope with being college juniors.

Seeing as how coping stories about high school seniors, college freshmen,
graduate students, and drop-outs had been done to death, it stood to reason
that one about college juniors just piddling around was a natural.

And whereas all four of Howie Kite's films had been wacky or zany—or,
in the case of *Beer Bust*, wacky *and* zany— there was absolutely no doubt
in his mind that he could handle a story that might probe deeper into the
human condition than a vibrator.

"Nobody ever said Howie Kite was afraid to take a chance," Howie Kite
said.

"Goddamn it, Howard, stop that," Leo Marks said, leaning forward.

"Stop what?" Howie Kite said.

"Stop talking about yourself in the third person." Leo pushed his ball cap
back on his head. "It's like you're talking about somebody in the next room
when, in fact, son, you're right goddamn here."

Howie glanced at Jerry Friedman, who sighed.

"Leo Marks believes in communicating as simply as possible, Leo Marks
said," Leo Marks said. "Now tell me the truth, Howard, do I not sound
moronic?"

Jerry Friedman, who had been searching a long time for a story that could bring together one of the all-time great directors and one of the most promising young writers to create an up-tempo film rich in old-fashioned charm and new-fashioned accounting, stood up from his desk before Leo Marks and Howie Kite squared off.

Leo and Howie had been in the building to look at the outline for the Newton film. Jerry Friedman assumed they liked this story a lot better. Both men said that was the case.

Howie Kite said that once this story had been translated to the screen, life on earth would never be the same. Leo Marks said that the secret of great drama was the understatement.

They both said that if the numbers were right, they'd enjoy working on this project.

While Jerry Friedman went to call several rich people who had expressed an interest in investing in a great piece of literature that would make everybody concerned highly respected members of their respective communities, Leo Marks asked Howie Kite for a moment of his time. They walked down a hallway to a coffee machine. Before things got too far along, Leo Marks wanted to make sure that he and Howard were on the same wavelength with regard to something that had been bothering him ever since he saw *Beer Bust*.

"Right after that one kid started playing with himself," Leo Marks said, straightening the bill on his ball cap, "I had the overwhelming urge to be sick."

Howie Kite, who was tired of getting bitched at for being commercially successful, called Leo Marks's attention to the fact that the scene in question was the first time this particular character had ever masturbated, which in Howie's opinion justified its inclusion; then, of course, there were all the laughs the scene got from coast to coast.

"The mentally unfortunate will laugh at anything," Leo Marks said. "Let's just say that I am not a big fan of mindless screwing and fondling on the screen." He smiled overly sweetly. "In other words, Howard, you would be wasting a lot of time and energy writing such nonsense for me."

Howie Kite said you couldn't censor *life*—they were talking about non-fiction here. "And besides, what about *The Pioneers*?"

That was one of Leo Marks's biggest pictures.

"You've seen it, Howard?"

"Yes."

"I'm honored. What about it?"

"Well, John Wayne pissed in the Red River. If that's not a gratuitous shot, I don't know what is."

"I think you're a little confused, Howard. In the first place, that was the *Jila* River, not the Red. Secondly, John didn't relieve himself."

"When he was standing on that cliff with his back to the camera?"

"He was simply taking off his belt before he whipped the bastard who had stolen those babies."

"Everybody I saw the movie with thought he was going to the bathroom in the Jila River."

"You see how easy it is to stimulate thought, Howard. Just keep the camera off their private parts."

They all got together an hour later in the big conference room to serve and volley the numbers.

Mort Goldberg said hello to Leo Marks and Howie Kite—said it was a pleasure to be in the company of two all-stars. Jerry Friedman brought Mort up to date: Leo and Howie were interested in the story. A great story. Mort brought Leo and Howie up to date: "I'm here to take possession of a great sum of money."

Jerry Friedman ordered snacks from the ACC.

Then Jerry, Leo, and Howie expressed their concerns about certain aspects of this project.

Jerry Friedman was not pleased with the erratic manner in which John Grape had put together his material. Although the early scenes read all right, three of the middle chapters began with: *That bitch.*

"Proving that people change has been a very emotional experience," Mort Goldberg said. "Some of the punctuation was a little weird because he was using a typewriter made in 1908. Hire a teacher to fix the grammar. Next."

Howie Kite was concerned about being picketed by womens' groups. They had come after him when his first film, *Air Heads,* was released. *Air*

248 *Heads* was the story of four girls who cheated their way to masters degrees in psychology. He didn't want to be known as a woman hater.

"You're on," Mort Goldberg said to Leo Marks.

Leo said that this picture would cost a lost of money to make, with all the location work in different parts of the country.

"Got it," Mort said, putting a period after the note he had made concerning how expensive the film would be to make. "Jerry's worried the writing isn't quite up to Pulitzer standards. Howie's worried about divorced women getting pissed off. Leo's bitching about money. Well, let me tell you this. It's hard to concentrate with people cutting on you. I wholeheartedly agree with all of this. Now pay me."

"How much?" Jerry Friedman said.

"Three quarters of a million, not a penny less," Mort Goldberg said.

Jerry Friedman made several more calls, met in private with Leo Marks and Howie Kite, both of whom wanted to own an interest in the property, then he wrote figures on a piece of paper and slid it across the table to Mort Goldberg, who looked at the numbers and said, "What is this, an *installment,* a *downpayment?*"

"It's my offer."

"This says a quarter of a million dollars."

"Plus three percent of the gross."

"*That* does it," Mort Goldberg said, collecting his papers.

Jerry Friedman was going to have to talk to other people, and that was all there was to it.

He understood Mort's desire to get his client money quickly.

But he was going to have to make a few calls before he could make another offer.

He said that Mort Goldberg's asking price of $750,000 had almost caused him to terminate the negotiations, then and there.

"Call the movers, Jerry, you let this guy get away because of a measly few hundred thousand. The author is very old-fashioned. You say his life story is worth the same as some space creature's, some slasher's, he is liable to instruct me to find a better judge of heroes."

Mort Goldberg grudgingly agreed to meet again at eleven in the morning to see where things stood. "I'll be the one in tennis shoes and blinkers," he said. "At eleven-oh-one, I'm off to a *real* motion picture studio."

"It was my finest hour," Mort Goldberg said, pausing to tell the fellow from room service where to park the prime rib. "Followed by my finest hour, and so on and so forth until it got dark."

It had been his finest day.

John Grape said he was very pleased for Mort.

"For *me*? You're the one who's going to have a big boat."

"So it stands at two hundred and fifty thousand?"

"It's more like it crouches in the starting blocks," Mort Goldberg said.

"We can take the two and a half?"

"I can call Jerry at home. He'd run the two and a half over in his underwear. Otherwise, we can leave them to their cold sweats tonight."

"They really liked the story?"

John Grape lay on his bed with a cool washrag across his eyes.

"About the way male and female rabbits tend to like each other, yes, that was my distinct impression," Mort Goldberg said, washing down a bite of prime rib with wine. "They put the two and a half on the table like it was something out of Elizabeth Taylor's navel, some jewel. We're properly outraged. I tell them I'll talk to you. We're talking."

"These emotional extremes are very hard to deal with," John Grape said.

"Get them all on paper. Leo Marks will do you up right, he's always been very big on guts."

"Howie who?"

"K-i-t-e, hot name, no factor, Leo will have him going for pizza. Listen, John, the thing about getting Mace in your eyes concerns me. They're interested in something that tops the core of the human psyche, not some goddamn thing out of Chong and Dong."

"Out of *who*?"

"They're comedians."

"Tell me exactly how you read them," John Grape said.

"They're all exclamation points."

250

"What'll we take?"

"All we can get should do it."

"*Five* hundred thousand?"

"You're reading my mind. A penny less, I'll go to Disney, they're crazy for adult themes, something deep, we'll get the half million, plus a lifetime pass to all the rides and Tinker Bell's first-born."

"Maybe we should call it off," John Grape said.

"Call what off?"

"The whole thing."

"John," Mort Goldberg said, "I'm almost positive I know two or three paid killers."

Mort Goldberg went to a window and let cool air hit his face, then returned to the telephone and said, "Tell me what's worrying you, it's what I'm here for."

John Grape said he was still concerned about so many things, he didn't know where to begin.

"Wing it," Mort Goldberg told him.

"I can't finish this book *at home*."

"John, you remember Herbert Philbrick, the one on that old television show, *I Led Three Lives*?"

"Yes."

"That son of a bitch is a quadruple spy, running radios and sending smoke signals out of his attic. His wife thinks he's up there sticking butterflies to a board. You get yourself a little office somewhere, you finish the book there."

"Once the book is published, she'll throw me out all over again."

"John, listen to me."

"I am."

"Women in love don't do that kind of thing. And even if she does throw you out, you'll make the exit in a stretch limo. Getting thrown out is also a *great sequel*."

"Mort, I care for her deeply. It looks like the person I have become is incapable of hurting anyone." John Grape chuckled. "Isn't that ironic?"

"No, John, it's absurd. She took all your money and demolished your house. No matter how you look at this, there's a better chance she's going to knock your new teeth out now instead of later. John, I see you as kind of a standard-bearer for the many millions of poor guys who have gotten wiped out because nobody thought they could change. You're like the patron saint of the screwed set. And I'm telling you, it's all going to end just fine. Five years from now, we'll all look back at this and laugh, Deloris included."

"I just don't know, Mort. I feel obligated to do the right thing."

"You remember fiction writing?"

John Grape didn't reply.

"Murdering dead guys?"

John Grape cleared his throat.

"You want to return to those light-hearted days?"

"This is very confusing."

"I can see a lot of problems, John, trying to love that woman, using public housing as a base of operations."

John Grape simply breathed at this point.

Then he said, "Get us the half million."

"Have fun at the dance," Mort Goldberg said.

9

The headline across the top of the front page of *Variety* was:

WARBROS TO UNLEASH LIFE CHANGER

WARBROS stood for Warner Bros., the motion picture studio. A smaller headline beneath the big one: BIGWIGS EXPECT BRANDO TO DUMP INJUNS, PORTRAY LOVE-STRICKEN EX; STREEP SLATED FOR SWITCHEROO.

Variety was a newspaper that recorded the goings-on in the entertainment business.

It refused to let accepted English stand in the way of a good time.

This story made public the fact that Warner Bros. was planning to do a film starring Marlon Brando and Meryl Streep. The movie would be based on the true story of a man named Hugh Brandenberg who, after learning that the woman to whom he had been married for six years was gay, had a sex-change operation and became his ex-wife's lover—without her knowing it was him.

This would be Brando's first film in years and Streep's first film in weeks.

The last anybody heard, Marlon had been calling numbers for a big bingo game on an Indian reservation up north.

According to one executive at Warner Bros., this picture would be a modern love story that would probe the subtleties of the human condition as no other drama had.

"Somebody call me a hearse," Mort Goldberg said as he finished reading the article in *Variety* for the third time. "You *swear* you didn't have this printed up at one of those novelty stores?"

Jerry Friedman shook his head.

He felt like somebody who had just avoided a head-on collision by three inches. Last night, rather this morning at three, he had decided to go up to $650,000 for the rights to John Grape's story.

Then his *Variety* was delivered.

Thank the heavens for *Variety*.

Needless to say, Jerry Friedman's offer of a quarter of a million dollars was no longer on the table; it was in the receptacle next to the paper shredder.

"I'm not entirely convinced there's *that* much of a similarity," Mort Goldberg said. "This story is depressing, anyway, it's lewd. Ours is clean, it's a romance, it's like Mary Poppins meets Grizzly Adams."

"Mort," Jerry Friedman said, "try to be a man about this."

Leo Marks said, "Condolences, old friend. This is why you see so many remakes. You run no risk of being screwed with a remake, seeing as how you're prescrewed going in, you see the point?"

"Holy," Howie Kite said, "enchilada."

"I think we're going to be able to work together one day, son," Leo Marks told him.

Mort Goldberg and Jerry Friedman stood by the elevator.

Mort flipped through the pages of a worn notebook.

"I've got some old people taking over a nursing home," he said.

Jerry held out his right hand and rocked it from one side to another to indicate that he was not too thrilled with old people taking over a nursing home, even one that was badly managed—too downbeat.

"I've got a new variation on a slasher."

"Which is?"

"A woman does the slashing."

"Who does she slash?"

"You name it, she slashes it, mostly cops."

Jerry Friedman wrinkled his nose.

254 "There's another twist. It's not set in Los Angeles. It's set in North Dakota."

"Pass."

"I've got a fictionalized version of what happened to Amelia Earhart."

"What happened?"

"Well, she didn't die in the airplane crash, she became a missionary in Australia."

Jerry shook his head.

"I've got a perfect murder."

"You're *kidding*."

"No. This woman, uh, shoots this guy who dropped dead of a heart attack, makes a natural death look like a murder, how's *that* for an angle."

"Why would anybody want to make a natural death look like a murder, Mort?"

"Hell if I know," Mort said, flipping a page. "I've got a kid Gothic."

Jerry Friedman raised his eyebrows.

"It's the forgotten element of this genre. It's as though young people didn't have any problems during this period."

"Let the elevator go."

"They had problems," Mort Goldberg said, squinting at notes about Gloria What's-her-name's work-in-progress. "*Big* problems. Puberty has been around forever. Modern teen pictures have had it, Jerry. Here's a viable alternative."

"You've got the book with you?"

"Not quite, the author is wrapping it up, Jerry. I've got a woman out in Oklahoma, she must have been a skinny blond countess in a former life, she's nailing Gothics left and right. This kid Gothic is going to be the biggest ever."

Jerry Friedman told Mort Goldberg to let the *next* elevator go, too.

"Teen problems in the middle of all those rocks, pounding surf, all that goddamn wind whistling, I'm telling you, Jerry, it's a natural."

"When's it going to be finished?"

Mort looked at his notes, then his watch. "I'd guess about four-thirty tomorrow, that's prairie time."

"Why don't you Fed-Ex it to me."

Mort Goldberg nodded and stepped into the next elevator.

"I don't envy you the call to Mr. Grape," Jerry Friedman said, rolling up his copy of *Variety*.

"I may write him," Mort Goldberg said. He did not want to spoil John Grape's big date.

10

John Grape wore a rented tux to the ballet.

He was concerned because Mort hadn't called all day.

He had tried the Wilshire. Seven times. Somebody in the bar thought Mort had been in around noon. Maybe Mort was holding out for three quarters of a million. But you'd have thought he'd have called.

"You're awfully quiet," Deloris said.

Maybe Mort had been celebrating in the bar at noon. By himself. In a dark corner.

"Sorry."

Deloris wore something silver and covered with many sequins. When she moved, she clicked.

The silver dress was roughly symmetrical in that there was approximately the same amount of material above her waist as there was below it. The evening dress stopped about two thirds of the way over her breasts and five or so inches above her knees—an odd way to dress in front of a perfect stranger, John Grape thought.

Charley spent as much time the first few minutes looking at Deloris in the rear-view mirror as he did looking at the road.

Having discussed the weather for all it was worth—it was cool and cloudy, and there went forty-five seconds—John Grape suggested that they each scoot toward the middle of the back seat a little so they didn't have to shout.

Sitting by the doors like this, it didn't seem like they were on their way to a great ballet and a memorable dinner—it was like they were on their way to court to turn state's evidence, or something; sitting far apart seemed too businesslike.

So they each scooted in a little.

"That's a nice dress," John Grape said.

Deloris smiled and pulled the bottom toward her knees.

"But I don't like it *that* much," he said.

"Do you like sports?"

"Oh, a little," John Grape said.

"How about . . . football?"

"Not a lot, no."

"Are you *serious*?"

"I travel so much, it's difficult to become familiar with any one team. College football is corrupt. The professionals, all the games look the same."

"Baseball?"

"I watch the World Series sometimes."

"Horse racing?"

"That's a sport?"

Deloris shrugged.

"I don't gamble. Baccarat a time or two on a ship, that's about it."

Deloris crossed her legs. Her attempt at pulling the dress down was not as dedicated this time.

"I'm asking too many questions," she said.

"Better to hear about what somebody likes than to see it, sometimes."

Deloris nodded. "What sort of things do you enjoy doing?"

"Besides running and going to the ballet?"

"Yes."

"I press wildflowers. I'm very fond of astronomy. Hiking."

Deloris looked out of her window and sighed. She turned her knees toward her door. She said, "My therapist just published a paper about people who have *too much* in common."

258   John Grape wondered why he hadn't sent a limousine for Deloris that was empty in the back.

"The premise of the paper is that when you have too much in common with a person, you settle into a routine. In other words, the less you have in common, the more new interests you're likely to develop."

John Grape had left this message the last time he tried to reach Mort: *Let's take three seventy-five.* He'd call from the theater and scratch that. Three seventy-five was nowhere near enough. Loving somebody was hard work.

He asked Deloris if she liked rooster fights.

She turned from the window.

"One of the great moments in sport is when a chicken pecks an opponent's jugular vein."

"Are you *kidding*?"

John Grape said yes, he was only trying to get in good with her analyst.

As they approached the city, Deloris said, "Here's what *else* I think."

She finished her second glass of wine.

John Grape wondered how fast Charley was driving, seven miles an hour?

Not having spoken with Mort was making John Grape very nervous.

"You don't drink?" Deloris asked him.

"No," John Grape said.

"Well, bless your heart. I don't drink. Much. Or very well."

John Grape had a sip of soda with a twist of lemon.

"Do you know what being honest can tell you?"

John Grape had no earthly idea, but was sure he was about to find out what.

"It can tell you more about the person you're being honest with than it can tell you about yourself. If somebody doesn't *respect* honesty . . . I forgot what I was going to say."

"I think you already said it quite well."

"I *did*?"

"Being honest is very educational."

"*Exactly.*" Deloris poured herself some more wine.

"I have the urge to be very honest with you."

John Grape said he was ready.

"About something very personal, very *painful*. What I'm about to tell you probably would have kept you from coming tonight."

John Grape doubted that.

"I wonder if it's all the wine making me so damn *honest*."

John Grape said no, all the wine did was make her cheeks pleasantly pink.

Deloris closed her eyes and leaned back against the seat. "Promise you won't put me out by the side of the road?"

"There's no way."

Deloris took a deep breath and said, "Toward the end of my marriage, I had an affair."

The limousine jerked to the right.

Several drivers honked.

Charley pulled the wheel back left.

"Hole in the road," he said.

"It just . . . *happened*," Deloris said. She kept her eyes closed. She brought her wine glass to her lips and had a sip.

John Grape considered choking her.

"I'm so . . . ashamed."

If he did it now, he'd also have to strangle Charley, and he wouldn't know whom to strangle next—the man Deloris was talking about.

At least he could cancel his plans to be out of the country when his book was published; now, he'd be glad to share a laugh about the book with Phil Donahue.

"Actually, it wasn't an affair in the strict sense of the word."

Anybody who treated him this way deserved everything she got.

"There was no . . ." Deloris said, ". . . no . . ."

"*What?*" Charley said.

"No *sex*," Deloris said, opening her eyes.

"Thank God," Charley said, stepping up their speed to eleven.

When Deloris opened her eyes, John Grape's face was no more than a

260   foot from hers. His head was turned sideways. His bright new eyes were wide. He was smiling.

Deloris put her right hand to her throat and said, "Why are you looking at my neck that way?"

"I was admiring your pearls."

John Grape settled back into his seat.

"Anyway, about all we did was kiss," Deloris said.

About?

John Grape would enjoy hearing about *about* one day.

Charley began running red lights.

A female dancer who was all legs played a character called Divine Genius.

She was not able to save Paganini's soul.

Once you have sold your soul to the devil in the world of ballet, all sales are final.

John Grape could relate to that. But Divine Genius, a ghostlike character dressed in white, was able to save Paganini's music for posterity. He gave his sheet music to Divine Genius before he went to hell—something like that.

The score by Rachmaninoff was tuneful, which is not always the case at the ballet. Sometimes you can't always tell when the orchestra stops warming up and the overture starts.

Deloris was impressed with the tickets. So was her escort. They were in the ninth row of the orchestra. They had cost $205 apiece.

Deloris's favorite part of the ballet was the first act, when Paganini gave a violin concert in an old-fashioned music hall.

John Grape's favorite part was when a man in tails gave the ballerina roses.

But he got through it.

He made comments about graceful arms and strong feet. Deloris watched most of the ballet with her left hand on John Grape's right thigh. He found it difficult to concentrate on much except learning the identity of the man who had been chewing on his wife back when he was spending seventeen hours a day trying to write about things that made no sense.

Over bisque, he brought up the subject of affairs.

His point was that affairs probably got a lot of undeserved bad publicity.

This discussion happened at a restaurant called Humboldt's.

The owner had bought one of Deloris's paintings and was going to put it by the front door; *behind* the front door, John Grape guessed, like a door-stop.

"I told you, I did *not* have an affair," Deloris said, sorry she had brought the whole thing up on the way to the ballet. "You act like there was *raw sex*. And I'd just as soon not talk about it anymore."

John Grape had some of what Deloris had ordered for starters—the bisque.

"Wait a minute." Deloris put down her spoon. "I've been talking all night. Go ahead, tell me what you think."

"Well, I was just wondering if a lot of love wasn't lost because seeing somebody while you're still married is thought to be so, I don't know, immoral."

"Baloney," Deloris said.

A waiter lurking discreetly in the shadows took a step forward, then stopped; they didn't have any bologna here.

John Grape waved the waiter away.

"Those *things*," Deloris said, "seeing somebody *briefly*, it just reflects unhappiness, that's all. I *told* you, I was married to a real dog."

John Grape shrugged and dabbed at his mouth with a napkin.

"It's a matter of striking back, however weakly. The person I was married to *hated* Carl."

John Grape leaned forward, careful to stop before his forehead reached his soup, and said, "You're right, it's meaningless. Forget all that. Let's go again."

"Go where?"

"The ballet. Sit way up next time, get a different perspective about the sets and formations."

"Are you *serious*?"

"Is there some rule against it?"

Deloris doubted it.

"Good. It's settled."

John Grape finished his starter and said it was the best bisque he had ever tasted.

"It has a lot more lobster in it than you would think, the way it's all ground up."

John Grape touched Deloris's hand and said that this had been one of the most enjoyable nights of his life.

"And it's not even over yet," Deloris said, and blushed.

John Grape excused himself to use the restroom.

When he got back, Deloris said, she wanted to try out a few middle names she had thought of.

He stood in the men's room, near the sink, wearing only his black boxer shorts.

He stood with his arms held straight out.

His tuxedo hung over a door on one of the stalls.

"I feel another one," he said, moving his right shoulder.

"Jesus, I see it," a waiter said.

The waiter ran some cold water on a paper towel and carried it to John Grape's back, which was covered with large red lumps.

"By the shoulder blade."

"Yeah, there it is, all right."

"Don't *touch* it."

The waiter tore the paper towel in half and covered the hive on John Grape's shoulder blade.

The maître d' opened the door, stepped into the men's room, and felt for a wall for support. "We will comp the check," he said weakly.

"I'm allergic to shellfish," John Grape said, scratching his chest, which reddened noticeably on contact. "Shrimp, lobster, crab."

"Then why did you *eat* it?" the maitre'd asked.

"I didn't know what I was eating. My mind was somewhere else."

"We will *not* comp the check."

John Grape scratched his jaw, his chin, and his stomach.

"It would probably be a good idea if you quit that," the waiter said, holding another towel under cold water.

Suddenly John Grape was digging at his chest with both hands and staggering toward the sink, his stomach and back almost completely covered with nasty welts that turned white as they were scratched, purple when they were released. He grabbed the wet towel from the waiter and put it on his neck and stumbled backward to the rough wallpaper and began rubbing his shoulders left and right.

"This place have a back door?" he asked.

He began passing out bribes.

Deloris looked up and down the street.

"You don't think he came out this way?" she asked.

"No. But I can't be sure," Charley said. "You're saying he just *left?*"

"He went to use the restroom, it was the last I saw of him." Deloris looked at her watch. "More than a half hour ago."

"And it was going okay?"

"What?"

"Dinner, you know, the evening."

"*Very* well."

Charley had checked with the staff; nobody had noticed anything out of the ordinary.

"This is disgusting," Deloris said.

"Maybe not. Here's what I think. He slips and hits his head on a sink and is wandering around town with amnesia."

"He'd better have done that," Deloris said, looking back at the restaurant. "Stiffing me out of a check like this."

John Grape was stretched out on his bed at The Royale with his body wrapped in half a dozen damp bath towels.

The hives had lost some of their redness. They no longer itched. Now they stung.

His face was badly swollen; it appeared to have been struck recently by a professional boxer.

264   "Coming back from the dead is a lot harder than you would think," John Grape said.

"I'm sure," Marvin Hunsacker said, straightening things as he moved about John Grape's suite. "But I had such high hopes for you."

It was 5:10 A.M.

Despite the fact that they were never supposed to speak with one another until a contract for the motion picture rights had been signed, John Grape had called Marvin Hunsacker at two with the news that he had just experienced some very bad luck.

Marvin Hunsacker, who was separated from his wife and living in a cheap efficiency, had arrived twenty minutes ago.

He had spent the last eighteen minutes reminding John Grape about the tremendous amount of money that was at risk here—he had read the other day that a novel about somebody who had become invisible after falling into a tub of chemicals sold for *$1.2 million.*

"Marv," John Grape said.

"Marv*in*."

"Fix it or get out."

"What were you thinking about doing?"

"I call her and tell her that I left the restaurant because I was afraid of falling in love with her, but that I am no longer afraid of it."

"All we need is organ music," Marvin Hunsacker said. "That's horrid."

John Grape pulled a cool towel over his face.

Marvin Hunsacker sat on an antique loveseat and ate a banana and earned his 15 percent.

At 7:15 A.M. John Grape called Deloris.

She was stretched out on her bed, still wearing the silver evening dress. She answered the telephone quickly.

John Grape told her that he had been more or less kidnapped.

He said that he had been overwhelmed in the restroom by four men, and taken out the back way. The four men thought that John Grape had inside information about a merger that would send the price of a stock up.

He said he rolled out the back of a station wagon over in Brooklyn and was rescued by two men working on a busted sewer.

Deloris didn't know she had gone out with James Bond; but she was relieved, and pleased that he was all right.

They made plans for lunch, once John Grape had his strength back.

He thanked Marvin Hunsacker for the thought.

"Bear down," Marvin Hunsacker said, slamming the door behind him.

John Grape called Charley and told him about the hives and the kidnapping.

"And she bought it?" Charley said.

"Yes."

"Good for you. Amnesia was all I could think of."

"I just wanted you to know. You've been so kind through all this."

"Who couldn't be," Charley said.

An John Grape put the phone on its base, it rang.

He brought the receiver back to his ear.

"What?" he said. "Hello?"

"John, it's Mort. Now this isn't as bad as it's going to sound."

"Now, John," Mort Goldberg was saying, "they're not out of this for good, you have to remember that. They're going to wait and see how the Brando-Streep thing turns out. This gives us an important opening. We go right through it to something like Home Box Office, to somebody not afraid to take a chance. Who's to say, maybe Brando's forgotten how to act. Here's what we have to do. The book, it becomes all-important. What we've got to do is get our book out first. We've got to finish the son of a bitch fast."

John Grape looked around his suite.

He was going to miss it.

"I can't think anymore," he said.

"What they're going to do is a novelization of the screenplay, one of those cheesy things written by some Columbia School of Journalism flunky. There's no way in the *world* they can get their book done before, hell, at least a month. Tell me *that* doesn't lift your spirits. All we need is a happy ending. Theirs is a real downer. You know the Brandenberg I mentioned? The one who got the sex-change deal so he could get in good

266   with his gay wife? Well, the gay woman shot his ass off, once she found out. He'd dead, John, how's that for a morbid last scene. They run the credits over a corpse. A happy ending, we're back in this thing."

"I can't take any more," John Grape said.

"And there's always that great house of yours, don't forget that, your money, there are some fine things to look forward to."

"Mort?"

"I'm here, John."

"I have a question."

"I'm at your service, just like always."

"You're telling me we *really* didn't get hundreds of thousands of dollars for the movie?"

"Put the five grand you owe us out of your mind, we'll talk about that later."

11

John Grape tossed an envelope onto the marble counter and kept walking.

Maurice used a letter opener on it.

The message inside was:

I check out.

No kidding.

12

"The house, Charley, I have to keep thinking about the house."

"It's a fantastic house, I'll give you that. Nice and solid."

John Grape wore a black T-shirt, black slacks, and black shoes.

"I think we need to talk about this," Charley said.

He had parked the limousine around the corner from Carl Chamberlain's office. Carl was a veterinarian. His office was in a small shopping center a few miles from the Grape house.

It stood to reason, the dog had a hand in this.

"John, you yourself heard, nothing happened between them. A kiss or two."

"I'm trying to write a simple sentence, she and the dog are over here playing footsie, *that's* nothing?"

"I'm seeing a side of you I've never seen before."

"I'm fine," John Grape said, pulling on some dark gloves. "You can go if you want."

"And you'll what, scratch around in the woods like a commando?"

"I'll get by."

"Tell me again how far away the sheriff's office is?"

"Four or five miles."

"I'll wait three minutes," Charley said.

• • •

John Grape was not exactly Raffles. He entered the veterinarian's office by putting a brick through a window in the back.

An alarm went off immediately.

It caused a few dozen pets to begin howling, hissing, chirping, barking, growling, and singing. John Grape let some dogs and cats out of their cages. The cats ran en masse down a hall to the outer office, followed closely by the dogs, and took up positions far above the floor.

When John Grape headed for the limousine, a cocker spaniel and a bull-dog were trying to shake a yellow cat out of the curtains, a wire-haired ter-rier was on top of the cash register barking at a Persian that was swinging on an overhead light fixture, and a Pomeranian was being chased into the bathroom by a very big parrot.

Charley parked the limousine at the corner, half a block from The Moran, and turned to his long-term passenger.

"The people who own the company don't like us waiting around by places that might be construed as fronts," he said, turning off the motor. "Now . . . you'd like to *borrow some money from me?*"

"It's that or . . . I don't know what."

"The collateral being . . ."

"My good looks."

"Brother," Charley said, rubbing his eyes. "I can see why you don't want to try this at a bank."

His passenger nodded.

"How much do you want to borrow, John?"

"The collateral is my house, the book I'm writing, all of it."

"How much?"

"Five thousand. Ten."

"I *drive* these things, I don't make them. Tell me how everything is going. Tell me about the house that sold, the one south from you, the three-story."

"We've seen each other three times this week. It's going well. The house went for three hundred and seventy thousand dollars."

"And you two are getting along."

"It's like a perfume commercial."

"Tell me how the book is going."

270   "Fine."

"Do the words reach out and grab a person?"

John Grape hoped. "One of the tough things about writing is that you don't always know if what you're doing is any good."

"Interesting line of work."

"My agent says we could stand a happy ending."

"She knows you're staying *there*?" Charley glanced up the street at The Moran.

"I'm in and out of town a lot lately."

"I'll loan you three grand for thirty-eight hundred, due in one month."

Let's flip a coin for the interest, double or nothing, John Grape started to say, then he caught himself about to gamble: "Book it," he said.

13

They ran together. They saw some movies and plays together. They shopped together. He bought her a female Scottie, and was never growled at again.

He bought her a ring that cost $2,900, plus tax. That was the day they had a picnic and flew a kite.

It was a devastating experience.

They came upon the ring after buying some health food.

Deloris did a double-take as she spotted the ring in the window of a jewelry store.

It looked swell on the fourth finger of her right hand, just swell.

The ring was comprised of a number of diamonds—six or seven cut so they'd appear oblong. One reason why Deloris loved the ring was the way it caught the light from a variety of angles. It wasn't pretentious and could be worn with jeans or silks. But the main reason why Deloris loved the ring was that it reminded her of a flower, with the diamonds resembling the petals.

It reminded her of a fresh start.

At least, that's what she said.

She was probably trying to find out if he had any money.

John Grape had no choice but to open his checkbook and say, "It's yours."

• • •

272   Later that day, just before they went to hear poetry of a sort read at a festival of the arts in a community thirty five miles to the north, Deloris began yelling in the bathroom.

She was upset because she found a washcloth draped over the bathroom sink.

The washcloth, she said, had been folded diagonally, exactly the way the person she had been married to folded *his* washcloth.

Deloris believed in the supernatural and thought that her ex-husband really had died and that his spirit had returned to make her miserable.

Sometimes, she said, she could *feel* his presence.

John Grape went to the bathroom and reported back that he had found the washcloth on the floor, not hung diagonally on the sink. It was probably the Noel Coward play they had seen the other night that was responsible for what Deloris imagined. The play was *Blythe Spirit*.

Poetry was read for three and a half hours at the festival of the arts. Deloris contributed two thousand dollars so that it could become an annual event; twenty dollars would have probably done the trick.

Thus concluded one of the worst days of John Grape's life.

But tomorrow was another day.

14

The three-card monte dealer said his name was Jimmy.

Sure it was. He had fast eyes and faster hands. He was dealing his game on a cardboard box next to a tree in a part of the park away from all the roads.

"It's a very simple game," he said, shuffling the three cards around.

"Go slow," John Grape said. "I had a long bus ride in."

"So how have things been out in Idaho?"

"Lousy. We had a bad potato season."

"You're *really* from Idaho?"

"Yes."

Jimmy said he didn't know potatoes had seasons. "Here's the way the game works." He turned the three cards face-up on the box. Two cards were red queens. The other was the ace of spades. "What you do is follow the ace. You find it, you win."

"What do I win?"

"You win what you bet."

"*Money?*"

Jimmy turned the three cards down on the box and began moving them around.

"This is like the shell game," John Grape said.

"It's easier."

274   Jimmy stopped moving the cards and turned over the ace, which was where John Grape thought it would be—in the middle.

"I don't do this for experienced players," Jimmy said. He picked up the ace and bent it slightly, lengthwise. "Now you ought to be able to follow it real good," he said.

"That was awfully nice of you."

"So what's the bet?"

"Can I ask you a couple of questions first?"

"Anything."

"What's under the box?"

Jimmy squinted. "You questioning my . . ."

"All of it."

Jimmy picked up the cardboard box.

Nothing was under it.

Nothing was in it.

He put it down and replaced the red queens and the black ace.

"Mind pushing your sleeves up?"

"You must have a lot of criminals out in . . ."

"Idaho."

"Excuse me," a man standing well behind John Grape said, a man at the curb.

"Be right back."

"You can't win at this," the man in the suit said.

"Why's that?"

"Well, when you're playing for money, his hands move a lot faster."

"Thanks for the warning."

John Grape walked back to the cardboard box and said to Jimmy, "You finished screwing around?"

"Beg . . ."

"You ready to play?"

"Always."

John Grape reached into his pocket and produced a roll consisting of two hundred-dollar bills, eight twenties, three tens, and two fives.

He put it all on the box.

"Four potatoes," he said.

"Call," Jimmy said, putting four hundred-dollar bills on top of John Grape's bet.

Everybody pressed in for a look.

Jimmy started moving his hands, slowly at first, then at Fast Forward.

John Grape tried with all his might to follow the ace, and lost it five seconds into the game.

So he yawned and watched a few birds hopping around on nearby branches; he doubted if he could have followed the ace had it been turned face-up.

When Jimmy was finished, John Grape applauded politely, then pushed up his sleeves to show everybody he was not cheating, either.

Although he had no earthly idea where the ace of spades was, he had a pretty good idea where it wasn't. There was no way it was in the middle.

The card in the middle was bent slightly.

Only a tourist would pick it.

So John Grape said, "It's not in the middle."

Jimmy put his hands on his hips and said, "You're supposed to pick the one it *is*."

"That's what I'm doing. I reject the one in the middle. It's a red queen. Flip it."

"Go on," somebody standing behind John Grape said.

Jimmy flipped the card off the box.

It was the queen of hearts.

"Now it's fifty-fifty," John Grape said. "What do you think about that?"

"I don't think a goddamn thing about it, that's what I think."

"Care to up the bet?"

"A hundred," Jimmy said.

"Call, raise a hundred."

Each person put two hundred more on the cardboard box.

"Go ahead, pick it, you fuck shop," Jimmy said.

John Grape, who had never been called *that* before, said, "Jimmy, since you're right-handed, I say it's nine-to-five the ace of spades is on your safe side, your right. It's human nature. I think. The desire to have something valuable close at hand in case things get tough."

Jimmy pulled a knife from his front pocket. It was a small knife, but it was the thought that counted.

John Grape grabbed the $1,200 off the box.

The people who had been watching this amusing test of skill, quite a few of them now, suggested that the dealer get out of there.

Jimmy and two lookouts who had been watching for cops ran away.

John Grape treated the people who had been behind him to some soft drinks and hot dogs from a street vendor.

A person had to pay the rent.

It wasn't as if he had started gambling again.

It was like he had been stealing.

15

"Far be it from me to tell you how to run your life," Charley said, turning onto the street where Deloris lived. "But maybe it's time to get serious."

John Grape wore a white tennis outfit. He sat tapping a tennis racket on his knee.

"I understand these things take time, but all we seem to have been doing the last couple of weeks is spend our money on suntan lotion and yogurt."

"You can't rush it," John Grape said, checking his tote to make sure he had brought along his headband. "You can't push it."

"Before long, we're going to have to push something, let's hope it's not a gun into some bank guard's stomach."

Charley reminded John Grape that he would owe some money in four days. All this coming and going had to stop.

"I'm spending the night," John Grape said.

Charley said *that* was more like it. "She ask you?"

"She will. One hopes."

"No, *two hope*," Charley said, slowing down.

Marvin Hunsacker stopped talking when John Grape entered the den.

John Grape and Marvin Hunsacker looked at each other, then at the floor.

John Grape and Katie looked at each other, then at the ceiling.

278 "What terrible timing," Deloris said.

John Grape apologized for being a minute or two late.

"For *what?*"

"Tennis."

"To hell with tennis," Deloris said. "A deadbeat owes me money."

She stood and made quick introductions.

Marvin Hunsacker squeezed John Grape's hand very hard.

"I've heard a lot about you," Katie said.

"Go in the kitchen and make us some tea," Deloris said to John Grape.

"Where was I?" Deloris said to Marvin Hunsacker.

"Overcome with greed," Katie said, interrupting.

"Please be quiet," Deloris told her daughter.

"You were about to tell me how late he was with the alimony."

"*Again,*" Deloris said.

"Again," Marvin Hunsacker said.

"You said he would never be late again. I hold you responsible."

"Mother, you're making an ass of yourself."

"He's . . . how late?" Marvin Hunsacker asked.

"Two days."

"Day and a half," Katie said.

"Why don't you give him a break," John Grape said.

He stood like Jeeves between the kitchen and the den, carrying a silver tray full of cups and saucers.

Everybody looked at him.

Then Katie winked.

Then the color left Marvin Hunsacker's face.

Then Deloris said, "*What* did you say?"

"The man might not be feeling well," John Grape said.

"Who cares."

"Just leave him alone, *all right?*"

"I want you," Deloris said, rising and pointing at the front door, "out of my house."

Katie, who had clawed and scratched her way to a magnificent 2.1 grade

average—she made a 99 on the English final and raised her grade up to a
strong C—walked John Grape to the limousine.

She was home for a week before returning for summer school.

"I'll do all I can," she said. "You *really* quit smoking."

"Hard to believe, isn't it."

"I guess you should try to control what destiny you can."

Katie took a puff off her cigarette, then ground it out under her foot. She put her hands on her hips and waited for a nicotine fit. "Do you have what you owe her?"

"Close."

"Now, exactly what are you supposed to do if you want a cigarette?"

"Pretend you just had one."

Katie stretched. "So far so good."

"How's it going in there?" Charley said.

"He got kicked out again," Katie said.

16

Aqueduct; it was good to be back.

He'd fired his best clip, his best forty or fifty shots.

And what he had to show for it was a nice little self-help book. Surely, a few people would be interested in reading about what it felt like to be healthy and better looking than before.

Of course, he couldn't end it at the racetrack like this.

You couldn't sign off a self-help book with a corn dog in one hand and a beer in the other.

He'd lie about this part.

Aqueduct was an old racetrack for thoroughbreds. The horse-racing business was changing. Many tracks had upgraded their facilities in hopes of attracting a more upwardly mobile clientele. Many tracks gave away junk like tote bags, jackets, and those digital watches guaranteed to keep perfect time unless you moved your wrist suddenly. Many tracks had concerts after the races featuring, of all things, philharmonic orchestras. But to the racing purist, the fan who does not give a damn about movements that occur anywhere other than the top of the turn for home, all that window dressing was for the birds.

You couldn't drown bad luck with Beethoven's Fifth.

Fortunately, the area by the rail at Aqueduct had been spared the shine of progress. It was covered with beer cups—you took a step, it sounded like you were walking on crickets—and butts of all sizes, few of which would have any tobacco left by the ninth race.

The rail at Aqueduct was where the people who had the horse right here congregated.

John Grape selected a spot near the finish line as the horses were being led onto the track for the fifth race, a mile journey for ten-thousand-dollar claimers.

A horse that runs in a ten-grand claiming race is a horse that can be bought by a qualified person—an owner or a trainer—for the prescribed price.

Many ten-thousand-dollar claimers wound up with careers in the private sector as actors—they posed for snapshots in shopping centers after kids climbed onto their backs.

John Grape stood at the rail, talking to himself, wondering if anybody had ever been unluckier, and doubting it; experiencing bad luck *before* a race was beyond belief.

He looked at a horse he had bet good money on, one called Hail Fellow.

Then he looked at the tote board.

Hail Fellow had odds of 4 to 1. The favorite, a horse called Free Spirit, was 3 to 1. Hail Fellow had opened at odds of 25 to 1 and should have been 20 to 1 at the very least, not any *four*.

It had not won a race in five months.

It had not finished better than sixth in five weeks.

John Grape couldn't believe it was being bet so heavily.

He had to *do* something.

He leaned over the rail and yelled, "*Hey*," at the jockey riding Hail Fellow, some guy named Delgado.

Jockeys don't communicate much with people along the rail, for obvious reasons, the most obvious being that people who gather at the rail are not known for their manners. They're emotional. They hold grudges. They remember when jockeys fell off horses years ago.

But Delgado glanced out of the corner of his eye this time because John Grape had yelled so loudly.

282   "Will you *please* tell these people that the thing you're riding is no four-to-one shot," John Grape shouted.

Delgado nudged Hail Fellow in the ribs, and they trotted up the track. The odds on this horse clicked down to 7 to 2.

Ah ha, many people along the rail thought; then many went to bet on this sure thing.

"I want you people to *listen* to me," John Grape said, waving his hands over his head. "This is *extremely* important."

Only a few people looked at him.

"The three horse, Hail Fellow, *I* did that. I knocked the odds down, there at the first. Not some owner. Not some trainer. Nobody with inside information. *Me.*"

"Why don't you shut up so I can think," somebody with three teeth said.

John Grape told him, "I bet a grand on that thing when the window opened. It's dropping in class. It ran in the mud last time out, they're putting on blinkers, it looked like a possibility at twenty to one, not *this* nonsense."

He looked over his shoulder at the tote board.

Hail Fellow was now the favorite at 2 to 1.

"Put this twenty on him to win," a girl with a tattoo on her arm said to her escort, who had a tattoo on his neck.

John Grape squinted up at the high-rent district—the Turf Club—and he could almost hear all the rich people marching to the hundred-dollar window to bet on Hail Fellow because it was obvious that somebody knew something.

When a lot of money was suddenly bet on a horse that had moss growing on its west side, the masses assumed that somebody knew something. But the somebody who knew something in this particular case was John Grape. The something he knew was that nobody knew *a damn thing,* which was irony most foul.

Fifteen minutes later, jockey Delgado twirled his whip, smiled at his adoring fans, hopped down, and shrugged at the owner and trainer, who must have asked this question simultaneously: What the hell *happened?*

Hail Fellow had won the race by three lengths over Free Spirit.

He could have been propelled down the home stretch by the gusts of air caused by all the people leaning over the rail, waving their arms toward the finish line.

Hail Fellow jumped wildly when his picture was taken in the winner's circle—he had evidently forgotten what a flashgun was like.

He paid his groupies $3 to win, $2.60 to place, and $2.40 to show.

John Grape had bet $400 to win, $300 to place, and $300 to show.

He won $350.

He should have won many thousands of dollars.

"This is the screwing of the century," he said to the cashier, who then told him what happened to people who looked gift horses too closely in the mouth. They got bit.

Still and all, it was good to be home.

He waited until one minute before post time to make his bet for the sixth race, so he wouldn't cause another stampede.

This beautifully timed bet only knocked the odds of the horse he favored down from 15 to 1 to 14 to 1.

The Pirate broke alertly from the gate in a six-furlong sprint, moved from the middle of the track to the rail, and opened up a nice lead turning for home.

He led by six lengths at the top of the stretch.

Then he led by five lengths.

Then four.

Three.

There toward the end of it, it looked like they were going to have to carry the finish line up the track to the tiring—or expiring—Pirate.

Then he led by a nose.

Then he didn't.

An hour and a half later, two track security guards stood over John Grape.

One touched a shoe to his shoulder.

"It's about time," a horseplayer said.

"We've been out front watching for purse snatchers," a guard said.

"We'll all sleep easier," the horseplayer told him.

"Tell us about it," the other guard said.

"Well, you remember the sixth?"

"I don't gamble," said the guard who had put a shoe to John Grape's shoulder.

"What's remembering the sixth race got to do with gambling?" the horseplayer wondered.

"Abe's wife said she was going to divorce him if he pissed away any more money," the other guard said. "That's why he doesn't gamble."

"It's a good reason," Abe said.

"My friend down there has a good reason, too. He bets fifteen hundred on the one that led all but the last foot at fourteen to one, The Pirate."

"Ouch," Leo said.

"All to win, nothing to place or show."

Abe said, "So in other words, he's . . ."

"In any words," the horseplayer said.

Leo took his walkie-talkie from his belt and said into it, "Drunk at the rail."

17

The drunk tank was a big room with bars in front and cement walls on three sides.

It was the worst place Mort Goldberg had ever seen.

And he had been to Hilton Head, which was an island in South Carolina. He and his wife had gone there the summer before last to seek solace from the rigors of city life. What they found was a beach covered with punks carrying radios. There ought to be a law, the way there is in civilized places like London, with regard to radios. In London, you carry a radio into some of the better city parks, they take a club to you. Punks and radios, it was the most serious problem facing this nation today.

To get some peace and quiet in South Carolina, Mort Goldberg had to walk into the Atlantic Ocean until the water came over his head.

The most important call a person could make before going on vacation was to the local board of education.

Mort Goldberg's rule of thumb concerning carefree travel was: If school was in session, go. If school was out, forget it.

Still, the drunk tank was even worse than the beach at Hilton Head.

It was full of men in varying states of disarray. The floor was concrete and it sloped downward to a big drain in the middle, which was enough to make a person sick. There were benches along the walls. The tank was full of sleeping drunks, crying drunks, ranting and raving drunks, and worst of all, singing drunks.

"You should see it on weekends," the officer in charge of fishing drunks from the tank said. "Saturday at this time, it's wall-to-wall wailing."

"Who'd you run over to get put on this detail?" Mort Goldberg said.

"I forgot her name," the guard replied. He had spoken with Mort Goldberg after John Grape dialed the number on the fourth try, then went to sleep.

The drunk tank was also the worst place Charley had ever seen, and he had been to Houston, where the humidity could fill a shot glass left outside over the course of an average weekend.

The tank gave off an odor of considerable pungency, so Charley stood at the bars with his hat over his nose. This place was hell to Marvin Hunsacker, who stood with his eyes closed, taking shallow breaths.

"There he is," Mort Goldberg said, pointing at a bench by the left wall.

The guard's flashlight illuminated John Grape, who lay under the bench on his stomach, smiling back from wherever he was.

"Never fails," the guard said, entering the drunk tank. "The real pros are the first to get sprung. Nobody wants the loud ones."

The fine for being drunk in public was five hundred dollars.

There was no additional charge for being drunk in jail.

"Goddamn it," John Grape said, not quite certain what he was talking about, or to whom he was talking. His head bobbed like a toddler's. Mort Goldberg held his left shoulder; Charley his right.

Marvin Hunsacker stood five yards off, frowning at his investment.

"Generally, we like to see them leave in better shape than this," the officer at the check-out desk said, handing Mort Goldberg an envelope containing John Grape's belongings.

"You want to split the bail?" Charley asked.

"Unless you want to pay it all," Mort Goldberg said, "good Christian that you are."

"He's already into me for three grand."

"Add two, here."

Marvin Hunsacker said this was the end of an era, a depressing footnote in the evolution of man. This proved people *couldn't* change.

"Goddamn it, where's my *typewriter?*" John Grape snarled, squinting up at the police officer, who replied, "It wasn't in your pockets."

"How long has he been here, *ten minutes?*" Mort Goldberg asked, handing over his share of the fine.

The officer looked at a log book. "Two hours, fourteen minutes."

"I thought jail was supposed to sober a person up," Charley said.

"Depends." The officer wrote out a receipt. "Somebody catches jail on the way down, yeah, it can be a rude awakening. But a guy lands in the tank, it's a lateral move, there's a tendency to blend right in."

Catching a cab in front of jail, while holding up a man, was next to impossible after dark, so they half dragged, half carried John Grape a block, propped him against a fire hydrant, flagged down a taxi, and took him to The Moran.

During the ride, John Grape babbled incoherently, once asking which race was next, another time instructing Mort not to sell out for less than three hundred thousand dollars.

Two of the six people sitting in the lobby of The Moran looked up from their reading material when Mort Goldberg and Charley and Marvin Hunsacker carried John Grape to the elevator.

The two people who looked up seemed surprised not because one person was lapsing into and out of consciousness, but because the three people dragging him were not.

"So how's his book going?" Charley asked.

"I own fifteen percent of it," Marvin Hunsacker said.

"Lucky you."

Although they'd had to walk a block from jail to catch a cab, they figured that they'd have to walk *two* blocks from The Moran in order to get a ride.

"Touch and go," Mort Goldberg said about John Grape's work-in-progress. He said he'd had some interest last week from a small publisher that did paperback originals. "But this update might wipe the smiles off their faces."

"How's the part in the book about me?" Charley wondered.

288   "Very sympathetic," Mort Goldberg told him. "You come off looking like a real friend of the needy."

"I'd appreciate it very much if you'd scratch out the part where I loaned him the three grand."

They stopped walking at the corner.

Mort Goldberg looked back at The Moran. He told Charley that if somebody offered a couple of thousand dollars and a few chickens for John Grape's book, he'd take it. He said that what they seemed to have at this point was the equivalent of a diet book where the author died of malnutrition in the third chapter.

18

ohn Grape discovered that he was talking on the telephone.

"Hello," somebody on the other end was saying. "Hello. Hello."

John Grape said, "I feel bad."

"Mr. . . . *Hunter?*"

"What?"

"There is a lady waiting to see you."

"What?"

"And I thought it best to . . . *call up first.*"

"*What?*"

"If you say *what* one more time, I will hang up this telephone."

John Grape got out of bed and stepped onto what seemed to be a raft drifting. When he stood, things tilted terribly to the right, causing him to stumble that way and bang into a chair. He yanked the base of the telephone off a table and onto the floor. After bumping into the chair, he tried to get his feet beneath him, but couldn't. He found himself shuffling to the left like a bad act from a vaudeville show, making a fast exit.

He pulled his head back and to the left just before he blasted into the bathroom door, absorbing most of the shock with his right shoulder. He was knocked off his feet.

Crawling back to the telephone was easier.

"I'm very, very sick," John Grape said.

"This is Maurice," Maurice said for the tenth time.

"Maurice?"

"At The Royale."

"Maurice."

"There is a woman here to see you."

"Here?"

"No, *here*."

"Oh," John Grape said, sitting up. When he sat up, the world went dizzy, so he lay back down on the floor.

"Her name is Miss Worth."

"Here?"

"Listen to me. I'm trying to do you a *favor*."

"Me?"

John Grape sat up again and balanced himself by pressing his back against the side of the bed.

"We're limited to an *hour* on personal calls. Miss Worth is here to see you. I'm also here. We're here. You're *there*. I explained to Miss Worth that your floor was under repairs. I sent her to the restaurant, where you are to meet her momentarily. I don't doubt that in a matter of seconds, she will return to this desk and inquire about the delay."

John Grape sincerely tried to hang up, but missed four times.

Shaving was hard; it was almost impossible. Violent, even.

John Grape steadied his right hand by pressing his right elbow on the sink.

He steadied his chin by pressing his chin against his chest.

Dressing was also difficult. He first put his tie on under his shirt.

Seeing as how the elevator at The Moran was slow, he called for it ten minutes before he was ready to go.

He got a cab by running into the nearest intersection while waving a handful of money over his head.

Maurice retied John Grape's tie in the restroom on the far side of the lobby. "The fat half is supposed to be longer than the skinny half," he said. "What's that *god-awful* smell?"

"I seemed to have sprayed deodorant on my head," John Grape said.

"Socks?"

John Grape raised his trouser legs.

"Congratulations."

"Maurice, I am in your debt."

"I'll get in line." Maurice went to the sink to wash his hands. "Remember the day you checked out and checked in?"

"Vaguely."

"The computer began flashing *Fault*."

"I remember some of it."

"Because of that confusion, I had to send a bill out while you were still a guest, well, the gist of it is that we're no longer waiting until a person completes his or her stay before a credit card statement is sent back to the company and on to the customer."

John Grape rubbed the back of his neck and said he was not well enough to discuss supply-side economics just yet.

"The quicker the statements are processed, the quicker we are reimbursed by a credit card company, the better, do you understand that?"

John Grape nodded and straightened the knot on his tie.

Maurice smiled and said that his hotel was billing credit card companies every third day; and before too awfully long, it would probably happen every evening at midnight, not at the completion of a lengthy stay.

"You're saying that something good came of me checking out and in simultaneously?"

Maurice said yes, sending along a bill while the guest was still in the hotel turned out to be *very* good business.

He showed John Grape his new name tag that had *Employee of the Year* on it.

Deloris had ordered strips of smoked salmon on clouds of cream cheese, which caused John Grape's eyes to water and his stomach to gurgle. The way he saw it, he could either knock the food to the floor with his elbow, or down it in a couple of big gulps.

He had two glasses of water and a large orange juice and explained his vast thirst to a touch of the flu.

292   Deloris agreed, he seemed pale.

She pushed her smoked salmon and cream cheese aside, which gave John Grape the opening he was looking for; he pushed *his* salmon and cheese aside.

Deloris said she was confused.

She was at a point in her life when she couldn't tell *what* counted.

She was afraid of making more mistakes with relationships.

She said she'd had this big speech rehearsed, but she had decided to go right to the punch line, which was: "I'm sorry."

John Grape agreed as to how being thrown off a person's property could make you wonder about their future together.

Deloris leaned over the table, touched John Grape's hand, and said, "Let's go upstairs."

John Grape leaned over the table, touched Deloris's hand, and said nothing.

"Better yet," Deloris said, "why don't you check out of this place."

John Grape said it wouldn't take a second.

19

They made love in the dark.

There was no awkward moment where somebody wondered: Who goes first? There was no jockeying for position. They simply ripped off each other's clothes and made love like junkies after a fix.

Deloris made most of it. John Grape simply lay there on his back, which he had never done much before now. There wasn't a lot of foreplay, which made the lovemaking act too final, anyway.

Sometimes looking at somebody you had just made love to was like shopping for groceries after a seven-course Mexican dinner.

Sometimes enough was enough.

Such was not the case here, however.

They made love twice in less than an hour, and were pretty smug about the whole thing.

So John Grape didn't know what to think when Deloris started crying. She came from the bathroom off the master bedroom wearing a robe pulled together from her neck to her ankles.

John Grape fluffed up a pillow and told Deloris there was nothing to feel guilty about.

"I am *not* guilty," she said, squaring her shoulders. "Much."

She yanked the robe so tightly together in front, some stitches in the right shoulder pulled loose. Then she cried some more. She cried herself pink.

Then she hiccuped for a few minutes and put on sunglasses to cover her swollen eyes.

Anyway, it was *finally* official. Sex aside, she had something very important to say.

Sex aside, running aside, personal enrichment aside, great food aside, art aside, wit aside, charm aside, intelligence aside, respect and consideration aside, money aside, good looks, fun and dance—the whole damn *mess* aside.

These sounded like opening remarks to a jury, so John Grape sat up in bed.

"Will you please *cover yourself,*" Deloris said.

The sheet came to rest at his waist.

He covered his trim stomach with a pillow.

"Come here," he said.

Deloris said, "I can't."

Some things, she said, pacing by the foot of the bed, you just couldn't explain.

Oh, maybe you could *explain* them; you just couldn't *justify* them.

Deloris opened the curtains in front of the sliding glass doors that were near the creek. John Grape ducked the sudden shafts of sunlight.

Deloris said the unfortunate thing about coming to understand yourself was that it always took a toll. She apologized if she had started to sound like a fortune cookie. Her point was that sometimes you learned about yourself at the expense of others; and for this, she was extremely sorry.

She opened the sliding glass doors to air out the place.

She asked John Grape if he was with her so far.

He said not quite.

"What?" Deloris couldn't hear his answer for the water breaking over the rocks in the clear creek out back.

John Grape said he didn't understand what Deloris was talking about.

She leaned against the frame of the door she had just opened.

A rose-breasted grosbeak flew by.

Deloris said, "You see, I miss my ex-husband."

John Grape . . .

. . . blinked.

ABOUT THE AUTHOR

JAY CRONLEY was born in Lincoln, Nebraska, in 1943. He attended the University of Oklahoma, where he played baseball and made All Conference, All Big Eight, at second base. He has been a columnist at the *Tulsa Tribune* for the past fifteen years, and has won the Playboy Prize for humor.